OVER YOUR DEAD BODY

TOR BOOKS BY DAN WELLS

I Am Not a Serial Killer

Mr. Monster

I Don't Want to Kill You

The Hollow City

The Devil's Only Friend

Over Your Dead Body

OVER YOUR DEAD BODY

DAN WELLS

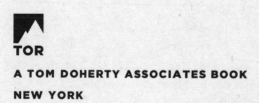

TOR

A TOM DOHERTY ASSOCIATES BOOK

NEW YORK

This is a work of fiction. All of the characters, organizations, and events portrayed in this novel are either products of the author's imagination or are used fictitiously.

OVER YOUR DEAD BODY

A Tor Book
Published by Tom Doherty Associates, LLC
175 Fifth Avenue
New York, NY 10010

www.tor-forge.com

Tor® is a registered trademark of Tom Doherty Associates, LLC.

The Library of Congress Cataloging-in-Publication Data is available upon request.

ISBN 978-0-7653-8068-5 (hardcover)
ISBN 978-0-7653-8069-2 (trade paperback)
ISBN 978-1-4668-7498-5 (e-book)

Our books may be purchased in bulk for promotional, educational, or business use. Please contact your local bookseller or the Macmillan Corporate and Premium Sales Department at 1-800-221-7945, extension 5442, or by e-mail at MacmillanSpecialMarkets@macmillan .com.

First Edition: May 2016

Printed in the United States of America

0 9 8 7 6 5 4 3 2 1

TO MY CHILDREN.
THIS COUNTS AS YOUR CHRISTMAS PRESENT.

ACKNOWLEDGMENTS

I hate writing these, as evidenced by the fact that in the last book I completely forgot. It's not that I don't like thanking people or that I don't have anyone to thank; it's quite the opposite: I'm always terrified that I won't thank enough people, and someone vital to my art or life will be completely forgotten. That's why this time I'm going small and thanking only a tiny handful of people in this public setting. If you're not mentioned in here, well, neither is almost anybody else. See what good company you're in?

This book owes its existence to my wife, Dawn; my assistant, Chersti Nieveen; my agent, Sara Crowe; and my editors at Tor and Piper: Moshe Feder, Whitney Ross, and Carsten Polzin. Those six people are the ones, more than anyone else, who convinced me that a second John Cleaver book could work and be awesome, and they are, it follows, the ones who helped make it awesome. I couldn't ask for any better collaborators than these.

Come away, O human child!
To the waters and the wild
With a faery, hand in hand,
For the world's more full of weeping than
   you can understand.

—WILLIAM BUTLER YEATS,
"THE STOLEN CHILD"

OVER YOUR DEAD BODY

1

"A."

I looked up, holding the side of the truck bed as we rattled down the highway. Wind whistled in my face, changing its pitch as I raised my head. I'd fallen asleep, and my dreams—all blood soaked, all screaming—faded away in welcome relief. In a panic, I looked for Brooke, fearing the worst, but she sat beside me, her short hair whipping around her face, and she smiled. She hadn't jumped. She was fine. She pointed at a billboard as we passed it.

"Proud America Motel," she said. "Ten miles. I could get all the way up to E with that, but there's no B."

We were in farmland, by the look of it: low fences on either side of the road, the flat land beyond covered with wheat and sectioned into squares by fences and trees and old dirt roads. A cloud of dust hung in the air a few miles off to our left; some farmer or ranch hand driving a tractor on a dirt road. The truck jostled us again, and Boy Dog whined. He liked his floors stable, so they didn't disrupt his sleep, but hitchhikers have to take what they can get. Brooke put a hand on his head, scratching the fur behind his floppy, basset hound ears. I scanned the farms again, hoping for an orchard, but it looked like nothing but wheat as far as the eye could see. An orchard we could have eaten in, but wheat might as well be a field full of sticks.

"There we go," said Brooke, pointing at another sign. "This Highway Adopted by the Baker Community Church. B, C, D, E."

"Are there really enough signs to play your game?" I asked. "We're in the middle of nowhere."

"Ten miles from a motel," said Brooke. "That means we're ten miles from whatever town we're going to, maybe less."

"That's not too bad, then," I said—and even though I knew the number by heart I added up our money again in my head: one hundred thirty-seven dollars and twenty-eight cents. I remember when I used to never count the cents—round everything down to the nearest dollar and lose the change in the couch. These days that was a luxury too painful to think about. Save enough change and you eventually get another dollar. A dollar could buy a burger in a truck stop, or some apples if we found a roadside stand. My stomach rumbled, and I put the thought of food aside. *Don't think about it until it's close,* I thought, *you'll just torment yourself.*

Wind lashed my hair back and forth across my eyes. I needed to cut it. Brooke had cut hers short last month, a kind of page-boy cut that was easier to maintain on the road. I looked at her peering ahead, past the cab of the truck, searching for more road signs. She probably needed another cut soon, too. We both needed a shower.

"What's the name of it?" she asked.

"Of what?"

"The town we're going to."

"I told you already," I said, and instantly felt badly about it. The edges of her mouth tipped down in a frown, from frustration or embarrassment, or maybe both. "Baker," I said softly. "Same as the church sign we just passed."

"I don't remember," she said. "You must have told one of the others."

I nodded, looking behind us at the road as it slipped away into the distance. Long and flat and lost in a faraway bend. One of the others. "Do you know which one?"

"F, G," she said, letting my question slip by without an answer. "Food and Gas, Five Miles. Now we need that hotel sign again; we could get H and I."

"And get stuck on J," I said. "We never see Js."

Brooke nodded, staring ahead, but her eyes looked blank—not searching, but simply staring, lost to the world and deep in some memory from another life. "Maybe Kveta," she said at last, answering my question from earlier. "I've been her a lot lately. Or Brooke. I think I'm her more often than not."

"That's because you—" I started, and then stopped myself. Brooke was her default state, or at least it used to be. If it wasn't anymore, bringing it up would only make her feel bad. It made me feel bad to think about it, because this whole problem was my fault. It was supposed to be Brooke's body; I was the one who'd let all those other memories in there.

I used to never feel bad about anything, but now . . .

Well, that's not true. I used to feel bad all the time. I guess the difference is that now, sometimes, I felt good, and the contrast made the bad times that much worse.

I kept my eyes on the road, avoiding her eyes. "Who are you now?"

She glanced at me, though in my peripheral vision I couldn't tell if she was hurt or surprised or simply curious. "You don't know?"

"Sorry," I said. Brooke had been possessed by a monster who had previously possessed tens of thousands of other girls, maybe hundreds of thousands, and all of their memories and personalities had fused with hers. Barely a fraction of the memories in Brooke's head were actually hers, and with numbers like that you could never tell which personality would rise to the surface in any given moment. "You all have Brooke's face, you know. You need to . . . announce yourselves or something."

"I'm Lucinda," said Brooke. "You remember me, right?"

I nodded. She was Lucinda a lot, especially while we were traveling, though the little I knew about Lucinda didn't suggest a lot of travel. "You died on your wedding day," I said, then paused, looking at her curiously. "Lucinda died hundreds of years ago. How do you know the alphabet billboard game?"

"I don't know," said Brooke/Lucinda with a shrug. "I just do."

I sat up straighter, curious, my back against the wall of the truck bed as I gripped it for balance. "Do you think that means anything? About how your personalities talk to each other?"

"We can't talk to each other," she said. "We just kind of share things—like, I know some things that Brooke knows, and some things that Aga knows, and different things from different girls. I don't know how it works."

"But do you want to?"

She said nothing for a long time, thinking and scratching Boy Dog's head. The truck slowed slightly, and Brooke shouted abruptly: "H, I, J, K! Baker Junior High!" She pumped her fist and leaned against the side of the truck bed to look ahead past the cab. "Yes! Js are impossible! Let's see what else we can find."

We were driving into the town itself now—still a mile or two out from the main drag, but close enough that buildings were starting to pop up more frequently. We passed the Proud America

Motel, but I hoped we didn't have to stay there; I thought about money differently now that I was carrying our entire worldly possessions in a pocket and two backpacks. We could *afford* a night in a motel—probably several, if it was as cheap as it looked—but then what? Having money wasn't the same as having income. If we spent it all today, where would we stay next week, and how would we eat?

One hundred thirty-seven dollars and twenty-eight cents. We could get more, sometimes, from the stashes Albert Potash had left here and there around the country. Money and guns and supplies, in bus station lockers and storage units and sometimes gyms or rec centers. We'd found the list in his gear after he'd died and it had kept us going for over a year now, but even that was running dry. There were only a few locations left, and the nearest one was thousands of miles away.

"L," said Brooke, skipping from letter to letter without slowing down to say where each had come from. "M." Pause. "N, O, P. Dangit, we'll never find a Q."

"Look for 'equipment,'" I said, closing my eyes and trying not to fixate on our dwindling funds. "Someone's bound to be selling farm equipment in this town. Or maybe there's a quality . . . something. Quality Hair Salon."

Brooke laughed. "You think they have hair salons that good in a town this small?"

"I think the scale of quality is relative," I said, permitting myself a small smile. Anything that made Brooke laugh was a good thing. "The best one in town is the quality one, regardless of the wider world of hair care."

"Maybe we'll get lucky and find a place that sells quality farm equipment," she said. "Then we'd have a Q for each of us."

"I'm not playing."

"But you could."

"I suck at this game."

"That's because you try to spell things out," she chided. "You can't just see a car and claim the letter C, you have to see the C written somewhere."

"But you never let me write it."

"Obviously you can't just write yourself, that's cheating."

I shrugged and looked at a passing restaurant. "I don't think I get the allure of this game." The restaurant was a greasy dive, some Dairy Queen knockoff called Dairy Keen. Probably out of our price range, unless there was literally nothing else in town. I saw a couple of teenagers in front of it, just hanging around, leaning on the front wall, and it reminded me of the old Friendly Burger back in Clayton. A tiny little place where nobody ate but the locals, and then only until a McDonald's opened up. Brooke and I had gone on a date there. And Marci and I, too. There weren't a lot of options in a town like Clayton. Or Baker, by the look of it.

I missed Marci. I tried not to think of her, but she was always with me, like a ghost in the back of the truck. Invisible and intangible yet relentlessly, inescapably present.

"No Q on the Dairy Keen," said Brooke. "Come on, guys, think about the alphabet game when you name your restaurants. Doesn't anybody plan ahead?"

I thought about our next moves. Our first stop would be a bus station, if we saw one, or a bank if we didn't—not because we had any use for a bank, but because it was a good place to ask about a bus station. We couldn't just ask anywhere in a little town like this; we looked so obviously homeless that if we walked into a store, word of the teenage beggars would spread too fast and we'd get locked out of any real assistance. Small-town shop owners looked out for each other. Bank tellers, on the other hand, tended to move in different circles, and we could talk to them without any real fear that they'd call the local grocery store to warn them. Our end goal, of course, was that bus station, where we could find either cheap showers or some fellow drifters who could tell us where the nearest shower might be. Drifters looked out for each other just as much as shop owners. Once we were clean and changed into some better clothes, we'd look like regular tourists passing through on the way somewhere else and we could walk around the town without setting off any mental alarms. We'd get some food and then look for the church—not Baker Community, but the other one. The commune. The reason we'd come here in the first place. I figured most of Baker's regular residents wouldn't want to talk about it, but they'd all know about it, and if we got lucky they'd point out one of the members.

"Quality Feed and Fertilizer," said Brooke. "Q and R. And over there's an S, T, U . . . V. Video Rental. They still rent videos in this town? Did we hitchhike into the past?"

"Looks closed," I said. We'd had a place like that in Clayton—it rode the home DVD boom, then crumbled when the Internet made their business obsolete. They'd closed a few years ago, and nothing had moved into the building. Looked like the same story here.

"At least they left the sign up," said Brooke. "I'm glad *somebody* in this town was thinking about my needs." She grimaced, and looked at me. "What's it called again?"

"The town?" I asked. She might have just switched personalities again; a lot of ideas transferred from one to the next, but some didn't, and she tried to hide the transitions by faking a poor memory. "Baker," I told her. "We're here to look for The Spirit of Light Collective."

"Yashodh," said Brooke, nodding. "We're going to kill him."

I felt the old, familiar pull of death. "Or he'll kill us."

"You say that every time."

"One of these days it'll be true."

The truck was slowing, probably looking for a good place to drop us off. I grabbed the strap of my backpack, getting ready to jump out, but saw that Brooke was ignoring hers, staring instead at the buildings we were driving past: tall brick storefronts with ornate, peaked facades on the second story. Some of them were painted, some were covered with wooden or vinyl siding, others were bare brick or bore the residue of old-timey signs too weathered to read. A barber shop. An antique store. A pizza place that looked way more modern than the rest of the street. I wondered if we could beg any food from the back door.

The truck pulled to the side of the road, by a bright green lawn in some kind of town plaza—city hall probably—and I was already over the side and reaching back for Brooke's bag when the driver rolled down his window. "This good? I could take you a few more blocks if you want."

"This is perfect," I said. A few more blocks would have been nice, through the town and out the other side where we could infiltrate at our own pace, but it never helped to ask the drivers for extras. Always make them feel generous, not put upon—like they would have done more if they could, instead of wishing they'd done less. Instead I pointed at the tailgate. "Do you mind if I open the back to get the dog out?"

"No problem," said the driver. He didn't offer to help, which meant I was probably right to refuse the extra ride. He was already forgetting us, free of his hitchhiker burden with his mind a mile down the road. I dropped the tailgate and lifted Boy Dog out, smelling the strong scent of dirt and hound. He needed a bath as much as I did. He sat on the sidewalk where I left him, scratching his ear with his stubby front leg, and I offered Brooke my hand. She seemed lost in some kind of reverie again, all too common for her, and I said her name to get her attention.

"Brooke?"

She turned to look at me, but her eyes showed no recognition. "Who?"

"Lucinda." I said, remembering. There was no response, so I tried another. "Kveta?"

"I'm . . . " She paused. "I'm so sorry, John."

The warning signs were all over her face—the disorientation, the downcast eyes, the subtle whine in her voice. I put on my biggest smile and grabbed her hand, knowing that physical contact was one of the best ways of bringing her out of a mood swing. "We got here early," I said, "everything's great."

"I don't want to be this way," she said, not moving. I tugged gently on her hand, trying not to glance at the driver for signs of impatience. If he yelled at her to hurry, it would only make her worse.

She remembered the lives of a hundred thousand girls, and she remembered dying as every single one of them. Suicide was as natural to Brooke as breathing.

"You want some pizza for dinner?" I asked. "I saw a good place about a block back."

"We can't afford pizza."

"We can splurge," I said, and pulled on her again. "Come on, let's go take a look. What do you think they have here, deep dish or New York style?"

She didn't respond to the conversational bait, but another gentle tug on her arm finally prompted her to climb down from the truck bed. She dusted herself off with a grimace, showing far more emotion than the dirt seemed to merit. I risked letting go of her for three precious seconds, closing the tailgate and shouting a thank you to the driver. He drove off without a word, and Boy Dog barked irritably at the cloud of exhaust that puffed into his face.

"My name is Pearl," said Brooke. "Pearly, they called me, and my father said I was the jewel of his life. I had a dozen suitors, and the finest horse in the county. We won all the races that year, but they let me win. I don't know why. I was horrible, and if I'd lived to know them better they'd have seen me for what I was—"

"I'm starving," I said, cutting her off instantly at the mention of death. I had one of her hands clasped in mine, and brought up the other quickly, looking closely at her eyes, not talking her out of it because that never worked, but talking around it. Distracting her from it. "My favorite pizza topping is mushrooms," I said. "I know a lot of people don't like them, but I think they're delicious—soft, savory, full of this incredible flavor. When you put them on a pizza they get roasted right there in the oven, hot and fresh, and they go perfectly with the tomato sauce. Do you like mushrooms?"

"I threw myself off of that horse," said Pearl. "I . . . don't even remember his name. He's not the one that killed me, anyway, it was the ones behind me. No one could swerve in time, and they trampled me right there in front of everybody."

"What about pepperoni?" I asked. "Everybody likes pepperoni. And that red pepper stuff you can shake on top—you think this place has that? Let's go check it out."

"Will you stop it!" she yelled. "I know what you're doing, and I hate it! You always treat me like this!"

I took a deep breath, trying not to look too worried—this wasn't exactly a bustling street, but if she attracted too much attention it could be disastrous. Even without a suicide attempt, there were people looking for us—people and things. Things we desperately didn't want to be found by. If she started fighting me, the police would get involved and we might be trapped for good. I spoke softly, rubbing her fingers with my thumb.

"You're tired," I said. "You're probably exhausted, and starving, and uncomfortable, and that's all my fault, and I'm sorry."

"Shut up!" She tried to yank her hands away, but I held tight.

"You need to rest," I continued, "and get some food, and change your clothes. And maybe we can sleep in a real motel tonight. Does that sound good?"

"You don't want to stay with me," she said, swinging in half a heartbeat from hating me to blaming herself. "I'm horrible. I screw everything up. You could be doing this so much better without me—"

"I couldn't be doing this at all without you," I said. "We're a team, remember? You're the brains and I'm the hands. Partners to the end. The only deadweight is Boy Dog." I cringed immediately after saying it, cursing whatever neural pathway had brought out the word "deadweight," but she didn't react. She stayed still, looking at the ground, and I looked up as a semi rumbled past, spitting gravel at us from under the tires. Boy Dog barked again, a short, halfhearted yelp. I changed tactics, and pointed at the receding truck. "Weller Shipping; there's your W. All we need now is an X, and there's bound to be a . . . saxophone shop around here somewhere, right? Axle repair? A pet store that specializes in oxes and foxes?"

I stepped toward the sidewalk, trying to pull her toward somewhere, anywhere, that she could sit down and eat and get some water, but she slipped out of my hand and ran toward the middle of the street—

—straight into the path of another semi. I spun on my heel and reached for her, missing her trailing fingers by half an inch. The truck blared its horn in angry warning, slamming on its brakes, and Brooke planted herself in front of it, spreading her arms and closing her eyes. I ran toward her, watching from the corner of my eye as the truck swerved, hoping I could get Brooke out of its way without even knowing what its new way was. I collided with her in a football tackle, pushing her toward the side of the road, stumbling and scrambling to stay on my feet, until finally we collapsed in the gutter on the far side, bouncing off a rusted fender as we fell between two cars. The semi roared past, correcting its course, avoiding a crash by the width of an eyelash. Brooke was sobbing, and I checked her quickly for injuries—scrapes on her arms, a tear in her jeans, but no broken bones or cuts that I could see. My own right arm was a mass of blood and gravel, which I brushed away gingerly.

"You okay?" asked a passing pedestrian. He looked down at us from over an armload of brown cardboard boxes.

"We're fine," I said, though my arm felt like it was on fire.

"You ought to get that looked at," he added, then hesitated, and continued walking.

Somebody else's problem.

Brooke was still crying, curled up in the gutter. I rested my hand on her arm, looking around to see who else, if anyone, had noticed our near miss. If anyone had, they weren't coming out of their shops to mention it. I wanted to scream at them, to rage against the entire world for allowing this scrawny, broken girl to be so coldly forgotten and ignored. I wanted to kill them all. But being ignored was the best thing we could hope for, and I couldn't risk making a scene. I turned back to Brooke. "It's okay," I said softly. "It's okay."

"You saved me," said Brooke.

"Every time," I said. "You know I always will."

"You shouldn't," she said. "I'm not worth it."

"Don't say that." The sky was growing darker; we needed to find shelter and a shower, now more than ever, and probably some antiseptic for my arm. I couldn't risk the clinic, though—they'd ask too many questions, and try to pry out information we couldn't give. A pharmacy, maybe. Even a little town like this ought to have one somewhere. *And the sign will have an RX on it*, I thought. *Maybe that will cheer her up.* I stood slowly, reaching for her with my good arm, but she caught me and pulled me back down to the curb, clutching me in a sad, desperate hug.

She sat up, wiping the tears and dirt from her face. "I love you, John," she said.

"I know you do." I tried to say it back—I always tried to say it back—but I couldn't make the words come out. I'd only ever loved one person, but Nobody had possessed Marci and killed her before moving on to Brooke, now almost two years ago. The monster had come for her, and I was one victim too late to save her. At least I'd saved Brooke.

And guessed I was going to keep saving her until the day I died.

2

I woke up with Boy Dog's back in my face, warm and itchy. His body expanded slowly as he breathed in, pressing against my nose, driving the little hairs into my skin. I rolled over, feeling a stiff ache in my muscles and a sudden sense of disorientation at the hard, flat ground beneath me. Where were the bumps and the roots and the . . . ? I opened my eyes wider. I was shrouded in darkness with, somehow, a perfectly vertical line of bright light off to the side. I focused on it and remembered the curtains. We were in a motel. The curtains were closed. I sat up and Boy Dog twitched, his stubby legs moving three times and then falling still again. We were on the floor.

I looked at the bed and saw Brooke, the covers kicked off her body but twisted around one leg. Her chest rose and fell, just like Boy Dog's. How much nicer, I thought, to have woken up with that pressed against me instead?

I corrected myself immediately: with *her* pressed against me. And then I corrected myself again: I couldn't touch her at all. She thought she loved me, but I couldn't love her back. I had broken her before, by failing to catch the demon called Nobody, and now it was all I could do to keep her from breaking again. She was my responsibility, not my girlfriend.

I saw the shape of her body under her clothes, the hint of pale skin at her waist.

I went to the bathroom, keeping the light off, and washed my face in the dark. The towels were thin, like dishrags. I stared at my silhouette in the mirror, a dark outline barely separate from the dark room behind it. The corner of the glass was cracked and the mirrored surface was flaking away.

Brooke and I had been on the road for seven months now, hunting monsters. I had always called them demons, but they called themselves Withered or Gifted, depending on whether they saw their lives as a curse or a blessing. I'd killed the first one on my own, almost four years ago now. And while I'd tried to keep the rest of the world out of it, this dark, hidden underworld had started pulling others in, killing or corrupting everyone I knew. Everything I touched. My mother had died, and Marci, and Brooke had been saved but only by the barest definition. I sometimes wondered if she would have been better off dead.

I saw the shape of her body again like an afterimage in my mind, so still and silent in the bed.

I sat down on the old chair in the corner of the room, pulling on my shoes as the wood creaked softly with each tiny movement. I'd been sleeping in front of the door—Brooke sometimes walked in her sleep—so Boy Dog was there now as well, blocking me from opening it more than a foot. I undid the chain and tried to slip through, but Boy Dog woke up and scrambled to his feet, shaking and rattling his collar. I hushed him, putting my hand on his neck, and he followed me outside. The light seemed blinding, but as my eyes adjusted I saw that it was still early morning, the whole world bathed in predawn blue. I stretched and rubbed my arms. Across the parking lot someone was throwing a fat white bag in a garbage can. *The* garbage can, I supposed. That's how they thought of it, the people who lived here: it was their garbage can. Their home. To me it was just another place, just another parking lot, just another stop on the highway that was taking us . . . somewhere, I guess. We had no specific plans. We were hunting Withered and we went where they did, and whoever—or whatever—was hunting us came after. We had to stay one step ahead, or more if we could manage it. I honestly had no idea how many steps behind us they might be; if you run fast enough, you're so far ahead you have no idea who's chasing you.

I looked at the door to our room; I probably had a few minutes before Brooke woke up. I made sure it was locked, then walked toward the front desk to ask for information on the commune— motel clerks didn't freak out about drifters, or anything else it seemed. We were some of the most normal people they saw.

The man at the garbage can went back in through the rear door of whatever business he was opening for the day. A pawn shop, maybe. It was too early to be a bar. The town was quiet, only just waking up, and I wondered what it would be like to live here, to put down roots and stay here forever. Not much different than in Clayton, I supposed. What brought people here, instead of there— or there instead of here? Did they choose to live here, or were they just born here and never moved away?

The front office had a bell on the door that dinged as I walked in.

"Good morning, sir." He called me sir even though I was only eighteen and looked even younger. I'd tried growing a beard, hoping it would make me look like an adult, but it just came in wispy and thin—I was so obviously trying to look like an adult that I gave up and shaved it off. He glanced down at Boy Dog, who followed me in. "That room working out for you?"

"It's been great," I said. "Thanks for letting us keep the dog; a lot of places get picky about pets."

"No problem. What can I do for you?"

I needed information, and I was caught by the sudden urge to torture it out of him—to tie him down and cut him in strategic places, just a bit at first, then more and more until he told me everything I wanted—

No. I wasn't allowed to hurt people. I took a breath and spooled out the story I'd concocted instead. "Well, I'm looking for my sister—"

"That's the girl you were with last night?"

Did he suspect we were runaways? More to the point, had he turned us in? I fed him some more of my made-up backstory, hoping some extra information would cool his suspicions. "No, that's my wife—we're taking a semester off of college to try to find my sister, who last I heard was hanging around this part of the state. Kind of drifting, you know?" I grimaced, as if the thought was painful. "My sister's a little younger, still in high school; she ran away from home last year."

"That's too bad," said the clerk. He leaned on the counter; a good sign that I'd caught his attention with the story. He might take it seriously enough to actually help me. "You think she's in Baker, specifically? You have family around here?"

"We don't," I said, "but I'd heard . . . " I trailed off, like I was too embarrassed to say it, and when he nodded I knew that I had him. Suddenly I wasn't a suspicious outsider asking about the local cult, I was a concerned family man, one of the normals, someone he could gossip with about those weirdos on the farm. I looked out the window, checking for Brooke, but our door was still closed.

"The cult," said the clerk, nodding again. "Spirit of Light? You think she's fallen in with them?"

"I hope not," I said, and paused just a moment before saying, "So it's real, then? They're actually here?"

"Sad to say," said the clerk. "A friend of mine joined up with them a few years back; local boy. We figured he was smarter than that but I guess nobody ever got rich overestimating the intelligence of rednecks. Them Light-Brights come into town for groceries and medicine and stuff like that, whatever they can't make on the farm I guess, toilet paper and whatnot, and so Nick he starts chatting with this one girl every time he sees her, bagging her things in the checkout aisle and whatever. We all told him them folks was nothing but trouble, and he insisted, right hand to God, he was just trying to talk her out of the cult, not himself into it. Inviting her to the Dairy Keen and asking her to movies and such. She keeps saying maybe and then saying no, and then finally one day the big man comes in: the High Chief Light-Bright or whatever they call him. The Messiah. You don't see him often, but he comes in now and then looking for this or that, and every time someone follows him back out. This time it was Nick. Didn't even finish his shift. Now he's the one comes into town buying toilet paper, and we talk to him sometimes and he says hi but he's gone—nothing in his head but songs and stories and ain't-it-great-to-be-alives. He smiles and nods and I'm not even sure he recognizes us anymore. Which I guess is just a long, depressing way of saying that if your sister's in there, you've got a long, empty road ahead getting her back out, and that road don't even lead out, so you'd best not take it in the first place."

"Has anyone ever left the cult?" I asked. "Voluntarily, I mean?"

"Not that I recall."

I asked the next question carefully, trying to sound awed by the mystery instead of desperate for concrete details. "Does anybody ever disappear?" If the cult leader was really a Withered, like Brooke's memories said he was, he had to be killing them somehow. Learning how could be the first step to finding Yashodh's weak points.

The clerk squinted. "From Baker, you mean? Sometimes, but they always show up as Light-Brights sooner or later."

"But from the commune, I mean," I said quickly. "The Light-Brights themselves, they're not being . . . killed or anything?" I glanced outside again. Brooke was still in the room.

The clerk shook his head. "Trust me, kid, there's not a person in this town doesn't know somebody out on that farm. If they was disappearing we'd be out there with torches and pitchforks, but this ain't the kind of cult that people disappear from. Every single one of them's still there, growing their own food and sewing their own clothes and praising whatever non-Christian whosit they've decided to worship. They don't die, they don't leave, they don't . . . do anything."

I realized I was frowning, confused by the lack of deaths, so I changed my expression to what I thought was hope. "Thank you," I said. "At least that means she's still alive."

"If she's there at all," said the clerk.

"How would we get out there?" I asked.

"You don't."

"But obviously people do," I said. "Which road is it? Which farm?"

"You're not listening to me," said the clerk. "People who go there don't come back. The city, sometimes, or the police, but folks like you? Just Light-Brights waiting to happen."

This was interesting. "They're that persuasive?"

"They persuaded Nick, and he grew up more afraid of them than the boogeyman under his bed."

"Thanks," I said again. "We'll be careful." I took a step toward the door, but I still didn't know where to find them. I looked out-side, but still no Brooke. I turned back to the clerk. "How about a roadside stand? A lot of these places sell cheese or vegetables or whatever—does Spirit of Light? Maybe I could ask there, see if any-one knows my sister?"

"Head out on State Road 27," said the clerk. "Plenty of folks buy produce from them—it's safe enough. You don't have a car, though, right?"

"Just the bus."

"Bus don't run that way, but you can try hitching."

I tried to look serious, eager to convince him we were as normal as could be. "Isn't that dangerous?"

"You're heading out to the most dangerous part of Baker there is. Someone kidnaps you on the way there, it'll be a kindness."

I thanked him and left, trudging toward our room. It was good to have information, but most of it made me uneasy. Where were the deaths? Was Yashodh using some kind of mind control? Most of the Withered were too dangerous to confront head on; we had to lurk in the fringes, learning everything we could until we found a weakness we could exploit. This Withered sounded like he might be too dangerous to even meet.

I paused in front of our door, thinking. What if we just left? He wasn't killing anybody, apparently. We didn't have to kill him. Maybe we shouldn't. But I couldn't shake the sound of the clerk's voice as he warned us away, too scared to—

The door opened, and Brooke started in surprise to find me standing silently in front of it. "*Sranje! Šta radiš ovdje?*"

"English," I said softly.

She stared at me, confused, and then tilted her head to the side as her surprise turned to curiosity. "What language was I speaking?"

I stepped past her into the room and closed the door carefully behind me. "No idea. Something you've used before, I think, but I didn't recognize the words."

She walked back and sat on the bed. "I asked what you were doing there. Guarding me?"

I starting gathering our few belongings, repacking them in our backpacks. "No, just lost in thought and standing in a weird place. Tell me about Yashodh again." The Withered assumed human identities, but they had their own names. Nobody, the demon who'd taken Brooke, had been called Hulla. The Lord High Light-Bright, as the clerk called him, was named Yashodh.

Brooke shook her head. "You know I don't like talking about Yashodh."

"Well, we're going to meet him at some point, so we need to get over that." I zipped one pack closed and collected some discarded socks for the other one. Today was my last clean pair; we'd need to do laundry soon. "You knew this day was coming. We've done all the other Withered we can find, so it's time to do Yashodh."

"We haven't done Attina."

"This is on our way to Attina," I said. "We do it now, or we do it six months from now."

"I know," said Brooke, falling back on the bed, "I just . . . I don't know. Maybe I can remember some others." Her memory was riddled with holes, but it was also the only tool we had to find and hunt the Withered. She clenched her teeth. "You don't know him like I do."

"So tell me about him."

"I already told you everything I know."

"You can't have it both ways," I said. "Do you know him or not?"

"He hates himself," said Brooke, "even more than I do." I glanced at her; I'd known her long enough to see the real meaning behind that statement.

I corrected her softly. "You mean 'more than Nobody hates her-self,'" I said.

"I am Nobody," said Brooke. Or, I suppose, said Nobody.

I shrugged and zipped up the second backpack; she didn't show any warning signs of another depressive attack, so it wasn't worth arguing.

"Each of the Withered gave something up," said Nobody, and her eyes got that faraway look they sometimes had when she talked about the distant past. Nearly ten thousand years ago, if the FBI's researcher had guessed right. "I gave up my body," she continued, "because it was horrible and I hated it. Yashodh gave up himself."

"But what does that mean?" I asked. "We've been tossing that around for a year now, trying to figure out what he can do. Nobody gave up her body and gained the ability to take the bodies of others. Can Yashodh take the 'selves' of others? What does that even mean? It might explain the cult, if he's somehow subsuming their individuality into some kind of collective, but why? What does he possibly gain from doing that?"

"He's weak," said Nobody, her voice dripping with disdain. "He's lucky to get anything, let alone something he wants."

"He's a ten-thousand-year-old monster," I said, "one who can probably mind control people. The more we look into him, the more I think he can get *anything* he wants."

"Then why is he here in two-bit Crapville?" asked Nobody. "Everyone loves him, and he can have everything, and he doesn't even have to kill people, and all he does is sit here picking his nose—"

"Wait," I said, standing up in a rush. "That's new—you've talked about Yashodh for a year and this is the first time you've said he doesn't have to kill people."

"That's new?" Her eyes went wide and she looked down at

herself as if expecting to see something different. Almost immediately she shook her head and closed her eyes, squinting them shut as she thought. "Something new . . . think . . . " She clenched her teeth with the effort. "He doesn't kill people . . . he doesn't have to kill people. . . . "

"Do they worship him?" I asked. If he'd set himself up as a messiah figure in a backcountry cult, maybe it was the worship itself that sustained him. "You said everyone loves him, right? Is that a means to an end, or is that the end itself?"

"That would make sense," said Nobody, rubbing her fingers together as she spoke, staring at the wall.

"But is it true?"

"I don't know," she growled, "I'm trying to think." She focused on the wall like it was a portal to the past. "Come on, brain, spit it out. He doesn't need to kill people. Maybe he doesn't want to kill people. Maybe he can't kill people."

"He gave up himself," I said, trying to keep her thoughts focused; brainstorming new ideas wouldn't help us, we needed to dig deeper into the handful of truths we already had.

"He gave himself up," said Brooke. "Everybody loves him . . . because he gave himself up. He saved them."

This sounded wrong. "From what?"

"From sin," said Brooke, looking up at me. "He died for our sins."

I shook my head. "How many of your personalities are Christian?"

"I don't know," she said. "Lots. I'm just talking about Jesus now, aren't I?"

"Yashodh is not the messiah," I said, "but he needs to convince people that he is. For . . . something."

"So he can be happy," said Brooke.

"That's it?"

She looked at me with a frown. "What do you mean, that's it? That's everything."

"The Withered are not trying to be happy," I said, "they're trying to gain . . . power, money, something. They're trying to survive."

"That's what happiness is, John. It's how we survive. It's why."

I sighed and rubbed my face with my hands. "Whatever. We can think on the way." I grabbed my backpack, and looked down at Boy Dog. "Sorry, dog. You've got a long walk ahead."

3

"What's your favorite song?" asked Brooke. We'd found State Road 27 but hadn't managed to catch a ride yet so we were just walking along—slowly, so Boy Dog could keep up.

I answered without thinking. " 'Don't Stop Believin',' by Foreigner."

Brooke laughed. "No it's not."

"Sure it is," I said. "Why not?"

"The question isn't why not," she said. "It's why. What on earth about that song makes you like it?"

"You say that like it's impossible to like," I said. "That's one of the most popular songs of all time."

"Is that why you picked it?"

I glanced at her. "I picked it because I like it."

"So sing it."

"What, right now?"

She spun slowly in the empty country road, looking at the wide fields and dusty trees that surrounded us. "Are you shy? We could sing at the top of our lungs and no one would even hear us. So prove it, big guy: if 'Don't Stop Believin'' is your favorite song, sing it."

"I don't really sing."

Her eyes gleamed with mischief. "Then recite the words."

I sighed. "Fine, I don't actually know the words."

"Of course you don't," she said proudly. "You didn't even know who sang it—it's Journey, not Foreigner, and I should know because I went to their concerts. Several of me did."

"They're the same band," I said, and then frowned. "Aren't they?"

"They're not the same band, they're super different."

"No, seriously," I said, "isn't it just, like, they changed their name? Like how Jefferson Airplane became Jefferson Starship."

"Wow," said Brooke, "you're going all in on classic rock, aren't you?"

"What else am I going to listen to, modern stuff? Have you *heard* modern stuff?"

"More than you have," said Brooke, "which is my whole point. You don't listen to anything, classic or modern or anything else. I'm going to guess that somebody, probably your mom, listened to classic rock all the time, so you picked the most popular one as your 'look how normal I am' answer if anyone ever asked."

I sighed again and shrugged. "Fine, you got me. And it was my dad, actually—huge classic rock fan. I don't know if you remember him very well."

"He left when we were little, right?" Brooke had lived two doors down from me since elementary school. "I liked him."

"Most people did," I said. "People who didn't live with him at least." I heard a car behind us and turned to face it, sticking out my thumb to try to hitch a ride. The car ignored us, not even slowing down. I faced forward again, but Boy Dog had flopped down in the dirt by the side of the road, taking our brief pause as an excuse to rest. I gave him a moment.

"I don't know why I bother keeping up the pretense with you," I said softly. "You know everything about me."

"I don't think anyone knows everything about you," said Brooke.

"But you know that I'm . . . different," I said. I don't know why it was so hard to say; I used to wear it as a badge of honor. "I'm sociopathic. I don't feel things the way you do, the way anybody does. Everything I do is fake, to make people think I'm normal. This morning I lied to the motel clerk, trying to convince him we came to town on a bus. He doesn't care how we came to town. Some of the lies were to put him at ease and get info out of him, but even after he gave us the info I didn't want him to know we were drifters. I wanted him to think we were normal."

"You just want to fit in," said Brooke. "Everybody wants that."

"I never used to."

She shrugged and started walking again. Boy Dog heaved himself to his feet and started following. "People change," said Brooke. I caught up with her in a few long strides. "And circumstances change. When you were a kid you lived in a nice little house full of nice little people, and it was all nice and little and normal, and you wanted to stand out."

"I lived in an apartment over a mortuary," I said. "My dad beat us and then left."

"So why you'd pick his favorite music?"

I thought about it then shook my head. "I don't know."

"Either way," she said, "your old life was pretty friggin' normal compared to your current social circle: a possessed girl and a dog with the dumbest name in the history of dog names."

"A demon named him," I said. "So to be fair, that name is not the worst thing it's ever done."

Brooke laughed, and I couldn't help but smile at the sound. We walked for a while longer, listening to the wind rustle through the trees. After a minute or two Brooke spoke again. "What do you think my favorite song is?"

"I don't know."

"How could you not know? We lived next door to each other for sixteen years."

"Since we're being so open and honest," I said, "let's get this out of the way and say that I did, in fact, stalk you for several months—"

"That's creepy."

"Compared to what aspect of our current situation?"

"Fair point," said Brooke. She took a few more steps, then asked, "Because you liked me?"

"I told myself I was protecting you."

"Were you?"

"Well, you're not dead."

"I did get kidnapped because of you, though."

"And rescued."

"And possessed."

"Are you going to hold that against me forever?"

"I'm just teasing," said Brooke. "There's, like, a million girls in here, and you only ruined one of their lives."

"Listen," I said, "I am doing everything I can to—"

Brooke burst into laughter. "I'm just teasing!" she insisted. "Come on, John, you know I love you."

"And we know that that's, like, the worst thing that's ever happened to you."

"You're my best friend," said Brooke. "You're literally the only person who knows me—the real, current me, I mean. My family just remembers Mary."

"You mean Brooke."

"I mean all of them," said Brooke. "Mary and Brooke and Katherine . . . honestly, like at least a hundred Katherines. They're all gone—even Brooke—but whatever I am now, some kind of messed-up, emotional Voltron made out of old, discarded daughters, you're the only one who knows *that* me. This me. And I know you don't love me, but you like me. And . . . that means a lot."

"Well," I said, not knowing how to respond. "There you go."

She raised her eyebrow. "Very romantic."

"But my point is," I said, "that despite stalking you, I never paid attention to the music you listened to." I paused. "I remember hearing a Pink song once."

"How can a song be pink?"

"Pink was a singer," I said. "Well, still is, I guess. Sometimes I feel like we've left the world, but we're still in it, just . . . on the fringes."

"What was the name of the song?" she asked.

"I don't really know music," I said, feeling guilty that I couldn't tell her. "Sorry."

"It would be nice to have a favorite song," she said. A moment later she pointed ahead. "Is that it?"

I peered down the road; the distance was blurry, but there was definitely something there. People, and a large dark shape that could be the produce stand. "Did we walk the entire way?"

"Poor little Boy Dog," said Brooke, bending down to scratch his ears. "His legs are, like, eight inches long. He's taken ten times as many steps as we have."

"We have to be careful," I said, watching the dark shape slowly come into focus as we walked closer. "Yashodh can control minds, and we don't know how to kill him yet—we're going to have to find some way of staying close to him long enough to figure him out without getting brainwashed, and that's not going to be easy."

"What was the old trick you used to use?" asked Brooke. "When we had the whole team?"

The first year Brooke and I were on the road we'd been in the employment of the FBI and we'd managed to kill eight Withered before they'd starting fighting back. That whole team was dead now, except for the two of us, but we'd learned a lot before the end. One of the simplest tricks was the speed-bump test: most of the Withered had incredible regeneration powers, but not all, so step two, after we'd found one, was to find a way to hit them with truck. If they regenerated we buckled down for a long game of cat and mouse, figuring out exactly how to kill them and then planning the perfect way to do it. I was really good at that part. If the truck worked, though, then it was over—the Withered was dead, and we moved on to the next one.

"I don't know if we can arrange a speed-bump test," I said. "At least not one we can get away with afterward. Potash was a military-trained assassin; I'm just a creepy kid with a knife."

"And a gun," said Brooke.

"And a gun," I said. She knew where it was in my pack, but I always kept the bullets hidden. A gun wasn't a great thing to have handy during one of her suicidal mood swings.

"Hello, travelers!" One of the people at the stand was waving to us, and we waved back. I think I'd been expecting them to be dressed in white robes or something, but instead they looked like they'd stepped out of a western movie: homemade dresses of colorful gingham, linen shirts, hats they must have purchased from a store somewhere. They weren't dour, they weren't otherworldly, they were just . . . people. They greeted us with smiles, and I slowed my pace for the last several yards, trying to gauge the danger. Boy Dog walked straight to the shady triangle by the wall of the food stand and plopped down, panting in exhaustion. One of the cultists picked

OVER YOUR DEAD BODY

up a ceramic plate of zucchini, dumped them into a box of yellow squash, and set the empty plate in front of Boy Dog, filling it with water from a plastic jug. Boy Dog eagerly lapped it up.

"You're a long way out from the city," said a woman.

I nodded, shielding my eyes from the sun. "Yep. Haven't been able to hitch a ride all morning."

"Where were you headed?" asked a man.

"Here," said Brooke. She was never very good at deception.

"We were looking for the Spirit of Light," I said, trying to spin Brooke's up-front confession into the same cover story I'd given the clerk. "My sister was down here a few months ago," I said. "We thought maybe she'd joined your commune."

The woman tilted her head. "Sister Kara, maybe?"

"Her name is Lauren," said Brooke, before I had a chance to say yes. I bit my tongue, wondering how I could talk to them without her spoiling all my lies, but the man laughed.

"We all get new names when we join with the Light," he said. "I don't remember Sister Kara's old name, but she joined us two months ago, so it might be her."

"She won't want to leave with you," said the woman. "Sister Kara is happy here—we all are." Her face softened and she peered into my face with concern. "You don't look happy at all."

"He never does," said Brooke, and looked at me with an expression almost identical to the woman's. "He's happy sometimes, though. More often than you think."

"How can you tell?" the woman asked.

Brooke nodded sagely. "The dog's still alive."

It disturbed me how close Brooke seemed to the cultists—how eerily her attitude of cheerful innocence matched their vibe of brainwashed emptiness. I'd grown so accustomed to her over the last few months that I'd forgotten how damaged she really was.

"That's good to hear," said the man. "Isn't it great to be alive?"

"We were hoping we might have a chance to go back to your farm with you," I said. "Just to look for her? We don't want to try to take her away, so don't worry—we just want to make sure it's really her, make sure she's safe."

"I assure you that everyone in the Light is completely safe," said the woman firmly. "Christopher makes sure of it."

"Is that the leader?" I asked.

"The Vessel of the Light," said the woman. "If you'd like to meet him, you're welcome to join us for dinner."

"Thank you," said Brooke. "That's very kind."

"Pull up an apple crate," said the man. "It's a long day until then. Have some tomatoes—fresh off the vine this morning."

I nodded my head in thanks, still leery of the emptiness behind their eyes—or was I just imagining it?—but Brooke smiled brightly and shrugged off her backpack, sitting in the shade and accepting a tomato happily. After a moment I took off my pack as well, though I told them I preferred to stand, and watched as they went about their business with the vegetables. There were five of them at the stand: Sister Debbie and Brother Stan, the two who'd greeted us, and behind them were Sister Tracy, Sister Molly, and Brother Zeke. The names seemed strange to me—not really biblical, and not from any other religious tradition I could think of, either. They were just names, and the only benefit to getting a new one seemed to be the loss of the old one, a clean break from your former life, which tied you to this new community only in the sense that you weren't tied to anything else anymore.

We spent the day with them, most of it talking, because the stand did very little business. I planned out how to kill each one of them if I needed to: a stab here, a slash there, the entire group gone before they could fight back. But I couldn't just kill people. The road had some traffic, but not much, and the few customers who came seemed to be regulars—locals who knew the cultists by name and bought a bushel of carrots or potatoes without bothering to ask the price. They looked nervously at Brooke and me, perhaps wondering if they could save us from whatever indoctrination lay in store. But they didn't do anything and drove away, and we watched the sun arc lazily across the sky, pulling us slowly toward evening.

I was not, I decided, imagining the emptiness. Sister Debbie and the others were friendly, but there was nothing behind it—no real concern for us or for anything else, just a rote recitation of meaningless small talk. Sometime in the afternoon they started over, repeating the same pleasantries, the same jokes, the same cheerful affirmations that had filled the morning, and my sense of unease grew deeper. Brooke chattered along as if nothing were out of the ordinary, and I wondered how many personalities had come and gone during the day, holding the same conversations one after the other without ever realizing it. It made me angry—it made me furious—to think that these hollow shells of former people might be the perfect match for my only friend left in the world. I closed my eyes and counted, running through number sequences and old recipes, estimating how many pots of vegetable soup I could make with the ingredients here in the stand. Anything to take my mind off of Brooke and the hell I had put her through. She didn't deserve this—brain-dead small talk in the middle of nowhere. She deserved a house. A bed she could sleep in more than two nights in a row. An education in math and English and science, instead of just How to Wash Your Clothes in a Truck Stop Bathroom, How To Hide From The Demon Army Chasing Us. She deserved a boyfriend that loved her back. I was trying my best to give her what I could, but John Cleaver and Boy Dog are a sorry excuse for a family.

After we kill the Withered, I thought. *A normal life can wait—don't get distracted. Don't lose track of why we're really here.* The Withered were killers, they were torturers, they were supernatural monsters; everything we'd never wanted to believe was real. Yashodh, whatever his methods, had stolen these five people's lives so completely they didn't even realize it—five walking corpses, physically alive but mentally gone. People who did that to other people had to be stopped. Brooke was the best possible reminder of why, and her memory, faulty as it was, was my only way to find them. I wouldn't let them hurt anyone else like they'd hurt her.

But how much was I hurting her in the meantime?

It wasn't quite dusk yet when a flatbed truck pulled to a stop beside us, and a man stepped out and introduced himself as Brother Lance. The six of them started packing up the vegetables, and Brooke and I pitched in, leaving the old wooden stand empty until tomorrow. They climbed into the back with the crates of food, and I lifted Boy Dog up after them. We held tight to the metal handrails as the truck rocked gently back and forth through a three-point turn and then rattled back down the road where it had come from. I looked at Brooke, and she looked at me, and we watched each other quietly as the sun dropped out of sight and the bright blue sky turned yellow, then orange, then a blue so deep that all the other colors of the world seemed to fall into it and disappear. Brother Lance turned on his headlights, and we pulled off onto a dirt road, passing through a nondescript gate and driving toward an old white farmhouse that seemed to shine as the light beams hit it.

"Home again," said Sister Debbie, smiling with the same mellow emptiness she'd used earlier to point out a bird flying over the vegetable stand.

The truck stopped, and I jumped out before lifting Boy Dog down with a grunt. He explored the dirt driveway, sniffing the tire tracks and the tufts of night-black grass. I turned back to help

Brooke, but she was already down, and put a hand on my arm, pressing close to whisper in my ear.

"I'm sad."

Instantly I worried about another suicide attempt, but before I could even start the process of changing her mind, she shook her head, pressing closer and forcing me a few steps to the side, out of earshot of the cultists. "Not for me," she said. "For them."

I glanced at the six farmers unloading the truck, listless and cheerful all at once. "You think they're sad?"

"I don't think they can be sad," said Brooke. "So I'm being sad for them."

Brother Stan nodded toward us, his arms full of vegetable boxes. "Would you mind grabbing a crate each and following me up to the house? I can introduce you to Christopher."

"This is it," I whispered to Brooke. "I don't want you to freak out, but I want you to be ready to run if we have to. Okay?"

"Okay."

"We don't know what we're going to find in there, and we don't know what this Withered can do, so just . . . be ready for anything."

"I'm not going to freak out," she said, stooping to pick up a crate.

I picked up one of my own and followed her, ten or twenty steps behind Brother Stan. "I just don't want to take you by surprise, okay? We're partners in this."

"I'll take care of you," said Brooke.

Brother Stan waited for us by the door, propping it open with his foot. After a moment of terrified hesitation, I went in. It scared me to be here, so far from help, so far from anything, but the lights were on, and I could hear happy voices murmuring in a nearby room. The door led in to a kitchen, and we set the wooden crates on the floor where Brother Stan pointed.

"I'll go get Christopher," said Brother Stan, and I realized it was unsettling to hear him talk about someone, especially a fellow cult-ist, without "Brother" at the beginning. Christopher lived here, but he was fundamentally different from the others. I didn't know what to expect. Brother Stan left us alone in the kitchen, and I felt for the gun in the back of my waistband, hidden by my shirt. The magazine was hidden in one of my backpack straps, in a pocket I'd made by digging out the padding. There was no way we could kill a Withered with something as simple as a gun, but it might buy us enough time to get out.

"The dirt road was a straight shot in from the gate," I said. "Maybe a hundred yards at the most. If I say go, you go, okay? Don't wait for me, just get out, and I promise I'll be right behind you."

"Don't worry," she said, "I'll protect you."

"He can control people's minds," I said. "We don't know how, but we don't want to give him a chance to try it. Just—"

"Calm down," said Brooke. "I told you, I've got this."

Her assurance only made me more nervous. "What are you going to do?"

"I'm going to stop him from controlling our minds," said Brooke.

"You don't have . . . powers," I said. "You remember that, right?"

"Of course I know that," Brooke whispered. "But he doesn't."

"Brooke—"

Footsteps clomped toward us down the hall, and I ran through my story again, looking for any last minute ways to polish it, to craft the perfect lie that would help ingratiate us into his community, to give us the time to get to know him, to find his weaknesses, to stay under his radar until the perfect time to strike.

A short, dark man walked into the room. He was balding on top, with a wispy gray mullet behind his ears. Mid fifties, I guessed, with skin and features that suggested Middle Eastern heritage. He smiled when he saw us, not like the cultists did, but a broad, genuine smile that seemed almost shocking after a day full of pale imitations. "My name is Christopher," he said, and his voice was thin but firm. "Welcome to the Spirit of Light. I understand you're looking for Sister Kara?"

I opened my mouth to answer, but Brooke spoke first. "Actually we're looking for you," she said. "It's been a long time, Yashodh."

I tensed, moving my hand closer to the gun magazine. What was she doing?

Christopher blinked in surprise, then took a step back and eyed us suspiciously. "Who are you?"

"That's the trouble with these bodies," said Brooke. "No one ever recognizes me." She dropped her backpack to the floor, and spread her arms slightly, presenting herself like an old friend. "It's me: Hulla. I'm Nobody."

4

Yashodh watched us warily.

My hand itched to lunge for the gun.

"Brother Stan," said Yashodh. "Can you help get the rest of the truck unloaded?"

"Of course," said Brother Stan, walking past him toward the door. I stepped to the side, circling slightly so that he never blocked my view of Yashodh. I don't know what prompted Brooke to spill our secrets like that, but I wanted to be ready if it all went to hell. Brother Stan walked outside and off the porch, and the door banged closed behind him.

"Who are you with?" asked Yashodh softly.

"With each other," said Nobody.

"I mean which side," said Yashodh. "Rack's trying to raise an army. Are you here to press me into it?"

"No," I said quickly. If he used the word "press," then he didn't want to join the Withered army at all; we needed to seem like allies. "We're trying to stay out of the whole thing, like you."

Yashodh studied me a moment, then looked back at Nobody. "Who's he?"

"He's mine," said Nobody, "and you don't touch him."

"Fair enough," said Yashodh. "And you won't touch any of mine? We haven't had a death here in decades; I don't want to have to explain one of your suicides the next time the police come through for an inspection."

"No fuss from either side," said Nobody. "We just want to talk."

Yashodh paused again, watching us, until at last he nodded. "I have a private room. We can talk in there."

He led us through the house, past a sitting room full of a dozen or so cultists singing quietly to themselves. They beamed when they saw him, whispering his name in a sibilant chorus: "Christopher Christopher Christopher Christopher." He slowed and gestured to them but didn't stop, leading us up the stairs to a small office with an old kitchen table for a desk. The wooden chairs were mismatched, and the carpet was a spiral pattern woven from old scraps and rags. He closed the door behind us and sat with a heavy sigh.

"I knew it was only a matter of time," he said. "It was bad enough before Fort Bruce, but after . . . " He shook his head. "It's a horrible thing, to look at a massacre like that and not be able to tell who won."

"Twenty-three humans dead," I said.

"And not a word from Rack since," said Yashodh. "If that was a victory for the Withered, their recruitment efforts would have stepped up, not down."

"Did he come to you?" asked Nobody.

"Not yet," said Yashodh. "But I have friends who've sent me word of his plans. Though even them I haven't heard from lately."

"Nashuja," I said, venturing a guess. Nashuja we had killed last month, she was a grizzled woman who made her living as a long-haul trucker. She picked up hitchhikers and killed them in empty rest stops, cracking open their bones and sucking out the marrow, crying for the mothers who would never see their children again.

Yashodh shook his head. "Dag," he said. We had killed Dag four months earlier. "I haven't heard from Nashuja in . . . hundreds of years at least. I didn't know she kept in contact with anyone."

"Kanta found her a few years ago," said Nobody. "I worked with him before he died."

"Kanta was on Rack's side," said Yashodh, and his voice sounded tired. "He wanted to get us all together, like the old days—the god emperors come back at last." He gestured around his office. "This is where we are today. This is what we are. Not gods anymore, just . . . " He shook his head. "They want to recruit me? They want *this* for their kingdom? Forty-six walking coma patients, smart enough to pull weeds and sew a few shirts and . . . " he gestured in the air, searching for words, " . . . wave at each other in the room downstairs? I'd be useless in a war."

Yashodh hates himself, I thought. It wasn't much of a weakness, but it was a start.

"Rack's plan is what put us here in the first place," said Nobody. "We'd been fine for millennia, hidden and surviving, and then he tried to get back into power and the humans noticed us. They fought back. Rack killed twenty-three of them in Fort Bruce, but they killed five of us, and we can't survive those odds. We have to go back into hiding."

"So why are you here?" asked Yashodh. "You can go anywhere and be anyone, but I'm always me. I always have a cult. I can't survive anywhere else, or any way else. They'll find me, Rack or the humans or both. And if you're with me they'll find you, too."

Interesting. He'd said, "I'm always me." Did that mean he

couldn't change his shape the way so many Withered could? The FBI suspected that the Withered's ancient origins were in neolithic Turkey; what I had seen as a vaguely Middle Eastern appearance could easily be Turkish. Was this really the same body Yashodh had had for ten thousand years? What else did that suggest about him? I needed him to keep talking about himself, hoping it could suggest something useful about the way his powers worked. I thought of a new tactic and started talking.

"Strength in numbers," I said. "Rack's plan failed because he started poking the bear, causing trouble and getting noticed. But if we stay quiet, if we stay low, then we can survive in the shadows and help defend each other from Rack's recruiters. Whatever powers you have to fight back, two Withered are still better than one, right?"

Yashodh stared at me a moment, then turned back to Nobody. "What's with him, anyway? He knows an awful lot."

"We're partners," said Nobody.

"But that's not like you," said Yashodh. "You attach yourself to women because you want what they have, and sometimes that includes their men. But once you've got whatever it is, you're never satisfied with it. How long have you been with this kid, without another suicide?"

"People change," said Nobody.

"Not us," said Yashodh, shaking his head. "Certainly not you and me. We're the worst of them—the lowest, the weakest, the most repulsive—"

"But even a weak Withered is strong," I said. "You have to have something. Hulla's killed more girls than we can count, but they've all been herself. If Rack's army is still out there, and if they come for us, we can't fight back. We need your help."

Yashodh kept his eyes on Nobody, studying her as I talked. After a moment he pursed his lips. "Is that what it is?" he asked. "You've stopped killing altogether, so now you're weak and you think I can help you? Well let me tell you something, human." He turned to face me. "I'm even more worthless than she is. I can't fight, I can't kill, I can't do anything. I can make people love me, and if it works then life is tolerable; if it doesn't then no one loves me at all and I have nothing, and what is the point of living? I'll kill myself, just like she does. Except I won't come back." He opened his hands in a sudden burst. "Poof. I'm gone. You want me to fight a war, but it's all I can do to stay one step ahead of oblivion. You're better off without me, because at least you're alive—all I am is not dead yet."

I felt my hands trembling. *Does this mean what I think it does?* "You have to have something," I said. "How fast can you heal?"

He pulled back the sleeve of his shirt, exposing a dull red welt on his arm. "I got this scratch pruning pyracantha bushes last week." He covered it again. "I don't heal any faster than you do. And when the armies finally come, they'll hurt a lot more than a pyracantha."

"I'm so sorry," said Nobody. "I didn't know." She'd realized the same thing I had. A tear rolled down her face. "I'm so, so sorry."

I reached into the dug-out pocket in my backpack strap, extracted the loaded magazine, and then pulled the gun from the back of my belt.

"Wait," said Yashodh, "what's going on?"

I couldn't just kill people. Except for when I could. I slid the magazine into the gun, clicked it into place, and shot him in the chest. The gunshot rang in my ears, and Nobody covered hers, turning away and crying. Boy Dog howled, backing into the corner. Yashodh looked down at the bullet hole, moving his mouth, but no sound came out. He looked up, staring at me as if searching my face for answers, and then his body crumbled into thick, ashy sludge.

Soulstuff, they called it. In ten seconds he was gone, with nothing but dark, acrid muck sizzling holes in the chair and the rug.

The door opened, and Sister Debbie looked in. "What was that sound?"

"Nothing," I said. "I thought I saw a bug."

Nobody was still crying.

Sister Debbie looked at the sludge, then all around the room. "Where is Christopher?"

"He left," I said. I pulled the magazine clear of the gun, popped the extra bullet out of the chamber, and put them all away. I'd have to find a new hiding place now that Nobody had seen this one. "Who's in charge here when he's gone?"

"He's never gone," said Sister Debbie.

"But if he steps out for a bit," I said. "Like, if he goes into town for the day? Who's in charge?"

"He's always in charge," said Sister Debbie. "Always and everywhere, over everything there is. I love him so much." She smiled. "Isn't it great to be alive?"

"You're asking the wrong people," I said, pulling Nobody to her feet. "It's time for us to go."

We picked up our packs and left the house. No one followed us. We left the farm and followed the road until we could no longer see to walk, then curled up together against the trunk of a tree, my arm around Brooke's shoulders.

"I didn't like that," she whispered.

"Neither did I." I wanted to like it. Killing was an important thing to do; killing was necessary. Killing demons made the world a better place, and the actual act of killing, well . . . I knew I wasn't supposed to enjoy it, but I did. Usually. The sharp thrill of it, of watching a living person turn into a dead one. I'd grown up in a

mortuary, surrounded by my parents' work, more at home with the
dead than the living, but Withered didn't turn into dead bodies,
they just melted into ash. Everything I wanted, except none of it
at all.

I wanted to light a fire.

Had it really been that easy? Was Yashodh really gone forever?
All he'd wanted was for someone to love him because he couldn't
love himself. Ten thousand years staving off death one whispered
adulation at a time, only to end here. Shot in his own home by a
stranger he thought was a friend.

"I don't want to do this anymore," said Brooke.

"Only a few left," I said.

"There will always be a few more left."

"Attina," I said. "And then . . . whoever's chasing us."

"The FBI is chasing us," said Brooke. "Please don't kill them."

"Of course I'm not going to kill them," I said. "I've never killed
a human." Well, never a good one.

"But you want to," she said.

"That's how you know I'll never do it."

She started crying again. "Is this all there is? Dirt on old roads,
secret pockets full of bullets . . . "

"I want to give you a real life—"

"Because I can't handle this one," she said, and all the alarms in
my head went off.

"You were a superstar back there," I told her, trying to feed her
self-worth. "That could have taken us weeks, maybe months to figure out, but you got him talking in five minutes. In two. I never
would have just told him who we were—you're brilliant, Brooke."

She growled her answer through clenched teeth. "My name is
Nobody."

"You are brilliant," I said again. "You said you'd protect me and you did. Partners to the end. I could never do this alone."

"Do you think that's going to make me happy?" she asked. She wrenched away from me, and I could see her silhouette in the starlight, sitting in the dirt a foot away. "I just told you that I hate this, that I never want to do it again, that I don't want to be a killer and watch anybody die, human or demon or anything else, not a bird or a bug or germ in my blood, and all you can think of to tell me is how good I am at it, how responsible I am for all the blood on all our hands—"

"That's not what I meant," I said, "and you know it. You know how good this is. You saw those people, without . . . without a brain between them, and you know that if Yashodh had lived he'd have done it to more of them, that he'd already done it to tens, if not hundreds of thousands, of people, a giant parade of brainwashed nobodies stretching back to the beginning of time, and it ended tonight."

"That's not funny."

"I'm not trying to be f— What does funny have to do with it?"

"You called them brainwashed Nobodies," said Brooke. "I am not brainwashed."

"I wasn't talking about you—"

"Then don't use my name!" she shouted. She stood up, and I rose with her, terrified of what she might do. There were no trucks to jump in front of on this empty road, but the area might hold a dozen other ways to kill yourself. "I am Nobody!" she screamed. "It's my name and my job and my entire wasted life! I can't be you, John, I can't just . . . turn off my heart whenever it hurts."

"Neither can I."

"Then why don't you love me?"

I thought she would run, but she grabbed my arms, squeezing with her fingers and shaking us both. "Why am I so horrible that you won't even love me when I'm the only one around, the only friend you have, the last girl in your entire world and you still won't love me!"

I wrapped her in a hug, hoping the physical contact might help to bring her back and calm her down. I pressed my cheek against hers, felt her trembling and sobbing, felt cold tears on her skin. I held her and shushed her and calmed her, rocking her slowly, sitting us down again, trying to think of something I could do to make her happy again. I wanted to love her—I wanted it more than anything—but I couldn't tell her that. It would only make it worse that I didn't.

"I suck at loving people," I said at last. "I did it once, and she's dead now."

"That's why you can't give her up," Brooke croaked. "A corpse is your perfect woman."

"I'm the most screwed up loser you've ever met," I said. "My perfect woman is the last thing you want to be."

"One day I'm going to do it," she whispered. "I'm going to kill myself, and you won't be around to stop me."

"Then I'll go into Hell," I said, "and I'll bring you back."

We leaned against that tree for another hour before she finally fell asleep. I stared at the empty sky above us. She'd said couldn't do it anymore, and I honestly didn't know if I could, either. I needed to light a fire. I shifted her gently, inch by inch, until I was out from underneath her, and I laid her down with her head on my backpack. She moved in her sleep, finding a better position, but she didn't wake up. I crawled through the dirt on my knees, gathering twigs and pinecones fallen from the branches above us, finding them all by touch in the darkness. I piled them up in a tent shape, barely the size of my fists, and pulled a matchbook from the pocket of my jeans. I lit a match and it flared to life, brilliant in the blackness. I tried it in the kindling but it didn't catch so I dropped it in the center of my pile and lit another, bright and orange, like a beacon of life in a sea of nothing. I shielded the flame with my hand and put it in the heart of the kindling, and this time it worked, spreading slowly from match to dead grass to stick. I tended the flame carefully, feeding it more fuel, watching the wood turn black and the grass curl up. It caught in the heart of a pinecone and burned it from the inside out, bits of wood and sap snapping and crackling in the heat. It wasn't a big fire, but I didn't need it for warmth. I just needed it. I watched it burn and listened to its voice, and when it went to sleep I did too, curled up on the ground next to Brooke and Boy Dog, my messed up little family in the middle of nowhere.

When I woke up Brooke was still there, breathing softly. We'd made it through another night. I watched the sky grow lighter, the black mass of the horizon slowly resolving into a row of trees on the edge of a field. A crow hopped on a fencepost, watching us from the other side of the road, then cawed roughly and flapped away. I let Brooke sleep as long as I could, and when she stirred she looked at me blearily.

"Where to next?"

"Attina," I said.

She nodded. "No one's heard from him in decades, but the last contact was in a town called Dillon."

"What do you remember about him?" I asked.

"Nothing." Brooke watched the sky, though there wasn't anything in it. "Attina doesn't come from my past, just my memories of Kanta's notes—all I remember is one line: 'Last seen in Dillon, Oklahoma. Probably useless.' I don't know what he can do, how he can do it, or anything."

DAN WELLS

"That's not much to work with," I said.

"Sorry."

"It's not your fault," I said quickly. "We have a location, so we go there and start looking."

We walked along the back road for an hour before we reached a two-lane highway, and then walked another hour before a car picked us up. We told the driver we didn't care where he was going, we just needed a town, and he dropped us at a gas station on the edge of a town called Forest Dell. We cleaned up in the restroom, changed into our cleanest-looking clothes, and I spent some of our precious money on two bags of peanuts and bottle of vitamins. We drank from the hose before the owner drove us off, and while we waited for another ride I studied the worn map I kept in my bag. Dillon was close, relatively speaking. A few hundred miles, but a mostly straight shot. We found a trucker willing to take us to the highway junction, and hitched another ride from there to just outside of town. Brooke was quiet all day—not depressed but simply solemn, lost in thought. I fed Boy Dog beef jerky from my pack and watched the wide, flat country roll by.

When we reached Dillon it was night again, the sky black and the stars half-shrouded in wisps of cloud. The light from the moon turned the clouds a pale gray, and they were so transparent they seemed to hang behind the moon instead of in front of it, like the cold, slate wall of a closed universe. The driver asked if we had a place to stay, and I assured her we did, because the last thing we needed was a Good Samaritan calling Child Protective Services, trying to "help" us. We were eighteen years old and legally independent, but we didn't look it and we had no ID to prove it. The woman drove away, and I looked around at the nearest buildings: a low barn, a closed barbershop, an old drive-in movie theater. There was a high wooden wall around it, but the wooden screen was even higher; it loomed above the rest of the area like a pale giant. There was no movie playing on it, and white paper hung from it in wrinkled tears.

"We can stay there."

Brooke stood still, looking at her arms as if she'd never seen them before.

"There's probably an old concession stand inside," I said. "Or a ticket booth at the very least. If we can't get inside we can sleep in the lee of it—it'll block the wind."

"John," she said.

"Yeah?"

"John Cleaver?"

I looked at her more closely. "Who are you now?"

She smiled, more widely than I'd seen in weeks. "John, it's me. I mean, it doesn't look like me, and I don't know exactly what's going on, but . . . it's me inside." She ran toward me, and wrapped me in a hug. "You're back," she murmured. "Or I am."

I felt a cold fear wash through me. "Who are you?"

"This body has everyone Nobody ever killed. Every memory, every personality, right up until she left Brooke's body. This is Brooke's body, isn't it? I totally recognize it now."

I shook my head, seeing the truth, not knowing if I should shout for joy or turn and run away forever.

Not this. This was too much.

"It's me, John," said Brooke. "It's Marci."

5

I backed away from her.

"I know this is weird," said Marci.

"Weird is the least of what's wrong with this."

"It's so . . . dark in there," said Marci. "In *here*, I mean; in Brooke. There's so many of us, all trapped, all together but all alone. I remember when Nobody came to me that night—"

"Please don't."

"It was the night of the dance. You took me home, and you kissed me again, and it was the most perfect night of the world and I never wanted it to end, but then I went into my house and there she was. Some kind of big, black blob. Soulstuff, I guess they call it. It was behind me and around me and I fought it with everything I had but I couldn't make it stop, and I couldn't get away—"

"Please don't." I was crying now.

"She came in through my mouth, and my nose, and even my ears," said Marci. "You know what it's like, because she tried to take you, too, before your mom saved you. I know that because Brooke knows that. I didn't have anyone there to help me, so she came inside and . . . then I wasn't me anymore. I was just watching. It took her a while to get control, but I was lost right then. Right at the beginning. That was the worst part, really—being in there for days and hearing her talk to you, and I screamed to try to warn you, but nothing worked, and you never knew, and then she decided she wanted Brooke instead, and there was nothing I could do to stop her from killing us." She paused. "They're all in there, you know, just like that. Some of them can hear us, some of them can't. Maybe Brooke is listening—"

"Just stop!" I shouted. "Please just stop. I didn't want to hurt you, and I didn't want you to die, and I'm sorry I didn't see it coming sooner but please just . . . " I didn't know what to say. Marci was everything I'd ever wanted, but she was gone, and her absence defined my life. Having her back again like this, in my best friend's stolen body, was as wrenching a change as losing her had ever been.

"I'm sorry," she said, walking toward me, reaching out to hold me. I backed away, crying harder, swatting weakly at her hands—but when I touched her I thought of Marci's hands, and the peace I used to feel when I was holding them, and I closed my eyes and broke down in sobs. Brooke's body caught me and held me, soothing me like I'd soothed her last night.

Boy Dog whined at the stars, and I cried until my tears ran dry.

"You've changed," said Marci, stepping back to look at me but still holding my shoulders. I looked into Brooke's eyes and wondered how many girls were looking back out, trying to talk to me, screaming in the darkness. And how many were just lost, buried like Marci had been, waiting to wake up and look around and wonder where they'd been?

When would she wake up as a thousand-year-old girl I couldn't even talk to, and I'd lose both Brooke and Marci forever?

"You never used to cry," said Marci.

"You did that," I said. "Or my mom did, I guess. You died, and I broke, and now I feel things differently but I . . . am not really good at it."

"I'm sorry about your mom."

"She's not—" And then another wave of emotion gripped me. "She's not in there too, is she?"

"No," said Marci, shaking Brooke's head. "Nobody took your mom after she left Brooke—whatever new thoughts she had in those few seconds, and whatever she gained from your mom, was all lost in the fire." She put Brooke's hand on my face. "I'm sorry."

I pulled away, slower than before but still deliberate. I couldn't process this yet: Marci, back again. It had always been a possibility, of course, but I had never dared to think of it because I had never dared to think of Marci. I hadn't made a healthy personal connection in years, maybe in my whole life, but I had with her, and then I'd lost it, and now to have it back in the worst possible way. . . .

"Do we have a place to stay?" asked Marci. She looked around at the darkened town; we could see streetlights in the distance, closer to the center, but here on the edge it was lifeless and empty.

"How much do you know?" I asked. "A lot of the memories seem to blend together for Brooke; one personality dominates for a while, but they all seem to share certain—" And then I had to stop because I knew she was only going to leave me again. "How long will you be here?"

"As long as I can be," she said.

"How long is that?"

She spoke softly. "I don't know." She looked away again. "I think it's like you say: I have some of her memories, but nothing concrete. Impressions, mostly. The last thing I remember clearly was the suicide, when Nobody slit my wrists. But it's not like I jumped straight from that moment to this one, you know? I'm aware, some-how, that time has passed, and that I'm in another body, and that there are other girls in here with us."

"Did you . . . talk to them?"

"It's not like that," said Marci, "it's more of a . . . I don't know. I think I was aware of everything Nobody did in my body because it was my body, and I was still in there, but now I'm not . . . I'm not me, I guess. I'm my memories. Maybe I'm actually Brooke and I only think I'm Marci, but I remember everything—things Brooke never knew, things nobody ever knew—and I *feel* like me. The body's weird, I'll grant you—I was never this thin—but I really feel like *me*. My personality, my habits, my . . . self. I guess I just con-tradicted myself, like, five times in one breath, but . . . does that make sense?"

"No," I said quickly, then shook my head and sighed. "But none of this does, and it hasn't for years."

"We're hunting demons, right?" said Marci.

"We were," I said, "but that's because Brooke wanted to. If you're you now—"

"Come on," said Marci, "remember who you're talking to. The cop's daughter and the mortician's son, together again." She raised her eyebrows with a mischievous smile, then shrugged. "This isn't really how I imagined our TV series would go, though."

"Nothing's gone the way we wanted," I said.

Boy Dog wandered toward us, back from exploring the smells of the area, and I gestured toward him. "By the way, this is Boy Dog. Boy Dog, Marci."

"His name is Boy Dog?"

"I didn't name him," I said.

"Obviously you would have gone with Harvey."

"Obviously." She knew me better than I remembered.

She crouched down and Boy Dog padded toward her and licked her hands and face. "Good boy," she said, scratching his ears. "Good Boy Dog. This is . . . " Her voice trailed off, and she put her hand on the asphalt.

And held it there, seconds ticking by into minutes, closing her eyes and simply . . . being.

"The road's warm," she said at last. "Just a little, but you can feel it. Asphalt traps the heat from the sun. And the breeze is cool, and it smells like . . . cows." She laughed, her eyes still closed. "Chlorophyll. I can smell cut grass and motor oil and lilacs. I haven't smelled a lilac in . . . how long has it been?"

"Two years," I whispered.

"Two years." She stood up slowly, opening her eyes to stare up at the sky. Boy Dog flopped to his belly, resting on her toes protectively. "Two years. The twins'll be six."

"You can't go back."

Her voice was a hoarse whisper. "I know." She stared at the sky for a moment longer, then looked at me and wiped her eyes. "Anyway. We're standing in the middle of the road in the middle of the night, with backpacks that I assume hold all our worldly possessions. Safe to assume we just got here?"

I nodded. "We hitchhiked."

"So now what?"

I stared at her helplessly. "I can't do this."

"Can't do what?"

"You know what," I said. "You . . . " I sighed, feeling like every word was a struggle. "I couldn't let Brooke get taken over by a demon, and now . . . "

"I'm not a demon."

You're the only person I ever loved, I thought, but I couldn't say it. I'd only ever said it to her corpse. "You're one of the most important people in my life," I said at last. "I want her to be herself, but I want you more than anything, and that's . . . this is too much."

"I won't be here forever," said Marci.

"You think that makes this better?"

"We can't just stand here in the street all night," said Marci. "I'm guessing we don't have a place to stay, so do we just . . . find one? Look for a motel, start knocking on doors—"

"We can't afford a motel," I said quickly. "We stayed in one two nights ago." One hundred and four dollars and eighty-six cents. The money we'd spent that night could have fed us for a week. I bit my lip, pained by the thought of Marci sleeping in the dirt, and tried to talk myself into splurging again. This was a special occasion, right? But no. At the rate Brooke flipped personalities, Marci might not even be around until morning. I rubbed my eyes and pointed toward the empty drive-in theater. "I was going to try that, but if you want to head further into town maybe we can find a . . . I don't know. A YMCA or something."

"In a place this small?" asked Marci. "Come on, John, I'm, like, the outdoor queen. We have a tent?"

"Just open air."

"Sweet," she said. "Let's do this."

We walked to the gate of the drive-in, and I couldn't help but study the way she moved. Was she walking like Marci? That slight sway of her hips—was that Marci or had Brooke always walked like that? In my memory Marci would swagger around, sensual and confident. Was that gone now, replaced by Brooke's physical mannerisms? Or had I exaggerated it all in my mind, remembering a girl who would never walk anywhere, ever again?

The gate was locked and not especially climbable, so we followed the fence around, looking for an easier access point. Despite Marci's statement that it was the middle of the night, it was only 9:30

or 10 at the latest; if the theater were still in use, there'd have been a movie playing. We found a pair of broken boards in the wooden wall and slipped through to find a wide, flat field full of four-foot metal poles, parking spaces between them. The top of each pole held a small speaker on a curled cord—or at least they did back when the drive-in was still operating; now most of them were broken, dangling, or missing altogether. The inside of the wooden fence was covered with graffiti—no murals or gang signs, just scrawled names and cuss words. The ground was littered with broken bottles.

"Looks like it's been abandoned for a while," said Marci.

"And we're not the only ones to use it since," I said, looking at the garbage. "Let's hope we're the only ones who use it tonight."

A low brick building stood in the back, just inside the gate, and I walked toward it. "Careful of the glass, Boy Dog," I said. We walked silently, worried about disturbing other squatters, but I couldn't imagine a little place like Dillon had a lot of those. The building was closed and locked. It had a metal door, and a wide metal plate with hinges at the top, which I assumed used to swing open for the concession window. The short wall closest to the gate had a ticket window; its glass was broken and the opening was blocked by metal bars. I rattled the padlocks, but they were all solid. "We need a—"

"Whooooooo!"

The loud holler soared across the empty lot, and I looked up just in time to see a glass bottle smash into the ground. Someone had thrown it over the wall, and a figure was coming in through the same fence hole we'd used.

"Stay quiet," I said, but Boy Dog barked at the intruder. "Dammit."

"Dog!" shouted a voice, and the figure by the hole stood up abruptly, looking for the animal.

"Since when do they have a guard dog?" asked another voice, and another figure climbed through the hole.

"Get behind the building," I whispered, but the first figure pointed to us.

"It's not a guard dog, it's just more people. Hey, people!" He waved, and a third person came through the hole. "You got any booze?"

"All three male," said Marci, though I couldn't see any of them clearly. "Teenage boys, it looks like."

"Be careful," I said, watching the figures approach. We were trapped, though they didn't appear to be intentionally cutting us off—as quickly as my paranoia had thought "someone followed us," I discarded the idea. This was just three teenage guys out for a good time.

Though that could be just as dangerous.

6

Boy Dog barked again, and Marci whispered under her breath, "I don't like this."

The three boys walked closer, coming slowly into focus. I guessed they were about our age, probably seniors in high school. The smell of alcohol was strong.

"You guys from Crosby?" asked one of them. He wore a baseball cap, though I didn't recognize the logo.

I remembered the map I'd used to find Dillon; Crosby was the next town over. "Just passing through," I said.

"I know Ms. Glassman has family in town," said the second boy, brushing his long blond hair out of his face. "You guys, like, grandkids or something?"

"Glassman doesn't have kids," said Ball Cap. "How's she gonna have grandkids?"

"She doesn't have legitimate kids," said Blondie, "that doesn't mean she doesn't have any. It's like the twenty-first century, man, get out of the dark ages."

"You're homeless," said the third boy. It wasn't a

question, but an observation. Despite the summer warmth he was wearing a dark jacket, though I couldn't tell what color it was.

"Not homeless," said Marci carefully, "but you're right that we don't have a place to stay. You know of anything here in town?"

"You can stay at my place," said Blondie, and he grinned wickedly. "I'll even let you stay in my bed."

I imagined myself stabbing him in the neck, right under the chin, behind the jaw and up through the skull into his brain. I twisted the knife to the side, and felt the crack of the bones. It was against my rules to entertain those kinds of thoughts and I knew I should push it out of my mind, but this was different—this was a direct threat to Marci, to Brooke, to the two most important people in my life.

"We're fine," I said. But I let my right hand hang loosely at my side, ready to stoop and pull my combat knife from where I kept it strapped to my shin, under my pant leg.

"Were you going to sleep here?" asked Ball Cap. "Dude, that's . . . that's kind of awesome. Are you, like, runaways or something?"

"Just travelers," I said. "Graduated high school last year, didn't want to start college yet, so we're just backpacking around for a while."

"Most people do that in Europe," said Ball Cap.

"I don't like flying," I said.

"This is crazy!" laughed Blondie. "Can you imagine going on vacation to friggin' Dillon? That's got to be the worst decision anyone's ever made." He jerked his chin at Marci. "Trip not really turning out as awesome as he said it would, am I right?"

Marci smiled. "Actually, Dillon was my idea. I picked it right off the map. Thought it looked cute."

"Cute," said Blondie, looking at Ball Cap. "We're cute." He

turned back to Marci. "I won't say it was the best decision of your life, but we can show you around if you want. We have a bowling alley, and the guy doesn't card for beer."

I had forgotten how smoothly Marci could manipulate people, boys especially. She knew how social interactions worked in a way that I had never understood and still didn't; she was as good at social deception as Brooke was bad at it. Blondie watched her expectantly. In one sentence Marci had turned his mocking joke into an offer of help.

But Blondie's help was the last thing I wanted right now. "We're fine," I said again. How could we get them to leave, or how could we leave without being followed?

"My name is Corey," said the boy in the jacket. He pointed his thumb at Ball Cap and Blondie in turn. "This is Paul and Derek." He looked around at the empty lot, then back at me. "We don't get a lot of new people in town."

"I'm Marci," said Marci, "and this is—"

"David," I said, cutting her off. Marci's name was fine, but Brooke and I were wanted by the FBI. David was the first name that came to mind, though I realized almost instantly that I had gotten it from David Berkowitz, the Son of Sam. Was that too much of a clue?

I was being paranoid.

My hand itched for the knife.

"So," said Ball Cap—Paul, the guy said his name was—"this is fascinating to me. You're just, what, hitchhiking around the country? Were you planning to sleep here?"

"That's what we were hoping," said Marci, "but there's an awful lot of broken glass."

"Yeah, sorry about that," said Blondie. *Derek.* "This place is a pretty common hangout for the kids at school—kind of hidden, kind of isolated. Not everyone's as cool as the dude at the bowling alley, so this is a great place to get drunk." He leered at Marci. "A lot of guys bring their girlfriends here too, it's kind of our Make-out Point."

"It's been a really long day," I said, trying to sound calm. "Do you guys mind—"

"The building is full of broken glass, too," said Paul, walking to the barred window. "Probably a couple of inches of it; people chuck bottles through the bars all the time."

"Come on," said Derek, "it's early! It's barely ten o'clock! Corey's got more beer in his bag, let's make this a party!"

I looked at Corey, standing so quietly in the back, and realized that he had a backpack I hadn't seen, hidden in the silhouette of his jacket. He stood a moment, watching us, then slowly shrugged the pack off and handed it to Derek. Was he looking at me or at Marci? Whichever it was, his eyes didn't leave us for a second.

"Beer!" shouted Derek, and he cracked one open, sucking the suds off the top of the can when it foamed. Paul took another can from the pack and offered it to Marci, but she declined. He held it out to me, and I shook my head.

"Suit yourself," he said, and he cracked it open.

Derek was chugging his entire can, which was now sticking straight up in the air above his mouth. He gulped it down loudly, then tilted his head down to look at us, smiling broadly. He belched and threw the can to the side, then went immediately for another.

I kept having to remind myself, over and over, that they didn't mean us harm, that they were just three dumb guys out looking for fun in a small town. I'd grown up in a small town and I knew how boring they could get. Drinking stolen beer at the old drive-in might literally be the most interesting part of their entire week—or least it would have been, if we weren't here. We were a novelty. Given the opportunity, they'd hang out with us all night.

I couldn't allow that, but I didn't know how to stop it without starting a fight.

"It's no fun unless you drink with us," said Paul, sipping his beer more moderately.

"But they're not with us," said Corey. He didn't seem to speak often, but when he did it was simple and to the point. "They're just here, purely by chance, and tomorrow they'll be somewhere else."

"All the more reason to drink right now," said Derek, opening his second can. "Man, I wish I was like you guys—free to go anywhere, do anything, just screw all the responsibilities and jobs and whatever the hell other stuff the rest of us are stuck with." He took a long pull on his beer, then pointed to me with his fingers wrapped around the can. "I bet you just steal stuff all the time, right? Like, whatever you need—pies off windowsills and Doritos off the shelf at a truck stop—because who's gonna find you? They look up and you're gone, and you're never going to see those idiots again."

"And no one ever sees him again," said Corey. "Or her."

They're not here to hurt us, I told myself again.

"That's a good point," said Paul, his speech slightly slurred. Either he'd already been drinking or he didn't hold his liquor well. "How does this work, like, mechanically? Do you choose where you go? Darcy said she picked this place on purpose—"

"Marci," said Derek.

"Marci," Paul corrected himself. "Why come here instead of just going where the cars take you? Like, how does hitchhiking work? Do you ask them to take you somewhere?"

"Have a beer," said Derek, handing another can to Marci.

"No thank you," she said again. Her voice was thin and even; she was as uncomfortable as I was.

"Come on," said Derek, "a hot girl like you needs to loosen up."

He stepped toward her. "Let me help you take that backpack off, it looks way heavy."

I stepped forward quickly, inserting myself between them, and Derek backed off, holding up his hands in innocence.

"Sorry, wow, touched a nerve there. Didn't mean to move in on your girlfriend."

"Please," Marci whispered, and I knew she was talking to me. *Don't start anything.*

"Do you coordinate with somebody?" asked Paul, oblivious to the mounting tension. "Like, does somebody know what route you're taking? Or is it literally just 'go where the wind takes you'? Like, does anyone even know where you are?"

"I doubt it," said Corey.

"Then what the hell is your problem?" demanded Derek, suddenly angry. Hadn't she gotten him on our side? Weren't they trying to impress her? Or had they already given up impressing her, and now it was time to punish her for not being interested?

Derek waved his hand at us, taking in our backpacks, our clothes, everything we had in the world. "A couple of homeless nobodies," he said, "sleeping in the friggin' Movie Time Theater, and you think you're better than us? Can't have a drink with us, can't even talk to us? You act like you can't wait for us to leave."

"Can you blame him?" asked Corey, and this time I knew he was looking at Marci.

Paul giggled, and I felt the hairs on the back of my neck stand up, as alert to the sudden danger as I would be to a cold breeze.

"Abso-damn-lutely!" shouted Derek, wagging his finger at me before taking another swig from his can. "You're not an a-hole, you're just trying to get lucky. You were hoping to tap this chick right here in the theater, while your friggin' dog watches, and now you can't because we're all up in your love nest." He threw the second beer can and opened a third.

"What'll you give us if we leave?" asked Paul.

Derek looked at Brooke's body. "What'll *you* give us?"

"I think it's time for you to go," said Marci.

"Oh man," said Derek. "She wants it too. Can't wait to be alone. Maybe we'll hang around and listen."

"Or watch," said Paul.

Corey was simply smiling, saying nothing.

I could feel my anger growing as they talked, incensed at the way they looked at the Marci, the way they leered and suggested and filled the air with filth. I wanted to hurt them, to make them scream in pain and terror, but then suddenly all my anger was gone, replaced by a cold, clinical calm. I had killed several Withered in the past few years, but only one human. I'd dreamed about it my whole life, or at least since the first time I made the connection between death and the dead. We don't always think about that connection, as obvious as it sounds, because death is so common in movies and games and stuff, and so sterilized, but it's like meat: there comes a time when you realize that bacon, for example, is literally the sliced up flesh of a living thing, an animal that used to walk around and do things and enjoy things, and now it's dead and you cut it into pieces. The body in the casket at your grandfather's funeral used to be your grandfather, not because of magic but because he died, because something—maybe old age or cancer or a car wreck or a murderer—killed him. I'm fascinated by that moment, that act of turning a live body into a dead one, and eight months ago I got to do it, and it was . . . nothing and everything all at once. Disappointing and amazing. Not what I thought it would be, but I couldn't wait to try again. They say your first time having sex is the same way, but I can't imagine it would have that level of intensity. People have sex all the time, but killing is . . . rare. Beautiful, in a way, and I know how that sounds, but think about it. It's like alchemy, a magic transmutation—not just of physical matter but of something ethereal. A spirit or a soul, turned from . . . something, into something else. I didn't know what that something was, but I wanted to. I lay awake some nights, most nights really, thinking about it, about how to do it, about how to slow down and do it right, and now here I had three people practically begging for it. What would it be like to shove my knife into Derek's chest? To cut out Paul's heart? To peel back Corey's skin and watch the muscles move underneath it, stretching and contracting and glistening in the starlight—

"Pay attention when I'm talking to you," said Derek, and I focused my eyes and saw him right in my face, so close I could feel the flecks of spit when he shouted. "There's three of us and one of you," he said. His voice came at me through a cloud of beer and halitosis. "How you gonna stop us from taking whatever we want from your little girl here?"

Which one should I start on? I bent down and pulled out my knife, and all three of them backed up in a rush.

I felt a hand on my arm, and looked down to see Brooke's fingers, travel stained and fragile. "You're not Potash," she said. Or was it Marci? Or was it one of the others? The thought made me angry, not being able to tell the difference, and I took a step forward, longing to finish the kill.

"He's friggin' nuts," said Derek.

Brooke's finger's tightened on my arm, and I heard her whisper: "You're not trained."

Corey's eyes were wide. "Trained?"

That's what she'd meant about Potash—not that I wasn't a killer, but that I wasn't a trained fighter. This was Potash's knife and he could have handled three teenage jerks without even breaking a sweat, but I couldn't. I had no combat training, no hope for a direct confrontation. My style was slow and methodical: to wait, to find a weakness, and then to exploit it with no warning and no chance for a counterattack. I couldn't win this fight with a knife, and if I used a gun it wouldn't . . . I felt my cold rage fading. A gun wouldn't have the same satisfaction, the visceral thrill that I needed this to have. I felt my emotions receding, backing out of the calm, passing down through the anger, returning to normal. I wasn't going to hurt them. She had said exactly what I needed, in exactly the way that worked—not protesting, not appealing to rightness or honor, but a simple, pragmatic statement of ability.

"Thank you," I said. I looked up at the three. "You can go now."

"What's wrong with you?" asked Paul.

"Let's go," said Corey, and the other two followed like obedient dogs. I'd assumed that Paul was the leader and Derek was the loudmouth buddy, but now I could see that Corey had been in charge all along, quietly manipulating everything the other two had done. It concerned me that I hadn't seen it. We watched them go, first backing away, then turning and muttering among themselves as they walked the rest of the way to the fence. Derek turned around and shouted a final insult, cussing us out as the others went through the fence, then he followed them out.

"Come over here," I whispered to Marci, and we walked away from the building, away from the closed wooden gate we'd been standing near. Sure enough, one last beer can came sailing over the fence, then another, then a whole barrage of cans and rocks and gravel, all targeting the spot we'd been standing. After a moment the volley stopped, and I heard them snicker as they ran away.

"Put the knife away," said Marci. I realized I was still holding it, my knuckles white around the grip.

I looked at it, not knowing what to say. "I wanted to kill them."

"I know."

"They were going to hurt you, and then I was going to kill them," I said, though I knew it wasn't true. Protecting her had been the impetus, but then the sheer love of death had taken over and Brooke or Marci or whoever it was had stopped being a reason and become an excuse. I wanted to kill them because I wanted to kill. I wanted to stab and slice and destroy.

"We can't stay here," said Marci.

"We have to find Attina."

"I mean here," she said, gesturing around us, "in this theater. They might come back when we're asleep, or they might even go to the police."

"Drunk teenagers don't go to the police," I said, still feeling some kind of weird buzz from the experience. An adrenaline high I was only slowly coming down from, and which a part of me didn't want to let go.

I had them right here. . . .

I needed to light a fire.

"But the police might find them," said Marci. "If they get picked up for drunk and disorderly conduct or disturbing the peace or whatever thing they don't want to get in trouble for, the first thing they'll do is use us as a distraction, and it will work, because two out-of-town squatters with a big scary knife are exactly the kind of thing that a cop is going to pursue immediately."

"If he believes them," I said, though I knew she was right.

"We're not the kind of story three drunk teens would make up," said Marci, and I nodded.

"I know." I put the knife away and started walking toward the hole in the fence. "Let's see what else we can find to sleep under. Another tree."

"Another?"

"We slept under a tree last night."

Marci nodded Brooke's head. "I remember," she said, but I couldn't tell if she did or not. Brooke tried to cover her gaps in memory; maybe Marci did the same. I crawled through the hole, and in the few brief seconds before she followed me, I put my face against the wood of the fence, closing my eyes, trying to know what to do. As if *knowing* were an act of will. I couldn't understand her, I couldn't help her, and now I couldn't even protect her—and if I ever did, that protection might cause more problems than whatever danger I was trying to save her from.

She deserved more than I could give her.

"John?"

I turned around, and she was standing there, ready to go. I started walking, and she hurried to catch up, reaching for my hand as we walked. I pulled it away, and we walked in silence. After a few blocks we saw a low chain-link fence around a big backyard and what looked like a vegetable garden. I climbed over it as quietly as I could, keeping Marci and Boy Dog in sight, and crept through the furrows looking for food. I stole a pair of tomatoes and three fat summer squash, and we ate them as we walked farther, looking for a safe hiding place to spend the night. We ended up in the narrow space between a sagging fence and an old wooden shed—not a dead end, because I hated being trapped, but the ground was full of undisturbed weeds so I was pretty sure no one would come blundering through in the morning. There didn't seem to be any animal tracks or droppings, so I figured the owners didn't have a pet, either. I set up my backpack as an armrest and sat with my back against the shed. I wasn't sleepy but I was exhausted—my body bone weary, my mind too frantic to relax. Would we be safe here? Would we be safe in the town at all? Where was Attina, and how would we find

OVER YOUR DEAD BODY

him, and how would we get to know him well enough to kill him? How long would Marci stay, and which would hurt me more: Marci leaving, or Brooke never coming back? I had to take care of—

Marci sat down next to me—not just sat, but snuggled, pressing her thigh against mine, her side to my side, pulling up my arm so she could rest her shoulder in the crook of it and her head on my chest. "I missed you," she murmured.

"I missed you too," I said. I could feel the warmth of her body on mine, acutely aware of the exact location of every part: her left hand on my leg, just inside the knee, her right arm on my wrist, the perfect curve of her hip pressing close to my leg. She turned her head, and her breast brushed my chest, her mouth was just inches from mine.

She leaned in closer and her lips brushed my chin.

Brooke's lips.

I pulled my head back, turning away from her. "We can't do this."

"I haven't kissed you in two years—"

"It's not your body," I said. My arms were shaking and I balled my hands into fists to try to steady them. "It's not right."

She let out a breath, long and slow and sad. "Did you . . . ? I guess it makes sense that you moved on after two years, right? You and Brooke, now, I guess?"

"It's not like that."

"Somebody else?"

"It's not your body," I said. "It's you inside of it, maybe, but it's Brooke. If I kiss you I'd be kissing Brooke."

"And you've never kissed her?"

"Of course I've never kissed her," I said, "She's a . . . I don't know. Can't you see?"

"You're right," she said, pulling away from my side. "You're right, it's like . . . date rape or something. It's like she's unconscious and we're using her body."

"Yeah."

She pulled her knees up to her chin, wrapping her arms around them. "Well this sucks."

"I know."

"I've been waiting two years, and now you're here, but . . . "

"But you're not," I said gently. "Not really."

"This is stupid," she said. "This is stupid and it sucks and I hate it. I can't even . . . this isn't even my body, these aren't even my legs or my arms." She let go of her knees, swinging her arms wide, like she'd touched something that repulsed her. She stared at her knees for a minute and then stood up, shaking her hands back and forth in a blur. "How do I even walk around like this? How do I even live?"

"I'm sorry."

"I know, and it's not—" She pressed her hand into her face, then pulled them quickly away. She was crying. "It's not your fault," said Marci. She was silent for a long time, and I hugged myself to stay warm. "How do you sleep, doing all of this? Knowing what you know?"

I shrugged and looked up at the narrow band of stars between the shed and the fence. "Most of the time I don't."

7

Dillon seemed larger during the day, probably because the light helped fill in the background, adding barns and hills to the middle distance, making the whole thing seem less isolated. The people helped as well. It wasn't exactly a bustling city, but there were cars on the roads, and people at the stores and churches. I realized that it must be Sunday and wondered if Brooke would insist on going to church, like she sometimes did. As we walked down the only major road in town, looking at the one stoplight far in the distance, we passed a church with a slowly filling parking lot. Brooke didn't say a thing and I realized she must be somebody else right now.

"Who are you?" I asked.

Brooke raised her eyebrow. "You mean, like, philosophically?"

"I mean, are you Brooke or . . . Lucinda, or whoever?"

A look of hurt flashed across her face, followed almost immediately by a sinking dejection; she looked down, her shoulders drooped, and she took a slow breath. "Sorry, I should have realized that would be a common question. But it's still me, it's still Marci."

I felt relief and despair and confusion, all at once, and tried to hide my grimace. "You've never been one person that long. Not since Fort Bruce, I mean."

"Dr. Trujillo helped keep her grounded," said Marci, then stopped in place for a moment, frowning. "Who's Dr. Trujillo?"

"He was our therapist in Fort Bruce," I said. "Looks like you're sharing memories, like we wondered last night."

I didn't know how to react to the idea that Marci was here long term. It had been hard enough to come to grips with her sudden appearance, and eventually I'd just given up and focused on solvable problems instead: how to get into the theater, how to get rid of the boys, where to find a new place, what to eat. When Marci had finally gone to sleep I'd laid awake for hours, clenching my fists and trying to sort through the situation, but nothing made sense. I didn't know what I wanted or how to get it; things had been so much easier when all I'd had to do was plan the next kill. Death was so much easier than life. It made me feel weak to prefer the easy one. I couldn't even light a fire to ease my tension because I didn't want those boys or the cops or the gardener to come looking for us. Now it was morning, and I'd hoped the problem of Marci's presence had solved itself, but here she was, and I was at war with myself. I couldn't live with her but I never wanted her to leave.

And all the while, Brooke was trapped inside, looking out.

Marci raised Brooke's hand to a sudden breeze, feeling the cushion of air as it swept past our faces. It would be hot today, I could tell by the sky, but the morning was still comfortable. "I like Brooke's memories," said Marci, walking forward again. I kept pace with her, watching the town carefully for signs of trouble—the last thing we needed was for Corey or Paul or Derek to see us. Marci mused out loud: "She had a good life, with a good family. And I mean, so did I, but . . . now I have more, you know? Now I can remember my happiness and hers, without letting go of either one. It's like . . . watching a really happy movie."

"Brooke's life hasn't been a very happy movie," I said.

"Not all of it," Marci agreed. "But more of it than you think. We're eighteen years old and she's only been chased by demons for three of those years. And there's gaps in the middle when things were calm, and she . . . got to be with you."

"I didn't mean to drag her into this—"

"I like it," said Marci, reaching for my hand. "I only knew you— only really knew you—for a few months. She's known you for years and spent every day with you for the last two of them."

I had never been a physical person, I was leery of personal contact, but when I'd finally held Marci's hand all those years ago, it had been one of the simplest, most comforting things I'd ever felt. I looked down now at her hand in mine and tried to conjure up those same emotions, but it was still wrong, just like last night. I pulled my hand away. She looked sad, or I thought she did. I wondered how I looked.

"We need to find a bus station," I said, trying to bring my mind back to more pressing issues. "I seriously doubt they have one in a town this small, but you never know. Normally I'd ask in a bank, because there are fewer repercussions that way, but nothing's going to be open on a Sunday."

"So let's ask back there," said Marci, turning and pointing at the church.

"We can't just ask anybody," I said, realizing I would have to explain my system. "People in small towns—"

"Are nice," said Marci.

"Not to outsiders."

"The ones in a church will be."

"Why?" I asked. "Because they're in a church?"

"Have you ever been to church?"

"I lived upstairs from a chapel," I said. "I can quote the Bible all day. But people don't go to—"

"Only the verses about death," said Marci.

I stopped, staring at her. "What?"

"You can only quote the verses about death," Marci repeated. "And, I assume, resurrection, which is really the same category."

I wanted to argue with her, but for every counter I thought of, I was able to prove myself wrong before I even said it out loud. Could I quote a verse that wasn't about death? No. Weren't those the only verses in the Bible? Of course not; there had to be other verses about other topics, I'd just only ever heard the ones they use in funerals. *For a time is coming when all who are in their graves will hear his voice and come out.* Death. "I've never thought about religion enough to take it seriously," I said. "But I don't remember you being religious, either."

"Christmas and Easter," said Marci. "That's enough to know that the people in a church are good people."

"But they don't go to church because they believe it," I said. "They go because someone died, or because it's a holiday, or because they're a pastor and it's their job."

"Is it really that hard for you to accept that some people actually believe in something?" asked Marci. "You believe in things—big, build-your-life-around-them things, just like they do. You believe in the Withered. And death."

"Death's not a religion."

"It is for you."

I scowled and changed the subject. "You haven't been driven out of a dozen little towns just like this," I said. "Brooke and I have.

Look at us: we're filthy, we smell horrible, and even those idiots last night could tell we were homeless—what is an adult going to do the instant he sees us like this?"

"Ask if we need help," Marci insisted.

"And then call the nearest social worker," I said. "Which means police, which means official reports, which means the FBI finds us."

"You just don't know the right people to talk to," said Marci, and she pulled me back down the street. "Come on, John, this is a church. Have faith."

I followed her slowly, resolved to run at the first sign of trouble. We had to stay in the town long enough to find a Withered; we had to lay low and arouse as little suspicion as possible, and I'd already threatened three guys with a knife. We needed to contact the locals, but how much contact could we afford?

The church sat on a corner lot, fronting onto the main street, which we were on, and a small cross street ran alongside it. The parking lot was on the far side from us, by the cross street, and I felt my heart rate speed up as we came around the near fence and saw a handful of people moving from their cars to the building.

"I don't like this," I said.

"Trust me," said Marci.

"I wish you'd let me do this my way," I said. "Brooke did things my way."

"No wonder you fell in love with me instead."

"Don't say that," I said, stopping at the corner of the fence.

She looked back at me. "Didn't you?"

I didn't want her to assume it, I wanted to say it. I wanted it to be *a moment*. But I'd only ever said it to her corpse, and saying it to someone who could hear me was something I totally wasn't ready for.

"I have a system worked out," I said, changing the subject again. "Exposing ourselves like this feels wrong."

"That's because it hurts," said Marci. "You're not used to it. It's risky and that hurts. But sometimes the thing that hurts most is the right thing to do."

I sighed. "Fine."

"So relax," said Marci. "Talking is what I do. I haven't done it in two years, and I'm dying to get . . . Sorry." She grinned sadly. "Poor choice of words."

I expected her to take us straight up the front walk to the main door, but instead she pulled me along the fence, across the lawn, and down the narrow passage between the side wall and the fence. We reached the back and came around the corner, bypassing another door and reaching the rear corner of the parking lot without running into anyone. Marci put a hand on my chest, holding me back, and whispered.

"Wait."

More people arrived in trucks and small cars: men in cowboy hats and bolo ties; women in bright blouses and floral skirts; little kids in dresses and collared shirts, their hair slicked and combed. I didn't know what Brooke was waiting for, so I watched the crowd and the way they moved, the way people smiled at neighbors or snapped at an unruly child.

"What if there's no Withered at all?" she asked softly.

"This town is where Brooke said to go."

"And is there always a Withered everywhere she says?"

I shook my head. "Her information is old. Some of them haven't had contact with each other in decades. Even if Attina was here once, he might have left."

"So then what do we do?"

I watched the people walking into church. Was it one of them?

"We leave," I whispered.

"And go where?"

"I don't know."

Soon the crowd thinned out, and I figured the meeting was either starting soon or had already started and these were the last few stragglers. An old woman pulled up in a wide sedan, her head tilted up so she could see over the dashboard. Marci pulled me out of the shadows.

"Here we go," she said. "Don't do anything creepy."

"Give me a little credit."

"I'm teasing." She walked toward the old woman, reaching her just as she was getting out of her car. "Let me help you." Marci held out her hand, and the old woman smiled and grasped it delicately, pulling herself out of the seat with a grunt.

"Thank you, young lady." The woman was short and plump, her hair mostly white, flecked here and there with gray. She turned back to reach for her purse, and Marci held the car door open.

"I'm sorry to bother you, ma'am," said Marci, "but we just got into town, and we don't really know anybody."

The woman smiled. "Well, dear, you've come at a beautiful time. Dillon in June is absolutely lovely." She closed the car door and faced us directly, getting her first really good look at our faces and clothes. I braced myself for a judgmental stare followed by a lecture or a curt dismissal, but instead she smiled again. "My," she said, "you're so young! It's nice to meet you, dear, what's your name?"

"Marci," said Marci, smiling back.

"Everyone in there will call me Mrs. Potter," said the woman, "but please just call me Ingrid. It's not my name, but I like it so much."

"I . . . okay," said Marci, apparently as surprised as I was by the comment. The old woman laughed.

"Of course it's my name, it's just a joke I like to tell because so many people don't. I've always loved it, but then, I got it from my grandmother, and I always loved her—and I figured any man who didn't like my name wasn't worth chasing anyway, no matter how good he looked in his uniform." She laughed again and looked at me. "And you, young man, what's your name?"

"David," I said, sticking to the same fake name I'd used the night before. I watched the woman in awe, wondering how Marci had managed to pick exactly the right person to talk to: she was kind, she was accepting or somehow ignorant of how filthy we were, and with the last few churchgoers streaming into the building, we were practically alone. If Ingrid was willing to talk, we could get all kinds of information out of her without raising any alarms or red flags.

"Like I said before," said Marci, "we're new here and we don't know anyone. Do you mind if we sit with you at church today?"

"No," I said, "we can't—"

"He's a little embarrassed that we haven't had a chance to clean up," said Marci, shushing me with a finger on my lips. I backed away from the contact but stayed silent. "Normally we'd never go to church without dressing up—he looks so handsome in a shirt and tie—but I think if we were sitting with someone nice, it might help us feel a little less self-conscious."

"Oh, for crying out loud," said Ingrid, "is that all you're worried about? Half the boys in there can't be bothered to cut their hair, let alone comb it. You'll be fine." She grabbed Marci's arm and started walking toward the door. "Stick with me, and if anyone starts anything, I'll fight them off with a cane."

"You don't have a cane," said Marci, looking back at the car. "Should we go back and get it?"

"Oh, I don't use a cane," said Ingrid. "But we're going to sit next to Beth and hers has a great big handle on the end. It fell on my foot once and I limped all day."

"We can't go inside," I said, as firmly as possible. "We have a dog."

"So does Pastor Nash," said Ingrid. "Come on!"

I clenched my teeth, following them with Boy Dog at my heels. This was stupid—this was reckless and dangerous and completely unnecessary. We could have asked all the questions we needed right there in the parking lot, then disappeared into a back street and never seen Ingrid again. Why expose ourselves like this? Ingrid walked to a bench near the back, where a skinny, wrinkled woman with a blue dress and a matching hat sat. There was even a flower on it. She had a cane, so I assumed this was Beth; she moved it for us and Ingrid sat down, pulling Marci with her. I sat on the end of the pew, shrugging off my backpack, and Boy Dog flopped gratefully to the floor.

I leaned close to Marci and whispered: "What are you doing?"

"We're going to be in Dillon for a while, right? I'm establishing connections."

"They don't want to connect with us," I said. "We're dirty and weird and we're here to *kill someone*." I said the last part so softly even I could barely hear it. "Don't think I haven't tried churches before—you ask them for information, and they give it because they're polite, but then they call their friends, and their friends call their friends, and soon everyone is going to know about the creepy vagrants slinking around town."

The man in the pew in front of us turned and glared; the pastor was droning on in the front of the room. I lowered my voice again, making sure absolutely no one could understand a word we were saying. "Getting shunned is a best-case scenario now—worst case: someone files a report or looks us up on a missing-persons database."

"So don't slink around town," Marci whispered back, "and people won't have anything to warn each other about. And if all you do is ask a bunch of questions and leave, it's no wonder people get suspicious. Church is about community: if you take from it, they resent you, but if you participate they protect you. We're part of the group now—"

"Shhhh!" We looked over and saw Beth raising a shaky finger to her lips. Several other people were glaring at us as well; they couldn't hear what we were saying, but they didn't want us whispering. I nodded and closed my mouth, staring at the pastor but ignoring his words while I analyzed our situation. Marci might be right—if we had to stay in Dillon for a while, being part of the community might make a lot of things easier, even if it did expose us. In the past we'd always stayed on the edges, studying things from the outside, trying to make sure that no one saw or heard us enough to think twice about us. But that strategy meant that when they *did* think about us it was always bad. This way we'd stay more visible, more present in people's minds, but they'd be more likely to think well about us, as friends or neighbors instead of suspicious travelers. It made me nervous, but these days everything made me nervous. I couldn't hunt demons and run from more demons and keep a low profile and pump people for information and find food and take care of a dog and a crazy girl all at the same time without something starting to crack. Even just sitting here, in an air-conditioned building, felt like a luxury, and that only made me more nervous. I couldn't afford to relax; I had to stay focused. For all I knew the demon was right here in this room, and more demons were converging on the building. I had to be alert and ready.

I closed my eyes, forcing myself to surrender, just for a moment, and relax. I didn't have to do everything, all the time, completely by myself. Marci was showing herself to be just as competent as I remembered, maybe even more so, and even Brooke had surprised me with her cleverness in Yashodh's farmhouse. I needed to treat them . . . or her . . . like a partner and not a burden. I had to let go.

OVER YOUR DEAD BODY

I opened my eyes, checking the windows and the doors with one quick sweep of my head. Letting go sounded good in theory, right up until we were captured or killed. I could relax when our enemies were dead.

The sermon went on for about a half an hour, interspersed with hymns that sounded every bit as dirgelike as the ones we'd sung in the mortuary. When the meeting ended we split into groups, the kids going to a basement room and the adults breaking out into groups for Sunday school. I even saw Corey, but if he saw us he didn't say anything. We stayed with Ingrid, and she introduced us to her friends, most of them as old as she was. The pastor walked over to shake our hands as well, and we lied our way through a minute or two of small talk while our dogs sniffed each other's butts. I mostly stayed quiet, speaking only to answer direct questions, letting Marci charm the crowd with her easy wit and Brooke's clear smile. Most of the questions were simple—where were we from, why were we in town—and we answered them with the same vague story about taking a year off from college. Then the pastor asked the question I'd been dreading:

"Do you have a place to stay?"

It meant he'd seen how dirty we were and guessed we'd slept outside last night. It meant he knew we were homeless, and despite our stories, he was worried for our well-being. He might even be wondering if someone missed us, if our parents knew where we were, if we'd run away from something terrible and needed help, or even from something good because we were too young and foolish to see it for the blessing it was. Adults who were scared of me made my job harder, but adults who tried to help could make my job impossible.

Before we'd gone to Baker, we'd spent two months in a town

called Bunnell, close enough to a state park that it had a campground right outside of town. We'd gotten a tent from one of Potash's depots, so we'd set it up in the campground and explained our long-term presence that way, which had been enough for most people to ignore us. Dillon didn't have anything like that, and it was much smaller than most of the town's we'd visited, so I didn't think I could fall back on my "staying with a cousin" excuse. Everyone in this town was likely to know everyone else.

"We're just passing through," I said. "We're doing fine."

"You don't have a place to stay?" asked a woman on the edge of the circle. "Does that mean you don't have anything to eat?"

"We're fine," I said, feeling like a noose was tightening around our necks. "Thank you, but we're actually totally set up, and you don't need to worry about us at all—"

"Ridiculous," said the woman. She was younger than the others, with black hair that had only just started to gray, strands of wispy silver floating above the rest like a halo. "You're eating at my house today. I made a bacon-pecan pie last night, and it'd be a downright shame if I had to eat it all myself."

"I'm vegetarian," I said quickly.

"All the more for me," said Marci, and she turned to the woman. "Thank you, that's incredibly kind."

"It's the least I can do for a fellow child of God," said the woman, putting out her hand. "Sara Glassman, it's nice to meet you."

"She's the librarian," said Ingrid. "Used to run the bookstore, but nobody in this town buys books, so they closed it five years ago."

"That was when the new highway bypassed us," said Beth. "We used to be right on—"

"That was fifty years, not five," said Ingrid. "She gets lost in the past sometimes."

"I know how she feels," said Marci, and she looked at me with wide, helpless eyes. She looked scared, and I knew in an instant that she had flipped again—Marci had gone and a new personality had taken over, completely unaware of where we were or what we were doing.

Marci was gone.

I'd lost her again.

8

Marci was gone.

I struggled for words, sad and broken, furious that I had to go through this again and feeling more guilty than I could stand over the fact that I would even dare to think about myself instead of the girl standing in front me. She was lost and scared and she needed a friend, she needed some kind of stability, and here I was too gutted by a surge of emotions to even figure out who she was. I hated emotions so much—all they ever did was get in the way—*and now look at me, thinking about myself again.* I had to help her.

She was someone who recognized me, that much seemed clear. Was it Brooke? I almost said her name, but stopped. The people in the church knew her as Marci, and I didn't want to make them suspicious.

"Marci, dear," said Ingrid, "are you all right?"

"Marci," said Brooke, and her eyes never left me, melting slowly from confusion to pity. "Oh, John, I'm so sorry."

So much for quelling suspicion, but at least now I knew it was Brooke—she was the only other personality who knew about Marci.

"Who's John?" asked Ingrid. I shook my head.

"She needs medicine," I said, grabbing Brooke's arm. Medicine was a great excuse because nobody wanted to argue with it and few people knew enough about medicine to ask probing questions. It would explain her confusion, I hoped, but mostly it would get us out of there—and I had to get out of there *fast*. "Thank you for letting us sit with you," I mumbled. "Have a good day." I didn't want to make a scene but I couldn't stay there for another minute. I needed air. Brooke followed without argument.

"Is something wrong?" asked the pastor.

"She just needs her medicine," I said again. "We're fine, thank you."

"Number 42 Beck Street," Ms. Glassman called out after us. "Lunch'll be ready at noon."

I picked up my pace once we got outside, turning away from the main road to try to lose myself in the side streets, to get as far away from everyone as I could. Paul was in the parking lot, leaning against a car. He stared at us in shock as we walked past.

"Hey, Marci," he managed, just as we rounded the fence and hurried out of sight.

"How long was I gone?" asked Brooke. "Does the whole town know us?"

"Yes," I growled. "It was stupid to go in there, it was stupid to meet everyone, it was stupid to . . . " I walked faster, nervous and scared and angry all at once. "Everything is stupid. Everything is wrong and I don't know what I'm doing, and I'm—" I stopped, closing my eyes, freezing in place on the sidewalk. I couldn't talk like this; I was talking like Brooke did before a suicide attempt. I had to help her, not set her off.

I took a deep breath and turned, finding her standing behind me with deep concern etched into her face.

"I'm sorry," I said, "everything's fine."

"You're not fine."

"I'm just a little frazzled, but we're okay. You're okay."

"How long was I Marci?"

"Just last night and this morning," I said, trying to slow my breathing. My hands were shaking, and I clenched them into fists. "We've only been in town for thirteen hours at the most. You're fine."

"But you're not," she said again, and she stepped toward me, reaching for my face. "I've always known Marci might come out and I knew that it would be hard for you—"

"Don't touch me," I said, shying away from her hand. "Why do you all keep trying to touch me?"

"Because that's what humans do when we're sad," said Brooke. "We comfort each other."

I folded my arms tightly across my chest. "Just stop . . . touching me, I can't handle this right now, okay?"

"You hold me when I need it," she said softly, stepping toward me again. "You know that it helps with my episodes to have a hug or a touch or some kind of physical contact." She put her hand on my arm. "Let me do the same for you—"

"I'm not having an episode," I said, wrenching away from her, "I'm just trying to—I don't know!"

"What do you think an episode is if not this?"

"She was supposed to be dead," I said.

Brooke watched me for a moment, parsing this sudden change in direction. "Most people would beg for a chance to talk to their dead."

"Most people haven't done it," I said.

"I thought you loved her."

"Stop using that word!" I shouted. I looked around, worried that people would hear us, that people would look out their windows and watch us, that Paul would come around the corner and start talking to us again. I needed to run, not toward anything, but just run, as fast as I could. I squeezed my arms tighter around my chest.

"You're having a panic attack," said Brooke. "Dr. Trujillo taught me about them. Take a deep breath or you'll hyperventilate."

"An hour ago you didn't even remember Dr. Trujillo."

"Is that supposed to hurt me?"

"Of course not," I said, closing my eyes and crouching on the sidewalk. "I never want to hurt you, I'm sorry, but I can't . . . " I didn't know what to say.

I heard Brooke's shoes scraping on the pavement, felt the soft puff of her breath as she crouched next to me. "You can't what?"

"Nothing you can help me with."

"Just saying it out loud can help."

I shook my head. "Marci was the most important thing in my life."

"I know."

"Now you are," I whispered.

She paused a moment. "I know."

"And I can't have one without losing the other."

I heard footsteps and opened my eyes to see the pastor walking toward us with my backpack in one hand and Brooke's in the other. We'd left them in the church. I stood up, grateful that I hadn't been crying—and then a part of me grew disturbed that I hadn't been crying and filed it away as another inhuman fault. "Thank you," I said, trying to keep my voice from trembling. "We'd just noticed we'd forgotten them." It wasn't true; it was another knee-jerk lie. Why did I do that?

"Are you okay?" he asked again. "Is there something I can do?"

"No thank you," I said, taking the pack. What if he'd looked through it? What if he'd found the gun, or my notes about the Withered? What if he'd found something that could link us to our real identities?

"You said she needed medicine," said the pastor softly, "but you don't look well, either."

"I'm just sad, is all." That was true enough, though I realized that might be the first time I'd ever admitted the emotion out loud. "Someone very close to us died."

"I'm sorry to hear that," said the pastor. "Is that why you're . . . traveling?" He'd hesitated just a moment before saying the final word. What had he almost said instead? Running? Hiding? He'd definitely guessed that our story wasn't true.

"David and I . . . " Brooke said the names carefully, as if she were testing strange waters with her toe. "Our friend passed away last week—my friend, his brother. John."

"Something you said in there reminded us of him," I said, continuing the story. "That's all."

He eyed us carefully. "Is there something I can do to help? Even if it's just listening while you talk about it?"

" 'For a time is coming,' " I quoted, " 'when all who are in their graves will hear his voice and come out—those who have done good will rise to live, and those who have done evil will rise to be condemned.' "

"John 5," said the pastor. "Verses twenty-eight and twenty-nine."

"What if they're trapped?" I asked. "What if they can't rise to go anywhere?"

He paused a moment, as if he was trying to figure out what I was really asking, the question behind the question. "The world is full of terrible things," he said at last, "but I've never seen anything so terrible it could stop God from saving his own child."

"Sure you have," I said, thinking of the Withered hiding somewhere in this tiny, idyllic community. "You just didn't recognize it."

"Where is Beck Street?" asked Brooke, then she tilted her head. "Or do I know that already?"

She was getting flighty again, losing her grip on the real world as the other girls' memories bubbled up to the surface.

"Still needs her medicine," I said, but all I could think was *He's going to turn us in. He's worried, he thinks we're lost and sick and ran away from home, and he's going to call the police.* How could I put him at ease?

He nodded, looking at us a moment longer, then pointed behind us. "It's that next street—we don't have many, so it's easy to find the one you want. Runs parallel to Main Street, where the church is. Turn left toward the center of town, and Sara Glassman's house is about three blocks down."

"Thank you," I said, and I looked at the sky. "Just past eleven o'clock, it looks like?"

He pulled out a phone to check the time. "11:13."

"Then I'm late for a phone call," I said, concocting a lie that I hoped would keep him mollified. "My mother's kind of nervous, us being out here like this, so she wants me to call every day at eleven to let her know we're okay." Adults didn't usually take teens at their word, but sometimes all it took to calm them was to mention another adult. They respected imaginary authority more than the children right in front of them.

"Where did you say you were from?" asked the pastor. Was he genuinely trying to remember or was he testing us? I hadn't said anything, but Marci had. Stilton, or Stetson, or something like that. I'd only been half listening.

"Stillson," said Brooke.

"That's right," said the pastor, nodding. "I remember now. And you please remember, please: if there's anything you need, I'm right there in the chapel."

"Thanks," I said, and I waved politely as he turned to walk back to the church. His dog and Boy Dog sniffed their farewells.

"Okay," said Brooke, turning to me. "Let's talk about this—"

"Let's don't," I said, putting on my backpack. "I'm fine now."

"But we need to . . . " She trailed off as I turned away, ignoring her. I didn't know if she was respecting my wishes or just too cowed to continue.

We walked to Beck Street and followed it slowly, staying in the shade of the trees on the lawns. There was no sidewalk here, just one block away from Main Street, so we walked through the gravel on the side of the road, listening to it crunch beneath our feet. We identified Sara Glassman's house but walked past it, looking for somewhere to kill time without being close to other people. This turned out to be nearly impossible in a town that small; there were so few people around we stood out anywhere we went. The few people we did see waved and seemed friendly enough, but I wanted to get out of sight. Finally we found a culvert adjacent to a narrow stretch of lawn and a giant weeping willow, the branches so long and heavy that they reached to the ground. We pushed our way through the leaves like a curtain of chi beads, and found a small space in the center that felt isolated from the rest of the town.

"Hey," said Derek, who was sitting on the edge of the culvert. "It's you again."

9

"I figured you left town," said Derek.

There was something in the way he said it—not just with surprise, but eagerness. He was excited to see us again. He'd been looking for us.

"You went back to the drive-in," I guessed.

"What happened last night?" asked Brooke.

I wished she hadn't said that, exposing her lack of memory, but Derek seemed to misinterpret her meaning.

"I just wanted to see if you were still there," he said. He was sitting on the culvert—a big cement opening leading out into the ditch. His feet were up on the metal grate at the mouth of the hole, but as he spoke he shifted his weight, leaning back toward the hollow space I couldn't see on the far side of the culvert. If it were me, I'd have a weapon hidden there. Did he?

"Paul wanted to call the cops," he continued. "But he's an idiot, and once we convinced him he was too drunk to talk to any cops, we got him back to his house and in through his bedroom window. Corey told me to leave you alone, but he's always telling us what to do, so screw him. By the time I got back there you were gone."

"What did you want?" I asked.

He just smiled and rapped his knuckles on the cement culvert.

How quickly had he come back? That would tell me everything I needed to know; if it was quick, then he'd been trying to catch us before we went to sleep, either because he thought we'd be making out or because he wanted to finish the fight I'd almost started. If he'd waited a few hours and come back when he knew we'd be asleep . . . well, there were several things that might mean and none of them were good.

"My name is Marci," said Brooke, though I couldn't for the life of me figure out why. Was she actively trying to tell him she had mental issues? I said the first thing I could think of so she wouldn't keep talking.

"Did you have a gun?"

He didn't answer, and I knew that he had. He'd come back looking for us, drunk and angry and armed. I saw myself stabbing him again, like a strobed image flashing in my mind, and took a deep breath to calm myself. I put my hand on Brooke's arm, subtly guiding her back out of the tree. "Let's go."

"You want to see it?" asked Derek.

Brooke froze, and I looked back at Derek. His guilty smirk had turned into a wicked grin and he reached behind the culvert and pulled out a hunting rifle—not a handgun but a full, meter-long rifle. It seemed insane, but I supposed it was the only gun he had quick access to. He worked the bolt action, showing a long, bright bullet in the chamber, then pointed it at us. "I killed four deer last year; two does and two buck. Had to tell the ranger they were my dad's, because that's over the limit for a youth license and I was still just seventeen." I watched his eyes, wondering if he felt the same thrill in killing that I did, but I saw was nothing there but anger. His lips curled back in a sneer as he spoke, trying to terrify us with his monologue. "One of the bucks was four points," he said, "but the other was twelve point, one forty-two net score, so it's not quite trophy level, but we hung it on the wall anyway. I skinned them myself, and we're still eating the meat nine months later. You ever skinned a deer?"

"No," I said simply.

"There's way more blood than you think there's going to be," he said. "I was drenched in it. So please, don't assume for one second that I'm too squeamish to pull this trigger right now."

"Please don't," said Brooke.

I shrugged. "He won't."

"I told you," said Derek angrily, "I'm not afraid of some little pissant with a knife."

I thought about the knife and how much I wanted to use it right now, but I calmed myself. Scaring him would only give him the excuse he needed to pull the trigger. If I didn't give him that excuse, he'd never dare. He didn't want to kill us, just freak us out.

So instead of scaring him, I got to make fun of him. And I was ready to tear something apart.

"I don't think you're afraid to do it," I said. "As much as it shocks all three of us to hear this, I think you're too smart."

He raised the gun a bit, scowling. "You want to say that again?"

"You're too smart," I repeated. "Maybe not smart enough last night, drunk and embarrassed and out in the middle of nowhere, which is why you're lucky we were gone, or there'd be a cop collecting forensic evidence right now, tracing the bullets in our corpses right back to your rifle. Lucky for all of us, then. But now, today, in the middle of this bustling metropolis, not twenty yards from the nearest house, even you of all people are too smart to shoot us.

They wouldn't even have to collect forensic evidence because this whole town would see you running from the scene. And you wouldn't be able to argue self-defense because we're unarmed and just came from church. So no, I don't think you're smart enough to have thought this through, and I don't think you're smart enough to have avoided this situation without my help, but now that I've explained it all in short, easy words, yeah, I think you're smart enough not to kill us."

He growled. "You don't know anything about me—"

"What?" I asked, cutting him off. "Were you about to argue with me about how you actually *are* that stupid? Go ahead—I'm excited to hear this. Tell us all about how stupid you are—"

The gun fired, and my bravado turned to mindless terror in an instant, deafened by the blast. I scrambled backward through the willow branches, hands and feet churning the wet grass to mud. Brooke was already outside of the tree when I got there, running for safety, but she turned around to help me to my feet. We ran, too scared to stop and check ourselves for injuries, and all I could remember was Derek's face, laughing and laughing.

In hindsight, I didn't actually think he was going to chase us. He shot once to scare us, probably confident that, with no bodies or actual damage, he could talk his way out of whatever trouble he got into, saying it was only an accident. Or maybe people shot off guns in this town all the time and he wouldn't get in any trouble at all. But in the moment I was too scared to think clearly, still coming down from the emotional overstimulation I'd been going through all day, so we ran straight to the first safe haven we could think of: 42 Beck Street.

"Wait," said Brooke on the porch, grabbing my hand. She was bent over, her other hand on her knee, gasping for breath, and I had to stop and do the same. She looked behind us. "He's not chasing us. Let's take a minute."

"Be quiet then," I whispered. I studied the front of the house. "She'll hear us and come out." I hated Derek so much in that moment I could have screamed.

Boy Dog had somehow kept pace with us and now he was prowling back and forth across the porch, growling and darting his head at every new sound. He was just as scared as we were.

The house was smallish. It had a wooden porch big enough to hold a pair of rocking chairs and windows on either side of the door. There was car in the driveway, which hadn't been there when we'd passed the place earlier; it was old, and the brownish paint was flaking off in a pattern that looked surprisingly organic, like an alien beast crouching in the shade.

"This is someone from church?" asked Brooke.

I nodded. "Sara Glassman. She . . . " I paused, suddenly remembering something. "Those three dirtbags last night mentioned a Ms. Glassman; they said she had relatives in town."

"So?"

"So today when she invited us she said she'd made a pie and that she didn't want to eat it alone. If she has relatives in town she's not alone, so someone is lying."

Brooke panted a moment longer, then shook her head. "About a pie?"

"I'm . . . just nervous, is all. It's probably nothing, I know. But if I jump at enough shadows I'll eventually jump at something real and save our lives."

"Is that why you just mouthed off to an asshat with a rifle?"

I peered at her more closely. "Marci?"

She shook her head. "Still Brooke."

"You don't talk like that very often."

"I don't get shot at very often."

I nodded. "Considering how often our lives in danger, that's pretty surprising."

"Don't go back and hurt him," she said.

"What?" I straightened up, finally breathing at a normal rate. "Why would I go back?"

"Because he hurt you," said Brooke. "And you don't like it when people hurt you."

It wasn't me that I worried about, it was her. For daring to threaten her I'd cut Derek into a thousand pieces, I'd stab and slice and chop and mince until there was nothing left, nothing even recognizable as a mammal, let alone a human, but . . .

. . . then what? What would I do after his danger was gone, and another rose up to take its place. Just kill again? And what after that? I couldn't just murder my way to peace. There would always be another danger.

What would I give to just disappear back onto the road? To stick out my thumb and be gone again, leaving only a fading memory of Those Weird Kids Who Came To Church.

We'd had nothing but trouble since we'd gotten here. Since Marci had gotten here. I took a deep breath, then shook my head. "It's free food," I said, addressing my own doubts out loud. "We'll take that wherever we can get it; no sense running. And it can't be any worse than anything else that's happened today."

Brooke nodded. "What kind of pie?"

The door opened, and Ms. Glassman beamed from the doorway. "I thought I heard voices out here! Come on in, I'm so glad you came! Oh, and you brought your adorable dog!"

"Thank you," said Brooke, smiling politely. We passed inside while Ms. Glassman held the door. The house smelled delicious.

"Did you get your medicine okay?" she asked.

"Yes," said Brooke, lying better than usual. "I'm feeling much better."

Ms. Glassman crouched to scratch Boy Dog's head. "What's his name?"

"Boy Dog," I said. "We didn't name him."

"Ha! You can leave your packs on the couch," said Ms. Glassman, pointing to a sagging sofa. She bustled into the kitchen, and I took the chance to study the room—art on the walls, mostly nature scenes, and a pair of old black-and-white photos hanging over the mantel. There were no other photos. "Is it a mental thing?" she called from the other room.

"Depression," said Brooke. "It comes and goes, but I'm okay now."

"I'm sorry to hear it," said Ms. Glassman. "My aunt was like that, but this was back in the day, when they didn't consider things like depression to be a condition. It was just a thing that you felt and got over. I'm just guessing, of course, but I kind of wish she'd had some of the modern medicines like yours. Coke or apple?"

"What?" I stepped into kitchen and saw her setting the table with thick ceramic dishes.

"To drink," she explained. "My brother buys this apple soda all the time, and I've still got some in the fridge. But I have Coke, too, if you'd rather."

"Apple sounds great," said Brooke.

"Just water for me," I said.

"Absolutely," said Ms. Glassman. "You can wash up in the sink there."

We obediently washed our hands, and I counted the settings at the table: only three. I still couldn't help myself from looking around the house for more people.

"Have a seat," she said, dishing some kind of green vegetable from a saucepan to a serving dish. "You said you were vegetarian, so I made beet greens. It's a southern thing, which we don't do a lot of in these parts, but I used to have family out that way, so I picked up a few recipes." She set the dish on the table and sat down, licking her fingertips. "Ready?"

"Is it just the three of us?" I asked.

"Just the three of us," she said. "Were you expecting more?"

"One of the kids in town told me you had relatives visiting."

"You make friends quickly," said Ms. Glassman. "But don't worry—Luke left yesterday. And he's a total bore, so you're lucky." She started dishing out beet greens, and Brooke did the same with a bean salad in the center of the table. There was ham as well, though I didn't take any, and warm rolls and a green salad that seemed like it was mostly just lettuce and cucumbers. I wondered how the rolls could be warm—she hadn't had time to bake them since church, and it seemed strange that she would have baked a whole batch just for herself, before she'd even invited us.

"Marci," said Ms. Glassman kindly. "Would you say grace?"

"Of course," said Brooke, and bowed her head and asked for God's permission or forgiveness or whatever you're supposed to ask for in a prayer. Ms. Glassman put a slab of ham on a plate for Boy Dog, and then we started eating, but I couldn't concentrate on my food—all I saw was their forks jabbing into the ham, their knives slicing it open, the flesh separating under the blades, and I thought about Derek and everything I wanted to do to him.

I needed to burn something. It was my only release valve when the pressure built up like this.

"Dillon is lovely," said Brooke.

"Thank you," said Ms. Glassman. "Most visitors complain about how tiny it is, but we love it. What else do we need, anyway?"

"We come from a small town as well," said Brooke. "Not this small, but still. I couldn't wait to get out when we were in school, but now I miss it."

I looked at her while I chewed, trying to guess if she was talking about Clayton or some medieval village lost to time.

"Small towns are the best," said Ms. Glassman. "Big cities are noisy, they're dirty, they're full of crime." She punctuated each word with a short stab of her fork. "I drove through Tulsa once and thought I was going to get mugged at every stoplight. I can't even imagine going to a bigger place like New York."

"It's not as bad as people say," said Brooke. "Yes it is."

I looked at her again, wondering if she had just switched personalities in midsentence.

"Ha!" laughed Ms. Glassman. "I know how you feel, I argue with myself all the time. David, honey, how are those beet greens working out for you?"

"They're delicious," I said and I meant it. Either she was an excellent cook, or I was starving. *Probably both.* I took another bite, feeling even hungrier now that my body remembered what it had been missing, but as I chewed I started preparing some questions. This is why we'd gone to church in the first place, and now it was time to cash in that goodwill we'd earned and get some information.

I swallowed. "Every town is dangerous, though," I said. "Even Stillson had a crime problem."

"Not Dillon," said Ms. Glassman. "Last year I lost the key to the library so I couldn't lock up, and after freaking out all afternoon I decided to just close the door and pretend I was locking it and hope. Nothing happened. I didn't find that key again until the carpet cleaner moved my desk three months later—the front door was just unlocked for three whole months—and we didn't have a single break-in."

"Do people ever break into libraries?" asked Brooke. "You get the books for free anyway."

"And most of this town isn't even interested in that," said Ms. Glassman, slicing off another bite of ham.

Derek's heart, parting in two under the blade of my knife. . . .

" . . . but I mentioned this story to Bill Taylor, who runs the Terryl's, and he told me the same thing happened to him the year before."

"Terryl's is a . . . hairdresser?" Brooke asked.

"Grocery store," said Ms. Glassman. "Same story: not a single thing stolen. Not one grape."

"Then what about that gunshot we heard?" I asked, using the incident to press her further. There was a Withered in town, or at least there used to be, and though it probably wasn't Derek I had to get her talking about danger. *Something* here was dangerous. "Right before we got here? It sounded like a hunting rifle."

"Oh that happens all the time," she said. "But folks around here are gun people from way back, and we know what we're doing. Except for that one time five years ago when Clete Neilson shot himself in the foot there hasn't been a single gun-related injury since . . . well since the Old West, I suppose. And Clete was drunk, so it's his own dumb fault."

"What about non-gun-related injuries?" asked Brooke.

Ms. Glassman laughed. "My, you two are morbid, aren't you?"

Brooke laughed, which was perfect, because a laugh was exactly what the situation needed and I could never make it look natural. We needed her to keep talking about this—she was presenting Dillon as some kind of quiet paradise, where nothing ever went wrong, but that couldn't be true if there was a Withered here. We still didn't know what Attina could do, or how or why, but even a Withered who didn't kill—like Yashodh or Elijah—still caused problems. Elijah was an outright good person, and actively tried to help people and avoid problems, but he still couldn't survive without a constant stream of death. Even if other people caused it, the Withered needed death. They fed on us like parasites, and yet Dillon seemed completely healthy.

We'd come to Dillon because the memories Brooke had gained from Nobody located a Withered here decades ago, but what if it had left? The highway had bypassed the town, just like it had a thousand other little towns across the country, and the population had dwindled. There was no way the tiny population of Dillon could support a drive-in theater today. So the people had left, and the Withered had left with them. Dillon wasn't a viable food source anymore.

"These rolls are wonderful," said Brooke. "Did they just come out of the oven?"

"Thank you, dear," said Ms. Glassman. "That's so sweet. I mixed the batch this morning and let them rise while I was at church. Then I just threw them in the oven when I got home, easy peasy."

"But you didn't know we were coming," I said. "You didn't invite us until you were already an hour into church."

Ms. Glassman smiled. "I've been making a fresh batch of my grandmother's rolls first thing before church every week since she passed. Why do you think I had the ham all ready to go, or the bacon-pecan pie? I trust the Good Lord to put someone deserving in my path, and when he does, I have a lunch all ready for them."

"Does that happen a lot?" asked Brooke.

"Honey," said Ms. Glassman, "if you make a pie and ask people if they want to eat it with you, you're never going to eat alone."

Was Dillon really this nice? This quiet and peaceful, with nothing under the surface, no evil secrets, no hidden killers?

If it was, then I was the worst person here. Derek and his buddies were awful, but they'd backed down—even three to one, the mere glimpse of a knife had scared them off. They were harmless. I, on the other hand, wasn't even mad anymore and I still wanted to cut Derek into pieces, nice and slow, until he was in so much pain he couldn't even scream.

Robberies were one thing, but I needed to know about the real statistics. "How often do people die here?" I asked.

"Don't," Brooke hissed.

"That's a . . . shocking question," said Ms. Glassman.

"The last town we visited had a string of cancer deaths that they eventually attributed to nuclear testing," I said, making up a story as I talked. "They were downwind of a bomb site back in the fifties, and the radiation was still poisoning the water. Every place we've visited has had a story to tell, and I think when I get back to college I'd like to write a paper about it." I looked at Ms. Glassman closely, trying to ascertain if she was hiding any information from us. "So what does Dillon have? Suicides, unexplained illnesses, an abnormally high number of . . . I don't know, painting accidents?"

Ms. Glassman raised her hands in a helpless shrug, staring at the table as she tried to remember. "I have no idea. Aside from Clete's foot, and a boy that fell under a thresher that same year . . . we don't have anything. If they didn't take the ambulance to the elementary school every spring, we'd forget we even had one."

I looked at Brooke, and she looked back at me.

"Will you be staying long?" asked Ms. Glassman.

"No," said Brooke. "I think we're leaving later today."

10

"G, H, I," said Brooke, cupping her hand as she held it out over the side of the truck, catching the air as it rushed past. "Highway."

"You told me you can't just spell things you see," I said.

"There was a sign," said Brooke, pointing over my shoulder. "You gotta turn around, you're missing half the letters."

"Technically I don't have any letters."

" 'Highway' has an A in it," she said, "so you could have started there. Besides, I'm stuck on J now, so you've got a chance to catch up."

Ninety-nine dollars and sixty-one cents. We'd bought another pack of beef jerky before we left Dillon, to keep Boy Dog fed on the road. In a truck bed like this we probably could have fed him actual dog food, but you never know what's going to pick you up.

"We need a Jeep dealership," said Brooke. "Or a . . . jelly-bean factory."

"A jelly-bean factory?"

"They have to come from somewhere, right? Why not right here, in this empty desert wasteland?"

"Yeah," I said, looking out at the low, empty hills. "Why not?"

With Attina gone, there was only one other Withered we had a good lead on, but we didn't know much about him. Brooke called him Ron, or sometimes Rain, but I couldn't imagine either was his real name. Brooke was also scared of him, intensely so, which made getting information out of her harder than usual. He had some kind of power over . . . something. I still wasn't sure. Rain, maybe, but that seemed a little on-the-nose. Brooke had said two things on the subject over the last two years: one was "Ron helps people," and the other was " 'Run from Rain." Neither made any sense. The second one might not even be a warning, but rather a description of how one name had changed to another. Maybe his name was Run? Interpreting Brooke's flashes of insight was sometimes harder than finding the Withered themselves. She hadn't known much about Attina, either.

How were we supposed to hunt them now? After Ron, assuming that Ron wasn't just another dead end, where did we go next? Was that all of them? Maybe they were all dead and no one was chasing us, we were just running from shadows. We wouldn't know until they caught us, and then it would be too late. Maybe we could set a trap—give away our position, just a little bit, enough to draw attention and see who shows up. A demonic duck call, quacking in the marsh.

"Where are we?" asked Brooke.

I looked at her. Another personality shift, but she didn't seem upset. Someone who knew me, at least, and knew how we traveled. I wanted to ask who she was, but I didn't want her to feel bad.

"Highway 287," I said. "We're going to Dallas."

"Who's Dallas?"

One of the older ones, then. "Dallas is a city in America."

"I know that," she said softly.

"I know you do."

She touched Boy Dog's head, not scratching him but drawing her finger slowly down the center of his muzzle, forehead to nose. "Are we married?"

Lucinda, almost certainly—she asked me that almost every time she showed up. "We're not," I said, and tried to remember the details of Lucinda's life. "Your husband's name is Gaius, I think. Caius, maybe."

"Caius," she said, nodding. "But he's dead, isn't he?"

"For thousands of years."

"And so am I."

The warning flags went up, and I looked out at the highway, hoping to see something I could use to distract her. "A," I said. "On that license plate."

"That's an N."

"Are you sure?"

"John," she said, "your eyes are terrible."

"There's another crossroads," I said, pointing ahead. "Chevron station. Um, so, A."

She laughed, and I wondered if the moment had passed—snipped off before it could grow too fierce. "What word?"

"Station?" I said.

"Nope," she said, and laughed again. "You can't just guess about which words are up there, that's cheating."

"Then how about that big building?" I asked. Next to the pumps was a large white building, several times larger than a regular gas station. It was too far off the side of the highway for me to read clearly, but it was obviously a restaurant. I took the gamble that it said so on the sign. "A: Restaurant."

"That doesn't say 'restaurant,' it says 'The Armadillo Grill.' "

"I didn't say it said 'restaurant,' I said it was 'a restaurant.' Called the Armadillo Grill, which has an A in it."

"Fine," said Lucinda. "I'll give you that one. But no more freebies."

"What do you mean freebies? I had to fight for that A."

"J," she said triumphantly. "Right under the Armadillo Grill—it says 'Buster and Jackie,' or 'Beef and Jerky' or something like that."

"Boots and Jackets," I guessed. "B."

She peered at the sign. "And K, and L, and M, and N, and O, and . . . dangit, that's as far as I can go." She glanced at me from the corner of her eye. "See how easy it gets once you break past J?"

She seemed fine now, distracted from her momentary flash of darkness, but I didn't dare to just drop the game completely. If I'd been playing in the first place, she might not have started talking about death. "That same sign had C, D, and E," I said. Now that we were passed the crossroads, signs were scarce, but I saw a road sign and pointed it out. " 'Ogle Cattle.' I didn't realize we were that far removed from civilization."

"You did not actually see a sign like that."

"I totally did."

"It said Montague Jacksboro."

"Not the one I was looking at."

She swatted at me lightly, then whooped in terror as the truck bumped and we grabbed the sides, holding on as we caught just a millimeter of air. She laughed. "I missed this."

"They have a lot of pickup trucks in the Roman Empire?"

"Roman . . . who do you think I am?"

Had she shifted again? "You're not Lucinda?"

"Who's Lucinda?"

"You were, a few minutes ago."

"That must get really disconcerting," she said.

"Not as disconcerting as you refusing to tell me who you are."

"Sorry," she said. "I just assume you know."

There were only two personalities, aside from Brooke, who would expect that level of closeness. "Nobody?"

"I guess I was wrong," she said, and winked. "It's me again, babe. Marci."

All the levity drained away.

"Where are we going?" asked Marci. "And don't say 'to ogle cattle.'"

"To Dallas," I said. Marci was back. Would this happen all the time now?

"What's in Dallas?" she asked. "Another Withered?"

"We're going to pick up another supply drop."

She looked incredulous. "Someone's dropping us supplies?"

Apparently not one of the memories that transferred over. "One of the FBI agents we worked with was a former . . . something," I said. "Secret agent, Jason Bourne, man-of-mystery kind of person. He died in Fort Bruce, the night we ran away, and we took his go bag—like, all his fake IDs and passports and things like that. There was a list of other little stashes around the country—I assume not a complete list—with little care packages for himself. We've been hitting them when we're in the neighborhood, and Dallas is on the way to Gartner, where the next Withered is supposed to be, so we're going to stop and see what's in the stash."

Marci nodded, thinking about it. "What's usually there?"

"More IDs—you have no idea how many different IDs this guy had—and some money. It's our only real source of income. Usually a change of clothes, which never fit us but we can pawn them, and then a gun and some bullets, and sometimes other stuff. The one in Cincinnati had a whole wilderness survival kit: a shovel, a tent, some waterproof matches, a couple of wool blankets. All in a big duffle bag."

"What happened to it?"

"We still have some of it," I said. "We moved what we could to our backpacks, and used the tent a bit, but had to leave it behind one night to make a quick exit."

"Withered?"

"FBI."

She thought about that a moment. "So they found the campsite, and they know we were using a secret agent tent."

"*If* that was a standard-model tent commonly used by secret agents," I said. "I don't know if that's a thing. It was a pretty good tent, I guess; it folded up really small." I shrugged. "I don't know what that would tell them, though."

"As long as they don't know where any of your friend's stashes are," she said, "it doesn't tell them anything."

"They might be waiting for us," I admitted. It was a possibility I hadn't considered; Potash had always been so careful, I couldn't imagine even his bosses knew where he kept his supplies.

"Are we really that important?" asked Marci. "Why do they want us so bad—did you commit a crime you haven't told me about?"

"Only if the law protects ancient demons," I said. "I guess the car we took from Fort Bruce was technically government property, but we abandoned that in the next town, so they probably got it back."

"What happened in Fort Bruce?"

"Our war came out of the shadows," I said. "The only reason it didn't stay out is that everyone who saw it is dead: dozens of people and a handful of Withered. Brooke and I were the only ones who made it out alive. Well, and you, I guess. And Nobody. The media thinks it was organized crime, some kind of mob war or something, but nobody knows who did it or why."

"Including the FBI," said Marci. "You're the only one who knows what happened."

"They know what we were doing there and they know what we were planning the night it all went wrong. But then our whole team died, and without anyone to report back in, the FBI has no idea *how* they died. At least not in any detail. For all I know they think I did it." I paused. "And I did kill one human, so I guess they're partly right."

Marci looked at me for a moment, studying my face. "Was it self-defense?"

"Sort of." I looked out at the passing hills, brown scrub grass dotted here and there with trees. "If I hadn't killed him I would have died, so I decided that was close enough. But no, he wasn't actively threatening our lives at the time."

Marci paused a moment longer, but I couldn't tell if she was still looking at me or not. "Was he at least bad?"

"Would that make it better?"

"I don't know."

"I needed his heart," I said, looking back at her. There were parts of my life she knew so well, but she deserved to know everything. "The king of the demons was coming for us, and Nathan had already thrown in with it, so he was holding us until it came. I knew I could kill the Withered if I had a heart I could poison, so I killed Nathan and poisoned his."

She paused again, watching me while she formulated an answer. Eventually she just said, "That sucks." I wasn't sure if she meant the situation itself, or what I'd done to get out of it.

"You never really knew who I was," I said. "I wore a facade back in Clayton, and sometimes I still do, trying to look normal and act normal and pretend to be the person everyone thinks I should have been. That's who you liked, not me." I shrugged and looked away again. "Not the real me, at least."

"The John I liked was never normal," said Marci. "That's what I liked about him."

"He was still a lie."

"Maybe you're not as good a liar as you think you are."

"So you fell in love with a psychopath?" I turned toward her again, feeling angry for reasons I couldn't pin down. "Out of all the boys in school I was the only one with those dreamy, soulless eyes, and you said to yourself 'I want to date a boy who might kill me.'"

She pursed her lips before answering. "Maybe you're not as dangerous as you think you are, either."

"You want my resume?"

"I was an attractive teenage girl," said Marci. "No offense to Brooke, I think she's beautiful, but I'm not being arrogant when I say that a lot of boys lusted after me. A lot of men, too. Maybe because my boobs came in so young, maybe because my mom had a nice butt and the genes were on my side. Maybe because I liked the attention sometimes, so I learned how to do my hair just right and wear my clothes just right and talk to boys saying just the right words in just the right ways. One time in seventh grade—I was twelve years old—I turned in some homework late to Mr. K., and he told me he'd give me full credit because he liked my eyes."

"You gave me this speech before," I said. "You liked me because I didn't stare at you all the time like some kind of creep. Well, not staring doesn't change the fact that I'm a creep, that I'm worse than a creep. I didn't stare at you because I had rules designed to mimic the behavior of a normal, well-adjusted person. I actually counted the times I looked at you, per day: five times at your face, two times at your chest, one time at your hips. Is this really what you want to hear? I had dreams about killing you and Brooke and half a dozen other girls in school. Recurring, nightly dreams about cutting you open and listening to you scream. I set those rules because if I didn't, I'd start to obsess over you and then maybe I'd start following you, and then maybe I'd start thinking it was okay to act on some of those dreams. I'm not a good person, and you were a fool to ever think I was. And I was evil to ever make you think I was anything else."

"You didn't let me finish," she said softly. "Do you remember the first time I called you?"

"It was . . . during the trial," I said. "After Forman kidnapped me and the others, and Curt tried to convince everyone I was an ally instead of a victim."

"My father heard you testify in court," said Marci. "He told me what you did, that you saved those women's lives and hurt the man who hurt them. Brooke turned away from you, but I called you the very next day."

"Because you liked the danger?" I spat. "The thrill of thinking I might snap and attack someone who hurt you?"

"Maybe a little," she said. "After all the crap I've had to deal with I admit that has some appeal. But the real truth is that I knew you were the safest boy in that whole town."

"Have you not been listening—"

"Every girl gets leered at," said Marci, her voice fierce, Brooke's eyes practically glinting with inner steel. "Every girl gets harassed. In American high schools sixty percent of all girls get directly propositioned for some kind of sexual behavior—I did a report on it—and the only thing surprising about that number is that it isn't higher. One in eight teenage girls will be groped, and one in fifteen will be raped, usually by someone they know and often by the boys they trusted enough to date. One in fifteen: that's one girl in every class you ever had in school. I've listened to boys brag about what they've done to my friends, so loud and careless they didn't even look to see who was close enough to hear them." She shook her head. "I didn't date you because you were dangerous, I dated you because you were the only boy in school who *knew* he was dangerous, and was actively trying to stop it."

I looked back out at the highway and didn't say anything.

11

Our ride dropped us off in the outskirts of Dallas, then turned and headed to a suburb. Marci and I hung out by the freeway on-ramp for a while, hoping to hitch a ride deeper into the city, but nobody stopped. Hitching was always harder in big cities, especially at night, and though it wasn't dark yet, the sun was setting, and the streetlights were coming on, and the shapes rushing past us were changing from cars and trucks to black blobs and bright points of light. The highway wove through the city like two wide rivers, one of white lights and one of red, and we stood on the bank and wondered what to do. We asked at a gas station for directions to the nearest bus stop then hiked almost a mile to reach it. We bought two fares and sat silently in the fluorescent light as we rode downtown.

Ninety-four dollars and sixty-one cents. We hadn't eaten since Ms. Glassman's house, the day before.

The notes for Potash's Dallas stash had an address and

four numbers, one with three digits, and three with two digits. I assumed it was a locker number and combination, probably for a bus station, but when we finally arrived two transfers later, we found a storage facility: all internal, four stories high, and closed after 10 PM. It was nearly 11:00.

"Well," said Marci. "What are the odds they have a drive-in theater we could crash at for the night?"

"We want to stay off the street if we can," I said, watching scattered pedestrians still milling around in the darkness. Most of them looked ragged and filthy; homeless, or junkies, or close enough to make no difference. "Everything's more dangerous in a city like this."

"The small-town Withered would be offended."

"The Withered don't have a monopoly on evil," I said and I thought about Derek and his friends. "They're just the ones we've decided it's okay to kill."

"Where, then?" asked Marci. "If this was a bus station we could have slept on a bench inside and been fine."

"We could look for one," I said. "Or maybe a homeless shelter. We'd have to find one that doesn't split up men and women, though."

"Because you don't know if I'll still be me in the morning."

I nodded. It had happened before.

"I'm going to need some tampons, too," said Marci. "Does Brooke keep some in her bag?"

I nodded. "Just pads," I said. It was about time for this to happen again. "Tampons freak out most of the older girls—anyone who died more than fifty years ago, really."

"Ha!" said Marci. "I can only imagine."

"This is the life we lead."

Marci nodded, looking around. "Okay. We'll need to find somewhere I can change in private, the sooner the better."

OVER YOUR DEAD BODY

"We've got another half hour on these bus passes," I said. "Or we could look for a fast-food place with restrooms—most of those don't close 'til late."

"I'd rather have a bed than a booth in a taco place." She pointed across the street. "I don't suppose it's a good idea to ask one of those guys about the nearest shelter?"

"I prefer not to," I said. "Most of them are okay, but the bad ones are pretty bad, and you never know what you're going to get."

We ended up walking four blocks to a burger joint, just closing up for the night, and they let Marci in to use the restroom once she explained the situation to the girl at the drive thru. Boy Dog and I waited outside, and I asked the other worker about homeless shelters. He gave me some vague directions, but didn't know much. Marci came back out after a few minutes.

"We're going to need some more pads," she said. "She only has a couple, probably just an emergency stash to tide her over until she gets to a drug store."

"Can you make it through the night?"

"Probably."

We wandered over what felt like half the downtown area before finally finding a shelter called Second Chance. They stopped taking new residents at 7 PM, which seemed ridiculous to me, but pointed us toward a sobriety shelter that was open all night. We walked another mile to reach that only to find they required ID and an extensive registration form. I wanted to stay off the grid, and we didn't carry ID anyway, so we left and kept wandering. Eventually we broke down and went to a restaurant, one of these twenty-four-hour breakfast places, so Brooke's body could get some good food, if nothing else.

"I can't let y'all in," said the woman at the front desk. Her name tag said Delilah. "The manager says we can't take no beggars."

"We have money," I said, but she shook her head.

"It's the rules, I'm sorry, I wish I could."

The old familiar thought popped up, like a voice in the back of my mind: just kill her, and you can stay here all night. Kill her and the cook, then lock the door, eat your fill, sleep in the back, and get out before the next shift showed up for work. It was stupid, in addition to being evil, and I pushed the thought away without dwelling on it. And then, as I stood there, it struck me that I should be dwelling on it—that it *should* bother me, or disgust me, or at least worry me to have thought something like that. And yet it hadn't. The urge to kill whoever stood in our way was so common now, so second nature, I almost didn't even notice anymore.

I needed to be better. If that meant I needed to feel more pain, or more guilt, then that's what I needed to do. I had feelings now, right? What good were they if I didn't use them?

I found a solution to our problem and a penance for my coldness in one simple gesture. I pulled a stack of neatly folded ten dollar bills from my sock—we'd been mugged before, so I'd taken to hiding our money in small quantities all over my body—and held it up. "I have thirty dollars," I said, fanning the bills. "Let me give it to you now, in advance, and then you just take what we owe you and give the rest back." It was expensive, but Marci needed to sit, and we both needed to eat.

Delilah stared at us a moment, then sighed and took the money. "I guess if y'all have money you ain't no beggars. Your dog has to wait outside, though."

"That's fine," I said. Most restaurants had the same policy, so I kept a leash in my backpack for times just like this. I took Boy Dog outside and tied him to a square metal pole that marked the handicapped parking spaces. I gave him the rest of the beef jerky, and then Delilah led us to a booth in the back of the restaurant, where we wouldn't be visible from the street or the front door. It's the table I would have chosen anyway.

Marci sank into the benches with an exhausted sigh. "I can't remember the last time I sat on a cushion."

"Get something healthy," I said, picking up a menu. "Cheap, obviously, but something that's going to put some meat on your bones. Or her bones." I bought the cheapest meal on the menu, four bucks for some eggs and hash browns and a couple of sausages, which I took outside to Boy Dog; I was a vegetarian, but eggs didn't count. Marci ordered an omelet with plenty of vegetables, and an orange juice that we ended up splitting. Sixteen dollars and forty-five cents, plus a dollar thirty-six in tax and four dollars for the tip—a little more than twenty percent, but I wanted to keep Delilah happy so we could stay as long as possible. We ate quietly, though there was no one else in the restaurant. Delilah left our plates, playing into the pretense that we weren't quite finished yet, and after a while she came and leaned against the corner of the booth.

"Where are y'all from?"

"It's a town called Stillson," said Marci. "Don't worry, nobody else has heard of it, either."

"What brings you to Dallas?"

"Just traveling," I said. There was no sense trying to pass us off as itinerant college students at this point; we were obviously home-less drifters, and she knew it.

"Where'd you get that money?" asked Delilah. "You work?"

That was a red flag—did she think we'd stolen it? "It's the last of my savings," I said, looking down at my plate.

"We sold our phones," said Marci. "Didn't want to, but we gotta eat, right?"

"It's none of my business," said Delilah, holding up her hands as if to ward off the implication that she was prying. She showed no sign of stopping her prying, though, and phrased the next question as a subtle accusation: "Not a lot of homeless people with phones, though." In other words, *did you steal them?*

I started to answer, hoping to spin some story that would get her off our back, but Marci got there first. "We're not exactly homeless," she said. "Just on our way to a new one. Our uncle lives south of here."

I wished she hadn't said south—that's where Rain supposedly lived, and if whoever was following us managed to find this waitress and question her, she'd give the right direction.

"What happened to your old home?" asked Delilah, and I could see by the look on Brooke's face that Marci had an answer ready to go. She was getting into this.

"Our mother died when we were little," she said. "And dad . . . well I guess he drank before that, but I don't remember. He drinks a lot now, though, and it's only getting worse. And the beatings are getting worse."

"That's terrible!" said Delilah.

"Uncle Zach is Mom's brother, not his, so we'll be safe there."

I hated using the runaway story because it usually prompted adults to call in the authorities, but as I watched Delilah's face I suspected that Marci had read her right—she wasn't the kind to turn us in if she thought we'd get sent back to an abusive home.

Marci put the finishing touch on the sob story by grabbing her backpack and scooting out of the booth. "Time to, uh, visit the ladies room." She shot Delilah a quick glance. "You don't happen to have any ibuprofen, do you? I grabbed some pads when we left, but I forgot the painkillers."

"Oh for heaven's sakes," said Delilah, straightening up. "All that with your father, and it's shark week, too? You go along, I'll see what I have in my purse." She bustled away, and Marci winked at me.

"She'll let us stay here all night, now."

"Shark week?"

"You have no idea of the nicknames this has."

Marci went to the restroom, and after a moment Delilah came back with a couple of pills and a piece of chocolate cake.

"Always helps me," she said. "No charge." When Marci came back she swallowed the pills and ate the cake gratefully, offering me a few bites. I turned them down and let her have it all.

"Sleep now while you can," I said. "We're going to get thrown out sooner or later." She curled up in the corner and nodded off quickly; I tried to stay awake but eventually fell asleep as well at around four in the morning. I was awakened by an angry shout when the manager came in at 6 AM and threw us out. We gathered our things while he grumbled and snapped at how slow we were, and when we left the building he yelled at Delilah so loudly we could hear it from the parking lot.

"We should help her," said Marci.

"The best thing we can do for her is disappear."

Seventy-two dollars and eight cents left. *Let's hope Potash's supply drop has more cash.*

We stopped at a pharmacy on our way to the storage unit, leaving Boy Dog outside again. Eight dollars and eleven cents for pads, plus six eighteen for ibuprofen. Marci changed her pad again in their restroom while I pretended to browse the aisles out front. I saw a black SUV in the parking lot that I didn't remember seeing when we'd arrived a few minutes earlier, which seemed odd because no one else had come in the store. Why would the driver just sit in the parking lot? I watched it out of the corner of my eye, thumbing through some discount DVDs by the window. Eventually a woman came in, trying to return a bottle of shampoo, but I couldn't be certain she had come from the SUV.

Were we being followed? How had they found us?

"Ready," said Marci, walking up behind me.

"Look at that SUV," I said, still pretending to browse the DVD bargain bin. "Don't be obvious about it."

"Ah." She bent over as if to look at a movie and cast a perfectly subtle glance at the parking lot. "Think we're being followed?"

"I think you might be right about Potash's depots being watched," I said. "They may have seen us last night and tailed us here. We should go somewhere random and see if that SUV shows up again."

She nodded and we walked out, collecting Boy Dog and passing the SUV as if we hadn't even noticed it. There was a man in the driver's seat, but maybe he was just waiting for the woman in the store? I took a quick glance at the license plate—it was out of state, from Iowa of all places, but it didn't have government tags; 187 RCR, Mills County.

We walked for several blocks, staying on major roads, not acting conspicuous, but simply easy to follow. Dallas seemed to have a lot of parks, and we stopped in one and let Boy Dog drink from a fountain. It looked like it was going to be another scorching day, and the glass and concrete in the city would only make it worse. Brooke and I were already deeply tanned from our months of hitchhiking, and as I watched Marci play with Boy Dog I noticed how weathered Brooke's face had become, chapped cheeks and sun-bleached streaks in her already bright blond hair. I liked it short, the more I looked at it. Or maybe I just liked it when she smiled. Did Brooke smile this much, or was that all from Marci?

No black SUVs appeared, so we moved on, crossing the street and looking for something narrow we could duck into—a shopping district would be ideal, but even an alley would do. It was time to make ourselves harder to spot, and hopefully draw out anyone who might have to make a desperate move to keep up with us. We found a hotel and angled toward it.

"They're not going to like having Boy Dog in there," said Marci.

"They're not going to like us running, either," I said. "But at least we won't be there for long." Entering a building was tricky, because there were only a handful of exits we could use to get back out— they didn't have to follow us in, just wait by the doors and pick up the trail again when we emerged. But if we ran through it, getting to the exit before they did, we might bypass them completely and force a slip-up. We walked leisurely through the lobby, eyes alert for employees, and at the first corner I picked up Boy Dog and we sprinted through the halls, still mostly empty at this time of the morning, racing for the nearest door.

"You can't run in here!" shouted a maid, holding out her hand to stop us, but we darted past her without slowing.

"We're leaving anyway," I called back, and when we rounded the next corner we saw another glass door. We ran outside just in time to catch a bus. I paid the minimum fare (Fifty-two dollars and fifty-one cents left) and we crouched in the back, keeping our heads below the windows. If they hadn't seen us get on, they wouldn't have any idea where we were. After a couple of blocks I sat up and scanned the street for any sign of pursuit. There were plenty of black vehicles on the road, including a handful of SUVs, but none of them seemed to be following us—though the bus didn't have a rear window, so we couldn't see directly behind us.

"Two more blocks," said Marci, "then let's get off and transfer to another bus. It'll expose us again, just for a minute, and it'll give us a chance to see what else is out there."

"That's smart," I said. I walked to the front of the mostly empty bus and grabbed the pole nearest to the driver. "Where's the next major transfer stop?"

"Which line do you need?"

"Just a busy stop," I said. He glanced over his shoulder, saw my unwashed face and clothes, and looked ahead again with a low grumble.

"This one," he said. The bus rolled gently from side to side as we pulled into the curb, and the brakes hissed when we stopped. "Those passes you bought are good for two hours only."

"Thanks," I said, and I gestured for Marci and Boy Dog. We got off and a handful of commuters got on, and we waited. The stop only had signs for three bus lines; the driver had probably just wanted us off his bus. We watched the cars go by on the street, but there were no black SUVs.

"What if it's someone else following us?" I whispered. "What if we spend all this time looking for a black SUV, and really it's a . . . green Honda or something."

"A suspicious SUV is the only reason you think we're being followed in the first place," said Marci. "If it's not them, it's no one."

"I know I'm being paranoid," I said, never taking my eyes of the street. "Paranoia is what's keeping us alive."

Most of the traffic was trucks and minivans, almost all in the spectrum of white, silver, gray, and black. Actual colors were rare— a handful of red pickup trucks—so anyone trying to blend in would avoid those. Waiting at the light were two extended-cab pickups in dark silver; a white SUV; two long, black sedans; a gray minivan; a two-door sports car, probably a Mustang or a Camaro—I could never tell those two apart, though my old friend Max had been a Camaro enthusiast. I honestly didn't know the make or model of most of the cars I was looking at. The light changed, and the cars moved on, replaced by another batch stopped at the adjoining street: more pickup trucks; more minivans; another sedan, this one cream color; a bright yellow sports car with so modern it looked almost alien. "City cars have gotten weird while we've been out in the boonies," I said.

"Black SUV," said Marci. I followed her sight line to the far side of the intersection and saw the SUV waiting at the light, two cars back in the nearest lane.

"Don't look directly at it," I said, turning my head but keeping it in my peripheral vision. "How far are we from that drug store?"

"Couple of miles, maybe," said Marci. "Unless I'm totally turned around, that car's headed toward the drug store, not coming away from it."

"Yeah," I said. "I think you're right."

"So what do we do?"

I thought for a long moment, my mind racing the stoplight as I tried to come up with a plan. "We try the speed-bump test," I said at last.

"What's that?"

"The speed-bump test," I said, walking toward the corner, "is how we avoid a long, drawn-out mind game." I walked slowly, watching the lights turn yellow, being careful not to run or attract too much attention. The plan wouldn't work if everyone was watching me. "Identifying a tail isn't what we typically use it for, but it'll do the job." I reached the sidewalk right as the cars started moving.

"How does it work?"

"It's simple," I said, watching the first car move toward me. "We're going to hit him with a truck."

"What?"

"Pull me back." The first car passed me, and I stepped out suddenly in front of the black SUV, waving my arms wildly. Marci grabbed my backpack and yanked me backward, shouting my name in alarm, and the SUV slammed on its brakes, swerving wildly to the side, getting rear-ended by the truck behind it and clipped by another truck passing in the next lane. The SUV bounced toward us and we jumped back again; the truck driver slammed on his own brakes, and the traffic behind them piled up with a chorus of blaring horns. I looked at the license plate.

187 RCR, Mills County, Iowa.

"Run."

I picked up Boy Dog and we ran back through the people on the sidewalk, shocked commuters interrupted on their way to work, hearing the sounds of the accident and trying to catch a glimpse. How many of them had seen that I was the cause of it? Half a dozen, at least. I heard a few shouts behind us, calling out for us to stop, but no one tried to restrain us, and we ran for two blocks before Marci started slowing, clutching her abdomen and limping to a stop.

"You hurt?"

"Cramps," she said, and she grunted through clenched teeth. I looked behind me, but no one seemed to be chasing us. She nodded at a coffee shop nearby. "Can we just lay low for a bit?"

"I want to get out of the area."

"Then that's what they'll assume we'll do," she said, trying to straighten up. She winced and stayed slightly bent.

"Actually running is safer than trying to second-guess the people we're running from," I said. "Let's just make it to the next bus stop."

"Easy for you to say." She took another pained breath, then loped forward as fast as she could. I set down Boy Dog and let him waddle along behind us, and took Marci's arm to try to help her.

"Don't touch me," she hissed, and when I backed away she shook her head, still plowing forward. "Sorry, I'm not mad, I'm just . . . "

"There's a stop right up there," I said, pointing. "It leads away from the accident, and we'll be able to relax."

"Good."

We made it to the stop as quickly as we could, but still had to wait three minutes for a bus. Nobody followed us. We flashed our transfer tickets and dropped onto a rear bench, exhausted. Boy Dog was panting like I'd never seen him before, and I wished I had some water to give him. "Don't worry," I told him, between pants of my own, "we'll get you a drink as soon as we can."

"Angels in heaven," gasped Marci, practically doubled over. "I haven't hurt like this since the baby was born."

My eyes went wide. "You had a baby?" I hadn't known Marci well until we were sixteen—had she gotten pregnant in middle school? Is that why she was so . . . but no. Of course it wasn't Marci anymore.

"What do you mean, 'you had a baby?'" she grunted. "He's right here—" She stopped abruptly. "Where's the baby? Where am I?" She looked at me with haunted eyes. "You're not Anton."

"My name is John," I said softly. Marci was gone again, and this was a new personality, with no idea where she was or what was going on. Some of them shared memories, and some of them didn't. I took a deep breath. "I'm afraid I have very bad news for you."

"I was attacked," she whispered. She shuddered at the memory. "Some kind of . . . black thing. Like swamp water, but thicker, and it . . . moved on its own." She started to cry. "What's happening to me?"

"The black thing is gone," I said. I wanted to help her but I didn't know what to do besides just telling her the truth. I put my arm around Brooke's shoulders, hoping to keep the new personality calm and far away from a suicide episode. "Now someone else is chasing us, and I'm trying to keep you safe. We are safe, for now." I hoped it was true.

"Where's my baby?"

"Tell me your name," I whispered.

She hesitated a moment. "Regina," she said at last. "Why . . . why do I feel like I know you? Why do I trust you so much?"

"Because I am your best and only friend in the entire world, Regina." I closed my eyes, trying to convince myself that everything would be okay. "Do you remember what year it is?"

"The year of our Lord 1528."

I took another deep breath. "Regina, your baby lived a long and happy life and died more than four hundred years ago."

She broke down in tears again, and cried into my shoulder while the bus trundled across the city.

12

The great thing about fire is that it doesn't come from anywhere else—you light a piece of wood on fire, and the fire comes from the wood. Light a piece of paper, and fire comes from the paper. It's like the inner soul of an object is trapped in a physical form, and when you set it free as a flame it roars to life, reaching for the sky as its old husk shrivels and disappears behind it.

A piece of paper without a soul looks like a twisted, poison leaf, curled and warped and blackened, so thin it might fall to pieces when you touch it.

I flicked my lighter and lit another piece, watching the flame leap out while the paper retreated, recoiling and empty.

"What are you doing?" asked Regina.

I dropped the paper as the fire crept too close to my fingers, watching the bright orange flames drift slowly to the ground, weighed down by the ashy paper, still heavier than air. The orange tendrils reached up, flickering into the orange sky, tiny sparks drifting in their wake.

"I'm waiting," I said, and pulled another page from the newspaper. The lighter flicked, the flame jumped up, and another soul broke free.

"Waiting for what?" she asked.

I didn't answer because I didn't know.

The sun was slowly setting, making bright bands of color across the horizon—red and orange and pink and yellow, shining in the sky and painted on the clouds. Overhead the sky was dark—not the deep blue we saw in the country, because we were still close enough to the city that the lights drowned it out. Just a dark, matte black. Maybe later we'd see the blue, when night fell for real. We sat now in a kind of half-light, where everything was visible and dark at the same time.

"That building is ugly," said Regina, "But the sky is beautiful."

We were hiding out in the lee of a small ridgeline outside of the city, across a field from what I assumed was an oil refinery. Did they have oil refineries in Dallas? Maybe it was something else, I don't know. Squat metal buildings and round welded tanks and giant chimneys reaching up into the darkness, every surface covered with pipes and gantries and bright yellow warning signs. Most of the chimneys were belching out giant clouds of steam, but one of the smaller ones shot a pillar of fire into the sky, at least twelve feet tall, brilliant even in the fading daylight.

We'd walked at least a half a mile from the nearest road, and the small copse of trees nearby showed none of the litter that came with a common camping spot for the homeless. No one ever came here, and no one was likely to find us or even see us, even with my little fires.

I lit another one and watched it burn.

"You should have seen my baby," said Regina. "We named him

Anton, like his father, and he was the most beautiful thing I'd ever seen."

"I'm sure he was." I pulled out another piece of paper and, on a whim, I rolled it this time into a loose cone, to see if the flames would travel through the middle before the whole thing lit on fire.

"His hair was dark," said Regina. "Most babies have so little hair, bald, like little old men, but my Anton was hairy as an ox, and strong as one, too. I'm sure he grew up to be a good man, maybe a soldier."

Boy Dog whined, and I looked up. We were still alone, as far as I could see. I looked at Regina and saw her cradling something imaginary in her arms, a tiny baby made of memory and air. She was feeling better now, as amazed by the fast-acting ibuprofen as she had been by the horseless bus, the glass-and-steel skyscrapers, and the constant stream of airplanes that flew over us, to and from the airport. She had no idea what an oil refinery was, and I'd eventually given up trying to explain it; she just called it "that ugly thing," and I couldn't argue with the description. Now that we weren't running, her cramps had subsided, and she'd been able to figure out well enough how the pads worked when it was time to change them. She'd been convinced that they would never hold enough, but it looked like absorbency technology had improved in five hundred years.

Regina took the time gap pretty well, all things considered. I figured some of Brooke's memories were coming through, or Marci's. Enough to make Regina feel that her current situation, if not "right," was at least normal.

That put us on a pretty ridiculous scale of normality, didn't it? Maybe "understandable" was a better word, but no. "Tolerable?"

"Endurable." We'd push through it and survive and hope it got better.

I lit my little cone of paper and watched the flames swell and surge and flicker and die.

"What is she like?" asked Regina. I looked over at her again and saw that her face was half obscured by darkness now; night was falling in earnest, and soon we'd be lost in the black. I looked up at the pillar of fire, fierce and deadly even in the distance.

"Who?" I asked.

"Brooke Watson," she said. "The girl whose body I'm . . . sharing, I guess. Borrowing."

"She's . . . kind," I said. How could I encapsulate an entire person? "She's a lot of things, but that's the one I feel like I ought to say first. Kind. She's my friend now, because she has to be—we're the only people in each other's lives—but she was my friend before, too. She saw something . . . " I stopped. "I don't know."

"Was it the monster?" asked Regina. She scooted an inch or two closer, across the weeds. "Did she save you from it?"

"That's not what I meant," I said.

Regina sighed. "I would have liked to have been a hero, even if it was only in another hero's body."

"She is a hero," I said, and laid down on the ground, my head on my backpack. The stiff, dry grass scratched my neck. The sky was half clouded and starless, like a lid over the world. "I didn't mean to say that she saw a monster, but I guess she did. She saw me, first as a good person, and then as a bad person, and then . . . as whatever I really am, I guess."

"A good person again," said Regina.

"No." I shook my head, just millimeters to either side.

"You're helping her," said Regina. "Of course you're good. You're helping me, and you're helping all the other girls." I'd explained the situation as well as I could, and she'd understood it as easily and innately as all the other personalities that surfaced in Brooke's mind:

they accepted the core reality of their fractured existence. On some level it felt right to them, even in a case like this, where none of the memories had transferred. The reality had. I suppose that on some subconscious level they'd had centuries to come to terms with it.

I hadn't.

"I'm not helping Brooke because I'm good," I said, "I'm helping her because it's all my fault. I can't make it go away, so I do what I can to make it . . . endurable." It was the only word that worked.

Regina raised her eyebrow. "Is that how she sees it?"

"She's broken," I said. "She can't see it for what it is."

"You don't give her enough credit."

"You don't know what you're talking about," I said, staring up at the sky. I wanted one star—just one star—to peek out. None did.

Regina shifted, turning to face me, forcing Boy Dog to get up and reestablish himself in a new spot, his body pressed against her legs. "How can you spend so much time with the woman you love and know so little about her?"

"I don't love her."

"She loves you."

"I thought you couldn't talk to each other."

"I love you," she said. "And I've never met you until this morning. Who else could that emotion be coming from?"

I closed my eyes. "I don't want to talk about this."

"Aren't you married?" she asked.

"Of course we're not married."

"It's hardly proper of you to spend all this time alone together, then."

"Oh, come on," I said, and squeezed my eyelids tighter together.

"You're sharing your life with her," said Regina. "How can you do it so . . . coldly?"

"Because I'm cold," I said, opening my eyes again but carefully, purposefully, not looking at her. "I don't connect with people, and the people I connect with are dead."

"That's a contradiction," said Regina.

"How do you even know that word?"

"Don't change the subject."

"How do you even know English?"

"We're speaking French," said Regina. "Now: you said you don't connect with people, and then say that you did. Just because the people you connected with before are dead now doesn't mean you can't do it again."

"You don't know me—"

"Am I wrong?"

I stopped, not daring to answer. She was right, about part of it at least—all the people I'd connected with were dead.

"Am I?" she asked again.

"It's more than that," I said. "It's like . . . " I stopped, trying to put it into words. "Okay, imagine that you wanted to bake a loaf of bread. You've baked bread, right?"

"All the time."

"And you had . . . I don't know what kind of resources you had. A market or something where you could buy flour and yeast and all that."

"What's yeast?"

"The stuff that makes it rise," I said. "What's it called—leaven."

"Yes." She nodded. "We bought all of that at the market."

"So imagine that everyone else in town can just go to the market and get whatever they need and bake bread all . . . willy-nilly. All the bread they want, all the time. But you can't. You have to plow your own field, and grow your own wheat, and harvest it, and grind it, and then build your own oven out of stone or clay or whatever you built your ovens with, and then raise your own trees and chop them down for firewood, and then you get you own leaven from . . . wherever the hell leaven comes from—"

"We'd starve," said Regina.

"You would," I said. "You'd spend your whole life making two loaves of bread—just two loaves—and they would mean everything to you. All the effort it took to make them, all the time and the struggle and the thinking it would be impossible, watching everyone around you make bread every day all the time like it was nothing, and you just sit by yourself and wonder how any of it can even make sense, thinking maybe they're all just lying to you, like it's some huge joke that the whole world is playing on you, and then one day you finally do it. You make your two loaves. And then . . ." It was too much, and I trailed off.

Regina nodded and her voice was soft. She stroked Boy Dog's fur as she spoke. "And then you make another loaf, and it's easier than the first two, and it feels wrong, and you don't dare to touch it because the first two were special, and if you treat this one the same it will make the first two seem less special."

I stared at the sky, watching for stars that never came out. "Yeah."

She sat in silence for a moment, and we watched the clouds drift slowly overhead, dark shapes against the dark sky.

"Who were your loaves?" she asked.

"I don't want to talk about it."

"That's fair," she said. "What do you want to talk about?"

"Nothing."

"Okay. Then what do I want to talk about?"

I looked at her. "You don't know?"

"Of course I know," said Regina. "Do you?"

"Your kid, maybe? I don't know."

"Then find out."

I sighed and laid my head back down on my backpack. "Fine. What do you want to talk about?"

"You could be a little less blunt about it."

"You want me to trick you into telling me what you want to talk about?"

"I want us to have a conversation," she said. "Not just you talking at me, or me talking at you. We'll talk with each other."

"The other girls are never this much trouble."

"Are the other girls married?" asked Regina.

"Up until you came along I used to think none of them were," I said. "Nobody was always looking for perfection, for the prettiest girl with the best life."

"And somehow that means none of them are married?"

"She wanted . . . boyfriends," I said. "Nice clothes. Lots of friends. She wanted the dream."

"Most people's dream *is* being married," said Regina.

"Maybe she didn't want to be trapped."

"Maybe she wanted a strong relationship with someone who loved her," said Regina. "That's not a trap."

I thought about my own parents. "Sometimes it is."

"And sometimes you get a stone in your shoe," said Regina. "That doesn't mean all shoes are full of stones."

"I . . . guess I hadn't thought about that."

She smiled. "It sounds like there are a lot of things you haven't thought about."

"Not everyone gets to think about the things they want to think about," I said.

"Now there's an interesting topic," said Regina, leaning forward. "What does John Cleaver think about, when no one is forcing him to think about anything else?"

"Honestly?"

"Girls love to be lied to," she said.

I glanced at her, narrowing my eyes. "Really?"

"Of course not," she said with a smirk. "Tell me honestly."

I shrugged, though laying in the grass it was more of a shoulder flop than anything else. I looked back up at the sky. "I think about the next Withered on our list and how to kill it."

"That doesn't count," said Regina. "The mission you're on is focusing your thoughts down that path. Get beyond that, to just your own mind: what do you think about, when you have nothing else to think about?"

I thought back to my old life, to my quiet times, to the moments between the terror and the pain and the loss, when I could just be myself, with no one else and nothing else, and . . . that was really it, wasn't it? That's what I thought about. Alone in my room, or in the embalming room, in some quiet corner.

"I think about peace," I said.

"Is your country at war?"

"Not that kind of peace," I said. "Peace and quiet. The absence of noise and trouble and problems."

"You think about happy times you used to have," said Regina, but I shook my head.

"Happiness is just as bad as sadness," I said. "For most of my life I didn't even know what happiness was, or joy, or anything else. Feelings were hard for me, good or bad, and it was better to just not feel anything at all to avoid the complication."

"Then what else is there?"

"I . . . " I stopped myself. "I can't talk about that with you."

"With me?"

"With Brooke," I said, "or any of the minds inside of her."

Regina nodded Brooke's head and stared at the ground for a moment. After a while she spoke again, and her words were almost too quiet to hear. "That means it's death."

"Yeah," I said. Death was the greatest peace I'd ever seen, the greatest calm I'd ever felt. Dead bodies were quiet and still and perfect. I was never more comfortable, more peaceful, than when everything around me was dead. "You understand why I can't talk about that with Brooke, right?"

"Because she'll kill herself," said Regina.

"She's killed herself a hundred thousand times," I said. "It's as much a part of her as eating."

Regina nodded again. "I remember when Nobody killed me," she said. "She was convinced that another girl in our village was better—happier, prettier, that kind of thing. That her baby didn't cry and her husband talked more."

"She wanted her life to be perfect," I said again. "She lived a hundred thousand lives and it never was."

The sky was almost black now, deep as a bottomless pit above us, and I felt a moment of vertigo, thinking I should clutch the grass to keep from falling up, plummeting away from the Earth and out into that vast expanse of nothing. A part of me wanted to go, bracing for the rush of wind and speed and fear. I didn't grab anything but I didn't fall away.

"All of her lives were perfect," said Regina. "She just never saw it."

"Perfect until she got there," I said.

"No," said Regina. "That's not what I mean. There were problems in every life before she came into them, and there would have been problems after. What I mean is that life is work and pain and trial, and that's what makes it worth living. The only thing broken about Nobody was that she didn't want to admit it."

"I don't think anybody wants to admit that," I said.

"Everybody has to eventually," said Regina. "It's how we grow up."

I looked up at the sky again, looking for a light, but all I saw were the lights on the tops of the refinery chimneys, blinking on and off like tiny white eyes. One by one more lights came on, up and down the chimneys, glinting on the pipes, shining from every corner of every frame and lattice and walkway. They shone in the darkness like a city made of stars.

"It's a fairy castle," Regina whispered. The thousand tiny lights reflected in Brooke's eyes, and I looked away.

"Ten minutes ago it was the ugliest thing you'd ever seen," I said.

"I feel sorry for you," said Regina, "that you live in a world this beautiful and all you see are the bad parts."

"It's an oil refinery."

"And it's beautiful," she insisted. "Things can be more than one thing."

I turned back to the towers of light, sparkling like jewels—white and yellow, and here and there a red one, spires and balconies and sweeping arches against a background so dark it looked like the metal itself had faded away, and the lights were hovering in the air by magic.

"I wish Marci could be here to see this," I breathed.

"Who's Marci?"

"She's . . ." I paused, trying to think of how to answer. "One of my loaves."

"Go ahead and say it," she said softly. "It's okay."

My voice was a whisper. "She was someone I loved."

13

Regina was gone the next morning, and Brooke woke up, bleary-eyed, asking where we were. I filled her in while Boy Dog sniffed and huffed and walked around our makeshift campsite, chewing on things and peeing on things and making himself at home. We wouldn't stay long enough for any of it to matter.

"Where to next?" asked Brooke.

"Gartner," I said. "Rain's the only one left that we know how to find. Or at least where to start looking." I checked our money as I packed my things, wincing at the dwindling amount. "I wish we could go back for that stash of supplies."

"Iowa's probably watching it," said Brooke. When I'd told her about the SUV she'd decided it must have been from the FBI, but I wasn't so sure—we didn't know what the Withered could do, so it was entirely possible that one of them was tracking us somehow. Besides, if I picked one option I'd be ignoring the other, so I'd rather be afraid of both and ready for everything.

"Tell me about Rain," I said.

"Run from Rain," said Brooke, automatically, as if it was an instinctual reaction. It was the same thing she'd said before, and she said it the same way.

"Is Rain that frightening?" I asked.

"Yes," said Brooke. "I don't know why, I just know that I'm scared. Like it's a part of me, deep inside."

The same way Regina knew she loved me, I thought. The personalities shared emotions and core knowledge better than they shared specific thoughts or discrete information. Maybe I could use that.

"What kind of fear is it?" I asked. "When you think about Rain, do you feel trapped? Do you feel rushed, like someone's chasing you? Do you feel alone or helpless or . . . I don't know, disgusted?"

Brooke thought about it for a moment, tapping her finger on her half-packed backpack. After a while she said, "I feel small."

"So Rain is big?"

"Or I'm just small."

"Fair enough." I looked down at my own pack, refolding the blanket I'd used as a bedroll. We were on the northwest edge of Dallas, if I'd read the map correctly, which meant that hitching a ride down to Gartner would be tricky without going back through the middle of the city again. If they knew where we were coming from, did they know where we were going? Would they be watching the highways to see where we went? We were too conspicuous now— dirty enough to stand out in any crowd, with a recognizable dog and that distinct "all our worldly possessions are in this backpack" kind of look that made truly homeless people so easy to spot. The FBI was looking for us, and the Withered, and probably the local cops as well after I'd caused that car accident the day before. We needed to change our look and our methods.

With fifty-two dollars and fifty-one cents.

"Do you remember that truck stop we passed right before the refinery?" asked Brooke.

I frowned at her. "Do you? You weren't even you when we passed it."

"Not really," she said. "But I know we passed one." She smiled. "You said something cute about it—what was it?"

"I don't remember, but I was just thinking—"

"Something about the name," said Brooke. "It was like a pun, it was really funny. I didn't get it then, because I didn't speak English, but I get it now. Was it a TA?"

"It was a Flying J," I said.

"Are you sure?"

"I want to go back there and shower," I said. "They even have a laundromat, so we won't have to wash our clothes in the sink."

"That sounds expensive," said Brooke.

"Ten bucks apiece," I said. "Plus two for the washer and two for the dryer. But we have to clean up or we'll never get anywhere."

"So that'll be . . . " she tilted her eyes back, adding in her head. "About twenty-eight dollars left." She wiggled her eyebrows, grinning at me.

"How on earth did you know that?"

"You talk in your sleep," she said. "I was hoping it would be something salacious, or at least something creepy, but apparently you just count money."

I finished packing my bag and stood up. Boy Dog stood with me. "I'm full of surprises."

She grinned slyly. "We could save ten bucks by showering together."

"No."

"I'm kidding," she said. "I'm totally kidding. But you get this really funny look on your face when I talk about sex. It's great."

"Sex is inextricably linked with violence in the vast majority of serial killers—"

"Ugh," said Brooke, finishing her own pack and standing up. "Please tell me more about your carefully calibrated psychological profile."

"I'm trying to keep you safe."

"I don't always want 'safe,'" she said.

"All the more reason for me to protect you."

"Thanks for keeping me alive," she said. "You know I really do appreciate it, right? Teasing aside?"

"I do," I said. "Thank you." She'd probably appreciate it more if I hadn't gotten her possessed in the first place, but there you go.

We hiked back to the highway and then six more miles to the truck stop. I didn't want to spend the money for showers, but we needed it, and it would help us hide. I gave Brooke the first turn, and while she was in the stall I threw all our clothes into the biggest washer they had and then wrote a short letter for Brooke's other personalities to read if they surfaced while we were apart:

My name is John, and you know me. I'm in the shower right now, and our clothes are in the washer. The basset hound you see roaming around is named Boy Dog, and no I didn't name him, but he's ours, and it's very important for you to stay with him and with the laundry. I'll be out as soon as I can. You are wonderful, and I'm excited to see you again.

That last bit was a suicide deterrent, just in case; the rest was to keep her from wandering off. She'd only left once in the last year, at a bus station somewhere in Nebraska, and I'd only just managed to find her, hitchhiking out in front. She was about to get into someone's truck when I ran up to her, half dressed and still soaked from my shower. Showers were the only time we were really apart, and I didn't want her to get confused and leave again, so I'd started writing her letters. She hadn't run off again, so I guess they worked.

I thought about her body in the shower, naked and wet and—

No.

She came out of the shower looking fresh scrubbed and satisfied, though she was dressed in her old dirty clothes again because everything else was in the wash. I talked with her just long enough to make sure she was still Brooke and that she knew what we were doing here, and then I gave her the letter and told her to keep it in her hand no matter what. I slipped into the shower stall I'd paid for and washed as quickly as I could, which turned out to be a solid eight minutes before I was convinced that I'd gotten all the dust and mud out of my hair. It was long, and I needed to cut it again, for ease of maintenance if nothing else. I threw my dirty clothes back on and stepped back into the hall, relieved to see Brooke still waiting for me.

"That was fast," she said. "Mine was, like, twice that long."

"We paid for it," I said. "You may as well get the most you can out of it."

"But not you?"

I did a quick visual check of the hall, making sure we still had all of our stuff. "I'm fine."

"The washer's still going," she said, pointing toward the laundry room down the hall. "How much longer do you think we have?"

"Ten minutes, maybe," I said. "Then another hour or so for the dryer."

"We could eat," she said.

I shook my head, thinking about our money. "Not in the restaurant."

"The burger place?"

"The most cost-effective source of nutrients in a truck stop is the snack aisle," I said. "We'll get pretzels sticks, sunflower seeds, and some baby carrots from the cooler section if they have them. We can drink out of the drinking fountain."

"You really know how to show a girl a good time."

"What?" I said, straightening up in mock offense. "You don't find thriftiness exciting?"

"Not as exciting as extravagance."

"Come on, then," I said. "We can watch some of the rich people eat sandwiches."

Ten minutes later we were back in the laundry room, spitting out sunflower shells and watching the news on a TV in the corner. I switched the washed clothes into the dryer and dropped in eight quarters. *Nineteen dollars and thirty-two cents.* The money was going too fast, and if we couldn't rely on Potash's depots to replenish it, we'd be completely broke in just a couple of weeks. What would we do after that?

"Somebody got shot," said Brooke, jutting her chin toward the TV.

"That happens," I said, but I wasn't really paying attention. What if Rain was the last Withered? We didn't really know how many there were and we thought some were chasing us, but we didn't know for sure. And Brooke couldn't find any more in Nobody's memories. If we could kill Rain inside of four weeks, we could go ahead and run out of money and then just . . . what? Settle down somewhere? Turn ourselves in? We couldn't keep this up forever.

"Drug bust," said Brooke.

"Cities suck," I said.

"It's not a city," she laughed, "it's like a . . . village. Look at that place, it's smaller than Clayton."

"Little towns suck, too," I said, looking up at the TV. Something about a tiny community in Kentucky.

"Everywhere sucks," said Brooke gruffly, crunching on a carrot. "The whole world is garbage." I looked at her, leery of any depressive language from her, but she was smiling, and laughed again when she saw me looking. "Rah, darkness, pain, rah." She laughed again.

I rolled my eyes as dramatically as possible and went back to my plans. Would it be so bad to turn ourselves in? Once all the Withered were dead, and we could go back to a normal life—whatever that meant? Could we just let whoever was chasing us catch up? Could we walk into a police station and tell them who we were? Even if there were warrants out for me, which I doubted, I'd just end up back at the FBI. They knew where I came from and they'd understand that I've only been doing exactly what they told me to do. After yelling at me a bit for doing it without them they'd calm down and let me get on with my life. Maybe. Or maybe I'd end up in prison for the rest of my life, and Brooke in a nut house. I couldn't let that happen. She needed me.

And if I was being honest, I think I needed her. Sitting here, talking, joking, I felt more normal than I had in ages. Even with all the running and hiding and stalking and killing, I felt more normal with her than I'd ever felt in my life. That said a lot. She was a friend like I'd never had before, not just a relative or a crush or a convenient acquaintance, but a real friend. Someone I could share everything with, and who shared everything with me. Sitting here, thinking about losing her and all of this ending, I realized that I didn't want it to. I didn't like who I was without her.

She made me less afraid of myself.

But was I as good for her as she was for me?

We needed to get back on the road, some way they couldn't

follow us. Hitchhiking wasn't working, but we couldn't afford anything else.

"Knife attack," said Brooke.

"Then somebody's having more fun than I am," I said.

"No," she said, and something in her voice was different. "John, look."

A new personality? I looked at her, and saw that her brow was deeply furrowed. Something was very wrong. I looked up at the TV and saw nighttime footage of some cops walking in and out of a small house. Brick with wooden siding. A gray pickup truck sat in the driveway.

"It's Dylan," she said. "That kid from the . . . with the gun."

"Dylan?" I peered at the screen, trying to read the titles along the bottom. "Dillon," I said, recognizing the shape of the word. "The town we were just in. The kid with the gun was Derek."

"He's dead," said Brooke, and the TV showed another shot—no body, just a room drenched in blood, the floor and the walls and everything else, parts of it covered with a blanket or marked with forensic tags. Whatever had happened had been brutal.

"Derek?" I asked, and then the news showed a picture of his face. It was definitely him.

Brooke nodded, her face pale. "Somebody cut him into pieces. The scroll on the bottom said it was almost a hundred."

Derek was dead. We'd been convinced that Dillon was clean, that there were no Withered there—but now Derek was dead. The first murder the little town had seen in . . .

Oh no.

"Somebody followed us," I said.

Brooke practically leaped off the bench, whirling around to look at the door. "How do we get out?"

"Not here," I said. "Or at least not yet." I gestured at the TV. "This happened last night, so whoever did it hasn't gotten this far."

"Then it wasn't Iowa, either," said Brooke.

I nodded. "Iowa's probably FBI, like you said. This is a Withered."

She glanced at the dryer, only a few minutes into its cycle. She swallowed and sat back down. "Which one?"

"You tell me," I said.

"Why aren't you terrified?"

"I am," I said. "I'm just reacting to it differently. We need to figure out what's going on and how to respond to it before we do anything rash."

"Rash?" she said, a little too loudly. We were the only two people in the laundry room, and when I glanced at the door I didn't see anyone looking in. Her voice was high pitched with worry. "What kind of word is 'rash?'"

Boy Dog was on his feet, aware that we were agitated even if he didn't know why.

"Stay calm," I said. The last thing we needed now was another mental-health episode. I put my hand on her arm. "Search your memory. We can do this. Wake up Nobody, if we have to. This Withered just cut a teenage boy into a hundred pieces: who does that sound like? What do we know about them?"

"It sounds like you," said Brooke.

I faltered a moment. "I've never cut anyone into pieces."

"But you want to," she said. "You told me."

"I told you I had dreams about it," I said. "I don't actually want to do it."

"Don't you?"

"Focus," I said. "Someone is following us, and we need to figure out who."

"I know," she said. "I'm just freaking out; it's hard to think."

My stomach roiled at her accusation, not because it offended me but because it felt so accurate: not only had I dreamed about cutting people up, I'd fantasized about cutting up Derek himself. Turning those smug leers into screams while I sliced through muscles and tendons and separated the bones like a butcher. Now someone had actually done it. What had it felt like? How long had it taken?

I was thinking about the wrong things—I needed to focus on the parts of the kill that would help us to figure it out. *Why* had a Withered cut Derek to pieces? They didn't kill out of annoyance, at least not that we'd ever seen. They killed because they were missing something—because they needed something that only that kill could give them. What had it been this time? Information? If something was tracking us, could it carve memories out of its victims like flesh?

Had this happened in every town we'd visited?

"Turn up the volume," I said, looking at the TV. "Have they talked about similar attacks? If this has happened before they'll think it's a serial killer, cutting its way across America."

"The story's already over," said Brooke.

"Crap," I said, rubbing my eyes as another realization washed over me. "If the FBI has followed us, then they know where we've been—and if there are kills in each place they'll think the killers were all us."

"That happened last night," Brooke reminded me. "You said it yourself. Iowa saw us in Dallas yesterday morning, so they know we didn't do this."

"*If* he's FBI," I said, shaking my head. "We're making too many assumptions. We need to *know*. We need to find out how many other times this has happened—there might be more information about the previous kills because they've had more time to investigate them."

"There's an Internet cafe by the restaurant," said Brooke.

"Good thinking," I said, and stood up. "Stay with the—no, come with me."

"Damn right I'm coming with you."

We gathered our food and our half-empty backpacks and left our laundry drying; we had another forty minutes, at least, before it was done. I took deep breaths to calm myself down and followed Brooke to the Internet cafe, which turned out to be three old desktop computers on a low counter. Each keyboard had a credit-card reader on it, and I threw back my head in disappointment.

"Crap."

"Maybe they're . . . " Brooke wiggled the nearest mouse and read the screen. "Yeah, cards only."

"Maybe they have something at the front," I said. We walked to the checkout counter in the convenience store, which served as the hub of the whole place, and I waited while the guy in front of us paid for his soda. The cashier was a short, stocky man, with a name-tag that said Carlos, and he looked puzzled when he saw us holding the half-eaten food we'd bought from him barely ten minutes earlier.

"Is there a problem?"

"Is there any way to use the Internet without a credit card?" I asked.

He shook his head. "Sorry, that's just how they are."

"Do you have a credit card?" asked Brooke.

"Everyone has a credit card," said Carlos.

I could kill him and take his credit card and—

Stop it.

"We just saw a news report about a friend of ours," said Brooke, and I thought *Don't connect us to Dillon!*—but she'd apparently already planned for that. "There was a drug bust on the news, and the house next door to it was my friend Rachel's. I need to find out if she's okay, but we don't have a phone or a credit card."

"There's pay phones in the hall by the game room," said Carlos.

"I'll still have to look up her number," said Brooke. "How much does an Internet session cost? Five bucks?"

"Four dollars for a half hour of low bandwidth," said Carlos. "Ten dollars for movies and stuff."

"If we give you four dollars cash," said Brooke, "can you use your card to get us online?"

Carlos stared at us through narrowed eyelids. "You're not going to look up porn or whatever, are you? I get in trouble if that gets traced back to me."

"News and search engines only," I said, and I dug out one of my stashes of cash. I counted out four ones and held them up. "Four dollars."

"Pretty please?" asked Brooke.

Carlos looked at us for a moment, then rolled his eyes and took the cash. He called over his shoulder as he walked to the end of the counter. "Carla, be back in thirty seconds."

"Carlos and Carla?" asked Brooke.

"It's not funny," said Carlos. We followed him to the computers, where he swiped his card and set up a short session. "This'll kick you off in thirty minutes exactly," he said. "No warning or nothing, so watch this timer in the bottom corner. And no porn."

We nodded, and he walked back to the front. I sat down, Brooke pulled over a chair, and we searched for "Dillon murder."

"Thomas Dillon," said Brooke, reading the top Wikipedia link. "A serial killer?"

"He hunted men like deer," I said, remembering him from some crime reenactment show. "He shot five that we know of." I scrolled past that, looking for current news, but none of the links looked recent enough to be about a murder from last night. I tried a new search for "Dillon murder news" and got another string about Thomas Dillon, and a few more about a murder in Dillon County, but that didn't look like the same place, and it was at least a year old. I tried again with "Dillon murder Derek," and got a hit. I clicked it and read the article, but it was just an announcement from the same news show we'd seen on the TV, with no new information. Last night's kill was too recent for anyone to know much about it.

Four minutes gone from our Internet session.

"Derek Stamper," said Brooke, reading over my shoulder. "I never knew his last name. It says he was their only child."

The article didn't say anything about other, similar murders, so I started searching for other towns we'd been in: "Baker murder." "Baker cut to pieces." I tried every combination I could think of, for every town we'd visited or traveled through, all the way back to Fort Bruce. "Fort Bruce murder," unsurprisingly, got a ton of hits, but they were all for the deaths we already knew about. There didn't seem to be any murders that fit the right profile, or indeed any profile, in any of the places we'd visited. *Eighteen minutes gone.* I checked the phrase "cut to pieces," to see if it turned up any similar crimes, but all I got was a quilting blog and a bunch of murders in other countries.

Twenty-two minutes gone.

"There's nothing," said Brooke.

"Or nothing people know about," I said. "Maybe he hides the bodies."

"Derek was killed in his living room," said Brooke, shaking her head. "He'd been there for at least an hour when his parents came home and found him. That's plenty of time to hide the body if the killer had wanted to, but he didn't."

I glanced at her, surprised. Brooke didn't usually talk so crisply about dead bodies.

I looked back at the screen. "Why so many pieces?" I asked. Nearly a hundred, the news had estimated, but the forensics team was still on the site. "Maybe the killer took some."

"Gross," said Brooke.

"We won't know if anything's gone until they do a full autopsy, and try to . . . put him back together."

"Look for missing persons," said Brooke. "If the other bodies were hidden, the stories we're looking for will just be about runaways or kidnappings or something."

I nodded and ran more searches for all the places we'd been, but none of them were reporting missing people, either.

Three minutes left.

"This doesn't make sense," said Brooke.

"So we look at what does," I said. "The town of Dillon has no violent crime, no untimely deaths, and no real problems whatsoever for decades. Some high school kids getting drunk at a bowling alley, some graffiti in the abandoned movie theater, and that's it. And then two days after we show up someone gets brutally, horrifically murdered."

"So we're the inciting factor," said Brooke.

I shot her another glance; she was speaking more coherently than usual and the terror she'd shown earlier had been replaced with a calm professionalism. Was Brooke gone again? Who'd come in her place? And how long had it taken me to notice?

"Two minutes left," said Brooke. "Search for . . . 'Dillon murder Facebook.'"

"Why?" I asked, though I was already typing. The results loaded, and Brooke took the mouse from my hand and started scrolling.

"Because if the killer didn't follow us to Dillon," she said, "but our presence in Dillon precipitated the kill, then the only explanation that makes sense is that the killer was already in town before we got there, lying low. We can't find evidence of a similar crime because the Withered we're looking for hasn't killed anyone in ages."

"So what are we going to find on Facebook?"

"That," said Brooke, and she clicked on a link. Corey Diamond—Derek's friend from the drive-in—had updated his status just after midnight:

It begins.

"No way," I said.

"We have to go back to Dillon," said Brooke. "We missed a Withered."

I nodded slowly, turning to look her in the eyes. "Who are you?"

"Who do you think?" she said, and her eyes showed a sign of hurt. "I'm Brooke."

14

We didn't want to be followed again, which meant we didn't want any friendly drivers who could look at a photo and say, "Yeah, I remember giving them a ride." Even if they didn't remember us, they'd remember the dog.

I thought again about getting rid of Boy Dog, just leaving him here or, even better, out in the countryside. He was too recognizable, and that made him a huge liability. But I had rules, and they wouldn't let me hurt an animal, even by neglect. Those rules kept me who I was. If I lost Boy Dog I lost my soul, so he came along.

We couldn't steal a car, either, for obvious reasons. That would get us more attention instead of less. So we sat in the shade of the truck-stop wall and watched the vehicles as they came in, waiting for just the right one. When it came we gathered our bags of newly washed clothes and got ready to run. An old pickup with a couch in the bed, flipped on its back and tied down with ropes and a tarp. It had come from the direction of the city, which meant it was headed out of the city. We watched the driver carefully; he topped off his tank, left the truck by the pump, and went inside the building, probably to use the restroom. We ran across the open lot, hefted Boy Dog into the bed beside the couch, and climbed in after him, hiding under the tarp as best we could. If the driver saw us, he'd raise a stink and maybe even call the police; if he didn't, he'd drive us away, and we'd be free.

We waited.

I was pressed almost chest to chest with Brooke, Boy Dog resting on top of us like a hundred-pound stuffed animal. He panted heavily, shifting to find a more comfortable spot, but he didn't bark. Brooke raised her hand and let him lick it, whispering *shhhh*, almost silently. I checked our feet again, making sure they were tucked inside of the tarp, and then closed my eyes and listened. The highway roared like the ocean. A brake squealed. An engine growled to life and drove away. A mother called to a child: "Hold my hand, Noah, there are cars here!"

Pressure on my face: lips; the barest hint of a kiss on the side of my nose. I opened my eyes and saw Brooke staring back, her eyes a wet reflection in the half-light under the tarp.

"Sorry," she said. "I couldn't help myself."

I have never considered that a comforting excuse.

I closed my eyes again and listened as the wind whipped at the edges of the tarp, as another engine moved across the lot, as a pair of heavy footsteps clomped on the concrete. Brooke's body went tense, and I knew she'd heard it too.

"Shhhh," she whispered, and Boy Dog licked her hand.

The door clicked open. The truck jostled, rolling slightly to the side as the driver climbed in. I looked at Brooke. "Here we go."

"Where?"

The engine started with a violent stutter, and the truck began to move.

"Doesn't matter where," I said. "It won't be too far before a truck this old needs to refuel, so we'll just wait 'til he stops, see if we can climb out in secret, and then start hitchhiking again, working our way back to Dillon. I don't know how the FBI is tailing us, but if they can't make the leap from Dallas to whatever random place we end up in, we might be able to lose them."

"And then just pick them up again in Dillon," said Brooke. "They're bound to investigate this murder."

"Maybe," I said. It was getting hard to hear as we pulled onto the highway and wind shook the tarp like a drum. "But it's like you said: they know it wasn't us, because we were in Dallas when it happened."

She flashed a wry smile. "Doesn't mean they won't be looking into it. We don't know what we're going to find there."

"If we're lucky," I said, "whatever we find won't know about us, either."

Her face was right in front of mine, mere inches away. I could feel her hips and her legs; her feet and mine were almost laced together in the tight space. Even with Boy Dog falling asleep on top of us, it was too close, and I needed to move. I closed my eyes and ran through my number sequence: one, one, two, three, five, eight, thirteen, twenty-one, thirty-four, fifty-five, eighty-nine, one hundred forty-four, two hundred thirty-three, three hundred seventy-seven . . .

Brooke exhaled, and I felt her breath on my face, warm and comforting like a pillow of air. I breathed deep, then shifted my legs and struggled to sit up, picking up Boy Dog with me. He flailed weakly in my arms, not fighting but simply looking for a new solid surface to replace the one he'd been sleeping on. I managed to maneuver him back into the slot I'd just risen from and crept toward the back of the truck, searching for fresh air.

The highway was full without being crowded, the cars and trucks and trailers moving seventy or eighty miles an hour at least, but nearly motionless in relation to each other. More vehicles were moving toward us from the side, another highway merging with ours, and I watched a bright orange semi glide toward us, growing larger and larger as it approached, until its road joined ours and we were right next to each other, barely three feet apart. I could see the pencil-thin scratches in the paint and read the tiny lettering on the signs and notices stuck to the side. The road behind us stretched out to the horizon line, a thousand cars in perfect formation.

An hour later they had all disappeared onto side roads and exits, and we were alone.

The truck drove for about five hours, all told, going deep into Arkansas. When he stopped again for gas and a restroom, we jumped out and hid, making sure he didn't see us, just in case. After he drove away we took a quick pit stop ourselves, filling old water bottles from the drinking fountain by the restrooms. I waited while Brooke used the restroom again, and then we walked back out to the on-ramp of the northbound freeway, hoping to circle around and head back to Dillon. We stuck to the back roads, and spent the night in a town called Longbend, somewhere near the border of Missouri. It rained all night, and we huddled together under an old rail car, wrapped in our thin blankets and catching scattered bits of sleep whenever our exhaustion managed to overwhelm our discomfort. I thought about our showers from that morning, all that cleanliness and nonthreatening approachability washing away into the gravel. At least our clean clothes were still packed; I made sure to keep the bags dry.

In the end, though, I supposed it didn't really matter. The people of Dillon had already seen us, if not at our worst then at least close to it. What would they say when they saw us? What would we say when we saw them? *Hi, we saw that dead kid on TV and rushed straight back just in case you didn't have enough suspects.* We had a perfect alibi—the man at the gas station had seen us buy snacks and then hitchhike out of town the day before the murder—but would that be enough? Would they interrogate us anyway? If they asked for ID, and maybe even if they didn't, they'd discover we were runaways. If they went so far as to fingerprint us, I was already in the system. Going back into this situation threatened to destroy every bit of secrecy and independence we'd managed to build up.

But staying away would mean letting a Withered keep killing. The local cops would be helpless—we'd seen that time and again. Killing a Withered took a different approach, soft and oblique, watching from the shadows until you discovered their secret and struck. Somehow we had prompted this Withered to kill after years of dormancy, and unless we could find a way to unprompt it, we had to assume it would keep killing. An object in bloodlust tends to remain in bloodlust. Cleaver's First Law.

I didn't like being the reason it had killed Derek. I refused to be the reason it killed anyone else.

"Do you think we can get all the way there tomorrow?" asked Brooke.

"Sorry," I said, shifting slightly away to avoid bothering her. "I didn't mean to wake you."

"I was already awake," she said. "Scoot back, you're warm."

I had only moved a fraction of an inch, but now I moved back, as grateful as she was for the added body heat. We pulled the blanket tighter around our shoulders and listened to the rain clatter against the rail car above us.

"I think we can get there in one day," she said. "If I'm remembering the map right, it's not too far."

"Kind of isolated, though," I said. "But you're probably right."

"What's your plan?"

I'd been puzzling over that myself. "If Attina is disguised as Corey Diamond, we need to find a way to talk to his friends."

"You mean the ones you pulled a knife on?"

"His parents, then," I said. "Or his teachers—someone who's known him for a while. Somewhere in his past, probably in the last three or four years, there'll be a moment when his behavior changed—when the real Corey died and a shape-shifting Withered took over. Honestly, it's probably easier for the Withered to take over teen lives than adult ones; the real person's likes and habits haven't really been established yet, so any inconsistencies can be passed off as puberty."

"That'll help us find out if it's really Corey," said Brooke. "How do we find out how to kill him?"

"A speed-bump test," I said, "if we can arrange without getting caught. Beyond that we just have to . . . get to know him really well."

"I didn't meet him," said Brooke, "but I have really uncomfortable feelings about him."

"He was pretty . . . uncomfortable," I said. "He stayed in the background, analyzing us while his friends cracked jokes. Honestly, he kind of reminded me of me."

"That's giving him too much credit," said Brooke.

"Talking to the other people first might give us an idea of how to talk to him," I said. "But how to get into his inner circle after starting off on such a bad foot?"

"This is going to be another long one, isn't it?" asked Brooke. "We'll need somewhere to stay."

"We're almost broke."

"We should go back to Sara Glassman's house."

I raised my eyebrow. "You think she'd feed us again?"

"I think she'd let us stay," said Brooke.

"You're kidding."

"Why not?" she said. "She has that whole house with nobody else in it, and she loved us."

"You, maybe."

"You too," said Brooke. "You're more charming than you think you are."

"I'm not charming."

"Charming's the wrong word," she said, nodding. She shot me a quick sideways look. "It's more of a . . . brooding loner thing."

I started to protest and then laughed out loud. "You want her to offer us rooms or hit on me?"

She shrugged. "I'm just saying. She likes us and she's a good person. She'll want to help us. And we know she has a guest room because she had family staying with her right before we showed up."

"I guess," I said, and I imagined Brooke in the shower again, naked and glistening. I closed my eyes and tried to push the thought away. Getting physical with Brooke would be like a . . . a betrayal, of her and Marci both. "You think she'll have two guest rooms?"

"You're forgetting our cover story," she said. "Everyone thinks we're a couple."

"Great," I said. I thought about her body next to mine, and started counting again. Two, three, five, eight, thirteen, twenty-one, fifty-five . . .

I counted all night.

In the morning we got as clean as we could, trying to look as normal and approachable as possible. I stood watch while Brooke changed her pad again; she said the flow was almost gone now and soon she'd be done altogether. I gave Boy Dog the rest of the food I'd been storing up for him, and we walked to the freeway to look for a ride. It took almost an hour before a small car pulled over;

a young woman smiled behind the wheel. She looked barely a few years older than we were. She leaned over and opened the passenger door.

"How far are you going?"

"As far as you'll take us," I said, holding the door for Brooke.

"That's pretty far," said the girl. Brooke closed her door, and I got in the back with Boy Dog. "Cute dog! What's his name?"

"Boy Dog," said Brooke.

"What?" asked the girl.

"That's his name," said Brooke. "Don't ask me, I didn't name him."

"He was a hand-me-down," I said. "We're going to eastern Oklahoma, but you can drop us off anywhere, thank you."

"I can do eastern Oklahoma," said the girl as she pulled back onto the road. "I'm Kate, by the way. Do you mind if I play the radio a bit?"

"Whatever you want," I said, buckling my seat belt. "Thanks again for the ride."

"Kate short for Katherine?" asked Brooke.

"Katelynn," said Kate, "with two N's. I hate it, though, so please just call me Kate."

"I'm Brooke," said Brooke. "Also with two N's." She frowned, looking concerned. "I mean—"

"Short for Brooklynn?" asked Kate.

"No," said Brooke, and she looked confused. Was she switching over to a new personality, or had one simply popped up, spelled its name, and then disappeared again?

"Just a joke," I said, hoping to soothe Brooke's worries. "Speaking of two N's, I'm Johnn." I dragged out the *n*. " Nice to meet you."

Kate laughed. "How far into eastern Oklahoma? I'm headed all the way to California—new semester, you know how it is. Or do you? You go to college at all?"

"We're taking a year off," said Brooke.

"Sounds fun," said Kate. She switched the radio station, skipping some commercials and settling on a bombastic country song, though she kept the volume so low it was mostly muffled thumps and the occasional twangy holler. "Where are you two from?"

"Kentucky," said Brooke quickly. Her confusion seemed to have dissipated, and I wondered if this was a lie or if she'd become a girl who was actually from Kentucky. She didn't look disoriented, but sometimes she didn't.

"Wow," said Kate, "I wouldn't have guessed that at all. 'Course, I don't really have an accent either. Our generation doesn't, really, right? All the TV and movies and stuff, we all sound like we're from . . . I don't know . . . Cleveland?"

"Comfortably Midwest," I said. I had no interest in small talk but I didn't want her to feel awkward, either, as the only one talking.

"Can I ask what brings you to Missouri?"

"Just traveling," said Brooke. "We thought about going to Europe, but decided there was so much of America we didn't even know, so why not get to know that better first?"

"There's no way," said Kate, shaking her head. "I'd never pick Missouri over Europe, are you kidding me? I mean, sure, I grew up here, so it's old hat and I've already seen it and all, but even . . . what else . . . Kansas? Tennessee? Maybe, what, Arizona and the Grand Canyon, or anywhere in the States is pretty enough, I guess, but they're not Venice. Weigh them on the scale and they don't stack up." She took her hands off the wheel, mimicking a scale with her palms. She grabbed the wheel again. "I'd give anything to go to Venice."

"It's beautiful," said Brooke.

Kate brightened. "You've been?"

"A long, long time ago," said Brooke. She stared out the window. "I'm sure it's changed a lot."

"Even if it's all touristy and whatever I still want to see it," said Kate. "Not just to take pictures, you know, but to stay there, to live there, even if it's only for a month or two. Maybe a summer, shacked up in a one-room apartment with nothing but a laptop to write poetry on. Or even better a typewriter. Old school."

"You're a writer?" asked Brooke.

"No, no, no," said Kate, shaking her head so vigorously I worried she'd drive us right off the side of the road. "Anthropology major—I'm going to join Doctors Without Borders or something like that. I'm hoping for an internship with them over Christmas, but, I mean, if you had the chance to just sit in Venice and write poetry, why wouldn't you? Just, like, sipping little demitasse cups of coffee and smoking in a plaza reading Byron. I don't even smoke but I would, because, come on."

I realized, listening to Kate talk, that no one would miss her for days if we killed her. She was in the first hours of a cross-country trip, with the kind of free-spirited independence that would explain away all kinds of silences. I could grab the back of her neck—soft and exposed, her hair pulled up except for a few wispy strands and the light blond down on her skin. She'd let two strangers into her car because she'd wanted the conversation, and because our status as drifters suggested a shared love of reckless romanticism. It was more likely that we were addicts, car thieves, or straight-up murderers looking for someone to chop into pieces. I thought of all the ways we could kill her, all the ways we could hide the body—dozens, if not hundreds, of ways that we could make her disappear without a single trace.

That slender neck, right in front of me. I could choke it, or stab it, or pull its hair and listen to it scream—

"It was really cool of you to pick us up," said Brooke. "Most people are scared of hitchhikers."

I looked at her and saw she was staring at me as she said it.

I closed my eyes and leaned back into my seat.

"I know, you hear all the stories," said Kate. "But seriously. I mean, you guys are great, and I think most people are great, you know?"

"It doesn't hurt to be careful though," said Brooke.

I never would have actually hurt her. I was just thinking about it because . . . because that's what I did. Killing wasn't a job, it was literally what I did for a living. To live. To help other people live. I couldn't just kill people, except sometimes I could.

That was the moral swamp I swam in and I was barely keeping my head above water.

Kate drove us through Tulsa without stopping, and then Oklahoma City, and finally stopped for gas somewhere west of there, in a land now almost entirely taken over by farms. It had been more than five hours, and Brooke had chatted with her for all of it. They'd even played the alphabet game, but with so much banter mixed in I'd lost track of who was winning. I checked my map, looking for which crossroads we needed to stop at, trying to remember if our next leg took us north or south.

"Want to stop for some food?" asked Kate, jerking her head toward the truck stop while she pumped gas. "They've got a burger place and a taco place, your pick."

"No thank you," I said quickly. "We're good."

Kate looked puzzled. "It's been hours—Brooke, I heard your stomach rumbling like five minutes ago."

"Honestly," said Brooke. "I'm not hungry. You get something if you want it."

"Do you not have any money?" asked Kate.

I wished she hadn't asked that. How could we possibly proceed from here? Either she offered to buy us food, in which case we were a burden, or she didn't, in which case she'd feel uncomfortable eating in front of us. Even if she ate in the truck stop without us watching, the difference in food possession would define the rest of the trip. She'd wonder if she should have given us some, or she'd wonder why we didn't get any, or she'd wonder if maybe we really were criminals. Were we running from something? Would we steal things from her car? Would we hurt her? In just a few sentences, her entire perception of us had changed.

"You know what?" I said, holding up the map. "This is where we get off anyway. I just found it."

"You sure?"

"We go north," I said, and looked around at the flat nothingness that surrounded us. "I told you we were headed for the country."

"I can take you farther if you want," she said.

"You're headed west," said Brooke, shrugging helplessly. "Thanks, though."

"Do you need food?" she asked, but she lowered her voice as she said it. It made her uncomfortable. What was she thinking about us? That we weren't equals anymore—that we were poor and possibly homeless. Whatever easy relationship we'd had was gone now.

But . . . who cared what she thought of us? We needed to eat, and if we made her uncomfortable, well, we'd never see each other again. "Sure," I said. She bought a burger each for the three of us, with fries and a drink, and we ate together in silence. Then she waved goodbye and drove away.

"I just hope she doesn't tell anyone about us," I said.

"She'll tell Becky," said Brooke. "A story like this is too good not to tell."

176

"Who's Becky?"

"Her roommate," said Brooke. "Weren't you listening?"

I watched the car drive away. "None of it really applied to me."

"That was the longest conversation I've had in two years," said Brooke. She stood silent for a moment, then started walking toward the freeway. "Let's go."

I followed, studying the map. Two more cars, give or take, and we'd be there.

15

We arrived in Dillon around noon the next day. A Wednesday. Just four days after we'd left, and three days since Derek was chopped into pieces.

The city was nearly silent and it was crawling with cops.

Our latest driver dropped us off at the same gas station where we'd bought our meager lunch the day we left. Brooke and I went straight to the restroom and locked ourselves inside, pulling out our cleanest clothes and washing our hair in the sink. I turned to the corner while she changed, counting off my number sequence and trying not to think about her skin, and then she did the same for me—though without, I assumed, the suppressed urge to flay me. Dark thoughts about Brooke had become so common and ignoring them had become such second nature, it was almost backwards at this point—my number sequence had become so firmly associated with thoughts of sex and violence that counting it off almost made it worse. One, one, two, three, five, eight, thirteen, twenty-one . . .

I needed a new coping strategy. My rules were like a lifeline for all three of us.

As quickly as we could, before the gas station clerk started asking questions, we repacked our bags and walked back out, looking for all the world like two normal teenagers with their dog. We walked down Main Street, looking at the store fronts and houses. With one or two exceptions—a man in a delivery van, a woman in a tow truck—the streets were empty. The children who would have been out playing were all inside, watching TV or, just as often, watching us through the cracks in the blinds. We could see them all through the town, little faces pecking out through the windows, wondering who would be next. And older faces behind them, looking out sternly, wondering which member of their community was a vicious killer.

We turned off Main Street and walked the block to Beck Street, keeping to the shade as we passed the rows of well-kept houses and neatly mown lawns. The streets were wide, probably a holdover from the days when frontier settlers used wagons with full teams of horses. The asphalt was old and crosshatched with lines of tar, the decades of wear and repair covering the streets in a kind of black, sticky lace. The sidewalks were dotted here and there with new slabs to replace older ones that had buckled over time.

We reached Ms. Glassman's house, but as Brooke started toward the porch, I put a hand on her arm. "Who are you?"

"Still Brooke."

"You're better with people than I am—"

"You're great with people."

"—and I need you to handle this, okay? I don't know how to ask a stranger to stay in her house." I stammered, searching for words. "I-I don't even know where to start."

"Don't worry," said Brooke, putting her hand on mine. I relished the touch, counting slowly to five, then pulled my hand away. She walked to the door, and Boy Dog and I followed.

Ms. Glassman opened the door with a frown of confusion. "Yes? Is there something I can . . . Marci!" Her eyes lit up with recognition. I'd forgotten we'd given her that name. "And David! I didn't expect to see you again! What brings you back to Dillon?" Her face fell immediately. "Oh, please tell me you've already heard the news; I couldn't bear to be the one to give it to you."

"We saw it on the TV," said Brooke, and she surprised me by opening her arms and stepping forward for a hug. Ms. Glassman hugged her back, cooing softly. "We met Derek the night we were here—I guess that would have been two days before he died. We hung out with him and his friends and I can't help but think that . . . that maybe if we'd stayed a few days longer he would have been somewhere else, or doing something else, and maybe he wouldn't have—"

"You stop that talk right now," said Ms. Glassman, stepping back and looking Brooke in the eyes. "It's not your fault, and don't think for one minute that it is."

"I know," said Brooke, "I know, but it's just . . . But I suppose it's been even harder on the rest of you."

"If it's anyone's fault it's mine," said Ms. Glassman, "for not dragging that family back to church when they stopped going."

"Was there a church event the night he was killed?" I asked.

Ms. Glassman looked at me oddly, as if surprised by the question. "The church is a help and a protection. If they'd had the Holy Spirit in their home this never would have happened."

"We thought it would be nice to come back for the funeral," said Brooke. "We're just drifting anyway, walking the land before we go back to college. Do you know when it's going to be?"

"Monday," said Ms. Glassman, "if the police are done with it by then. Luke says they will be."

"Luke," I said, remembering the name. She'd said it before . . . one of her relatives?

"We don't have a lot of money," said Brooke. "Is there a . . . really cheap motel in town?"

Ms. Glassman shook her head. "The Stay-Thru, but it's terrible—they charge too much for the garbage you get, and if they charged less it'd only be worse. There's a bed-and-breakfast, of course, but that's ridiculous, and I'm sure we can find you a place to stay. I'd offer you the spare bedroom here but Luke's in it, naturally, so that's out. Maybe Ingrid."

"Luke is your brother," I said. "He left right before we got here on Sunday."

"Good memory," said Ms. Glassman with a smile, turning to close and lock her door. "He came in for his birthday, since we're the only two left in the family, but now he's back, of course."

"He was a friend of Derek's family?" asked Brooke.

"Only in passing," said Ms. Glassman, walking toward the street and beckoning us to follow. "He's here for the investigation. He's with the state police."

I glanced at Brooke, and followed behind as she caught up to Ms. Glassman and made idle chatter. We didn't go far—the town was too small to have a "far"—though the eerie, empty streets made the walk seem longer than it was. I felt like the whole town was watching us through their windows and was glad we were with a known member of the community. Marci's point about how going to church would help us to be accepted into their community, instead of being outsiders, was comforting; I could only hope it turned out to be true.

And what about the church itself? Was Ms. Glassman's comment about protection just typical religious faith or something more? We didn't know what Attina did, or how; what if it was something like Yashodh and his cult? Was Derek's family punished for leaving the community? Did that mean the Withered we were looking for was the pastor?

This was nothing but idle speculation. I had no evidence, just vague, paranoid theories. There was a Withered demon somewhere in the shadows of this town, but only in one of them. The rest of the shadows were empty.

I hoped.

I recognized Ingrid's car in the driveway of an old, single-story house, but Ms. Glassman led us past it to the next house, and as we got closer I could see that the figure on the neighbor's porch was Ingrid herself. She banged on the door and called out in a voice that was thin but loud.

"Come out, Beth, you can't hide in there forever!"

"Scared?" asked Ms. Glassman, climbing the steps to the porch.

"She's dotty," said Ingrid, and glanced over her shoulder at Ms. Glassman. "I can't get her to—oh my, it's you two. Welcome back."

"David and Marci were friends of Derek," said Ms. Glassman. Ingrid nodded, as if she had only just now recognized us, and I wondered if she'd forgotten our names until Ms. Glassman mentioned them. Which would mean Ms. Glassman knew she'd forgotten and had reminded her smoothly and subtly. How long had they known each other to have such an established understanding? More and more every minute, I was getting the impression that no one ever moved out of this town, and no one ever moved in. Nothing had changed in Dillon in decades.

Someone inside the house muttered, though I couldn't hear it well enough to understand the words.

"She says she not coming out," said Ingrid. "Fool of a woman." She turned toward the door and raised her voice again. "You have to come out, there's a town meeting."

"Stay inside where it's safe!" said the voice.

"Beth's a little excitable," said Ms. Glassman. She walked up to stand next to Ingrid and shouted at the door. "We're in charge of the refreshments, Beth. Did you make brownies like I asked you to?"

"No one's going to the meeting," called Beth. "We have to stay in our homes and lock the doors! Do you want get sliced up?"

"She's worse every year," said Ingrid. "I don't know how much longer she can stay in this place alone, and that boy of hers certainly isn't going out of his way to check in on her. It's going to be us that puts her in a home, you know."

Ms. Glassman sighed and banged on the door again, though she didn't yell anything. She listened for a moment, then looked at Ingrid. "These two came back for the funeral. I'd put them up but Luke's at home. Can they stay with you?"

"Of course, of course," said Ingrid. "See what you can do with Beth, I need to pick up my banana bread anyway." She walked down the stairs, smiled at Brooke and me, and waved us toward the house. "Come on!"

I stared at Brooke, who grinned impishly. We fell into step behind Ingrid, crossing the lawn between houses. I whispered in Brooke's ear. "How on earth . . . ?"

"Nice people do nice things for nice people," Brooke whispered back.

"They don't know us."

"They think they do."

"That's not enough to invite strangers to stay in your home."

Brooke laughed under her breath. "Are you complaining?"

DAN WELLS

"I'm wondering how these people went so long *without* being murdered by a serial killer."

"This town is so small it makes Clayton look like Gotham City," said Brooke. "They know each other, they trust each other, and they always see the good in people."

"And look where that got Derek," I said.

"Yeah," said Brooke. "The only violent crime in at least fifty years. Theirs is truly a dangerous mindset."

Ingrid climbed the steps and opened her front door with a flourish. "Come in! I'm sorry it's such a mess, but I've been baking all morning for this town meeting."

The house smelled like fresh bread and warm cookies. "Don't worry," I said, "this is perfect. And thank you so much. We can . . . pay you with chores or something? Would that be okay? We don't have lot of money—"

"Obviously you're going to work," said Ingrid with a sly grin. "What am I, the US government? Room and board, though I'm afraid I'm a strict vegetarian, so there's no meat on the table."

"So am I," I said. "I told you this was perfect."

"The room's back here," said Ingrid, and she led us down the short hall to a trio of doors; the one in the middle turned out to be a linen closet, from which Ingrid pulled some clean sheets and towels. She opened the door on the left to reveal a guest room decorated in soft pink and lace; a queen-size bed sat in the middle of the room, covered with a pink comforter so thick and frilly I felt like I'd been miniaturized and stuck in a doll house. Pictures of cats and lighthouses filled the room like the world's most adorable fungal growth. I felt like turning around and running away. Brooke's face broke into a wide smile and she covered her mouth with her hand to hide the laughter already bubbling up to the surface.

"Oh yes," she said, with just a hint of a giggle in the back of her throat. "This is perfect."

"You can leave your things in here," said Ingrid. "And I'll ask you to keep the dog off the comforter—we can make him a bed with some of my old picnic blankets later tonight. For now, though, can you help me carry these things to the meeting? Consider it your first day's rent."

"Of course," said Brooke, and she set her backpack in a white wooden rocking chair. She pointed at the throw pillows decorating the head of the bed. "Honey, do you want the puppy side or the kitty side?"

"The puppy," I said, dropping my backpack on the hardwood floor. She'd have the pink fluffy bed to herself, and I'd sleep on the floor with Boy Dog, blocking the door. Just like always.

We followed Ingrid back to the kitchen and gathered up trays full of baked goods—sliced banana bread and zucchini bread, plates of frosted sugar cookies, pans full of sheet cakes and brownies and bar cookies packed with chocolate chips.

"This would have taken a dozen trips on my own," said Ingrid. "But now that I've got my own indentured servants, this whole process just got easier." We balanced the trays and pans and plates carefully and walked out to load them in the car. Other neighbors were emerging from their houses, furtively, like groundhogs looking for their shadows, but one by one they began streaming up the road, on foot and by car. Even Beth was opening her door, as if spurred on by the actions of her neighbors, though from the looks of it she had yet to step outside. We sat in Ingrid's car, holding the more precarious dishes in our laps, and she drove to the church.

"The town meeting's here?" asked Brooke.

"Where else?" asked Ingrid. "It's the biggest building in town outside of the school, and that doesn't have air conditioning. Here we go." She parked, and we carried the treats inside.

Corey Diamond was leaning against the wall, with Paul beside him, chatting with two girls about the same age.

Corey looked up as soon as we came in the room, watching us without any obvious emotion. *Just like I would,* I thought. He tracked us with his eyes as we walked across the room to a table and laid out Ingrid's treats. The other three teens didn't seem to notice his distraction.

"I'm going to head back and help Beth and Sara," said Ingrid. "You two wait here—go talk to Paul, he's a great kid. Did you meet him, too?"

"Briefly," I said.

"Great," said Ingrid. "Back in a jiff."

She left, and Brooke and I stood awkwardly for a moment, trying to identify which people might be Corey's parents. From the corner of my eye I could see him still staring at us.

"Does he know we know?" asked Brooke.

"We still don't know anything for sure," I said.

"Should we go talk to him?"

A hand clapped down on my shoulder, and I jumped a bit before turning and recognizing the pastor. "David and Marci," he said. "Welcome back. Though I have to admit I never thought I'd see you again."

Corey smiled at my startled jump and started walking toward us.

"We met Derek on Saturday night," said Brooke. "When we saw him on the news we . . . well, we didn't know him well, but he was nice to us. We thought we should come back and pay our respects."

"Sweet," said Corey. "That was really cool of you."

"Corey," said the pastor. "Have you met David and Marci?"

"Just once," said Corey, smiling kindly. "The same night Derek was so nice to them."

He knew we were lying and he wasn't exposing us. Why not? What did he stand to gain by covering for us? And why did he think we were here, if he knew our stated reason was false?

The pastor looked at us again. "I'd like to speak with you later, if I could. I have an office here at the church and I'm here pretty much all day. Will you stop in some time?"

I tried to keep myself from looking suspicious. "What for?"

"Just a chat," he said, and smiled again. "Looks like the police are here, I'm going to go get everything set up. You stick with Corey, he'll show around." The pastor walked toward the door, where four police officers had just arrived.

"So," said Corey. "What do you want me to show you? You've already seen the movie theater."

What should I say to him? I wasn't expecting a direct confrontation so soon. We needed him on our side, so we had to be nice. And despite our antagonistic feelings, he'd never actually threatened us, at least not overtly. I was the one who'd done that.

"I'm sorry about the other night," I said. "It had been a long, hard day."

"Nothing to be sorry about," said Corey. He was still speaking politely, though his smile was gone. "You pulled a knife on my friend a full two days before he got sliced to ribbons. There's nothing to be sorry for."

He spoke of the death—even joked about—so passively. Like it didn't bother him at all. *Just like I would.*

"We didn't do it," said Brooke.

"Obviously not," said Corey, and he smiled.

I stared at him, trying to decipher his thoughts. I was better at reading people now than I used to be, but that wasn't saying much. He was calm, confident, even teasing us slightly. In complete control of the situation. Was he trying to provoke us, or lord over us the power he wielded? The cops walked past us, so close one brushed my arm with his uniform. One sentence from Corey, and a corroborating testimony from Paul, would make us the prime suspects in a horrific murder. The cops walked by, and Corey said nothing. What was he doing? What did he want?

"Come over here," said Corey. "Let me introduce you to my friends." He started walking back toward Paul and the girls, but Brook and I stood still.

"What's going on?" she whispered.

"No idea."

Corey stopped and looked back. "Come on."

"Play along for now," I said. "This is what we came here for."

We walked toward the group and saw that the two girls Paul was talking to looked almost identical, though one was clearly older than the other. Sisters?

"Hey guys," said Corey. The three looked up at us, and Paul's eyes bugged out in surprise. "This is Dave and Marci," said Corey. "Can I call you Dave?"

"I prefer David," I said.

"Sweet," he said. "You already know Paul. This is his girlfriend, Brielle, and her sister Jessica."

"I'm not his girlfriend," said the older of the two girls. Brielle, then. She rolled her eyes, but laughed as she did it. She looked about our age, and I guessed that Jessica was closer to fourteen.

"Where are you from?" asked Jessica.

"Kentucky," said Brooke.

"That's pretty far away," said Corey. "What brings you here?"

"Just passing through," I said.

"That's what you told us Saturday," hissed Paul, his brow furrowed in anger. "Now our best friend is dead—"

"Easy," said Corey. "They weren't even here, they were in . . . ?" He left the sentence open for me to fill it in; I couldn't ignore it without making myself look even more suspicious.

"Oklahoma City," I said. I couldn't think of any smaller towns in the area fast enough, but I guessed a big city would be easier to lie about anyway. Nobody could disprove our story.

"They were making out in the drive-in Saturday night," said Paul, obviously still furious. "We showed up just goofing around and this bastard pulls a—"

"We got off on the wrong foot," said Corey. "And since you and Derek were more than a little drunk, that's perfectly understandable."

"Gross," said Brielle. "Again? No wonder you didn't answer my texts."

"We were just out walking around," said Paul. "It was nothing."

"Shh," said Jessica. "They're starting."

We looked toward the front, and saw Pastor Nash step up to the lectern and adjust the microphone. "Friends and neighbors," he said, "thank you for coming here today on this solemn and tragic occasion. We all mourn the passing of Derek Stamper, and we send our love to his parents, who are still at the police station working closely with the investigators. But we have work of our own to do, and for that I turn the time over to Officer Davis of the state police." The pastor stepped back and sat, and one of the officers stood up—older than the others, with close-cropped hair much more silver than black, and a beard about the same length and color wrapped around his face and chin.

"Is that Ms. Glassman's brother?" I whispered.

"No," said Corey. "Her brother's name is Officer Glassman."

I glanced at him, seeing just the hint of a smug smile. I supposed it was obvious enough, but only if you knew Ms. Glassman used her maiden name. Now we did. Did that tell us anything?

Most of the shadows are empty, I reminded myself.

Officer Davis stepped toward the lectern, looked at it uneasily, then took a few steps to the side.

"Sorry," he said. "Feels too weird to make like I'm a preacher. I'll just talk loud and you let me know if you can't hear me in the back. My name is Officer Davis and I'm heading up this investigation. I recognize that this crime is a horrible thing, a lot more horrible for you folks than it is for us; any death is heartbreaking, but you knew this boy, and you worked with him and played with him and taught him in school and so on. So I know this is hard, and we're doing our best to get it over with soon and to give you all some closure and some sense of safety again. But there are two things we need from you that are going to be a huge help, and we appreciate your cooperation. The first is that you stay calm. Don't freak out, don't cause any trouble that might hinder our efforts, and whatever you do, don't accuse each other. A small town like this can go completely insane if you start looking sideways at your neighbors, and you'd be surprised how quick a simple suspicion can turn into a mob or a witch hunt. So be careful."

I'd seen some of that mob mentality in Clayton, when the killing started all those years ago and we'd thought it was serial killer. The town had been ready to lynch some of the people they thought were behind it. I'd been worried at the time that everyone would accuse me, because I was the weird kid obsessed with death, but that's the kind of thing kids think when they don't understand the world very well. They think it all revolves around them. Most of the people in Clayton didn't even know who I was, and if they did, they didn't think twice about me. But now I was a visible outsider.

I needed to trim my hair, and try to look as clean-cut as I could. And I needed to figure out Corey's game before he hurt us with it.

"The second thing I need you to do is a little at odds with the first," said Officer Davis, "but it's a vital part of the investigation. I need you to talk to us—not here, not in a public forum, but privately, in our office at the police station or on the anonymous tip line that we've set up. Fliers with that information are by the door and posted around town, plus I'll be here in Pastor Nash's office for a bit after this meeting. If you know anything—anything at all—please tell us. We're starting pretty much from scratch on this one: there are no witnesses and no security cameras, so we have no description to start building a profile or even a sketch. We've collected a huge pile of forensic evidence from the crime scene itself, but that takes a lot longer to process than the TV makes it look, and it might not turn up anything useful. What's going to help us crack this open are your observations. If you see anything suspicious, or especially if you find any knives or blades discarded around the town, come to us immediately. I'm not asking you to accuse your neighbor because you think he's acting shifty, but I am asking you, if you know something concrete, to have the courage to come to us. More often than not these kinds of criminals are caught when someone close to them gets involved. We can protect you, we can keep you anonymous, we can do whatever you need us to do, but you have to come to us or we can't do anything."

He was walking a dangerous line in his speech, and I looked around the room to see how people were reacting to it. He was right about criminals being caught by the people close to them. Somewhere in this town, someone had ended their Monday night covered with blood, and that meant that somewhere there were bloody clothes, or even just a gap in somebody's closet. If it was Corey, catching him might be as simple as his mother wondering where that one pair of jeans ended up, or finding a crust of blood around the drain in the shower. Could I get into Corey's house? Would I even know what to look for? Not as well as his family would, but if he'd hidden his tracks well, they might not even look.

By the same token, coming right out and saying "family members of the killer are the best ones to catch him" would put those family members in immediate danger. If Attina was masquerading as a simple teenager, and he thought someone in the house suspected something, he might kill them to try to cover his tracks, passing it off as just another random attack. Even if Attina decided to skip town, he might hurt his pretend family on the way out, to stop them from sharing any more helpful information.

I looked at Corey, and found him looking at me. How much did he really know?

A tall man with slightly graying hair raised his hand. He spoke with a kind of angry confidence. "Do you think this killer's going to strike again?"

"It's too early to say," said Officer Davis. "And I urge you not to speculate on this—we can extrapolate a lot of probable details, but when we start extrapolating beyond our data points, all we get is baseless paranoia."

"But we hear about these kind of murders all the time," said the man. "You don't need a degree in criminology to know that this wasn't a crime of passion—whoever did it took their time, and that sounds a hell of a lot like a serial killer to me." There were murmurs of assent, and Officer Davis raised his voice to speak over them.

"The time the killer spent is definitely a factor in our investigation," he said. "But I remind you that without more information, that extra time might mean anything—it might be a serial killer, but it might just as easily be a moment of passion that got out of hand, followed by a desperate and failed attempt to hide the body. I apologize for speaking so bluntly, but this is important and I want to make sure you understand: there are multiple explanations for literally every aspect of this case, and we don't have enough information at this point to even narrow it down, let alone pick the one right answer. We're not here to guess what happened, we're here to find the truth—and you want to find the truth, too, so don't guess. Don't jump to conclusions. Don't start spinning out scenarios based on untested assumptions, because that will tear this town apart."

"Phrasing," murmured Corey.

"Thank you for coming," said Officer Davis. "I'll be in Pastor Nash's office for the next hour if anyone wants to talk to me. If you'd rather do it in private our tip line is open twenty-four hours a day. Please enjoy the refreshments." People shouted out questions, but he descended from the podium and walked with the pastor into the back room.

"This is just creepy," said Jessica.

"Duh," said Paul.

Brielle swatted his leg. "He was your best friend, idiot."

"That's what I'm saying," said Paul. "We don't have to say that my best friend's murder is creepy, because duh. What else would it be?"

"You can at least be nice about it," said Brielle. "Jessica didn't kill him, don't take it out on her."

"All I said was duh!" said Paul.

"Oh good," said Sara Glassman, walking up to us, "you've found some other kids already." A man was with her, but she seemed more annoyed by him than anything. "And these are good kids—I vouch for them all as their librarian."

"She's a great librarian!" said the man with a smile.

Sara ignored him. "Speaking of libraries, Jessica, have you finished Sherlock? It's overdue again."

"Finished it how many times?" asked Brielle.

"Can I hang on to it just a little bit longer?" asked Jessica. "I'm trying to write a script for one of the stories."

"Like, for a movie?" asked Brooke.

"I want to put it on YouTube," said Jessica, looking down at the floor and lowering her voice almost to a whisper.

"Cool," said the man. "Maybe we could show it in the library."

Sara sighed. "Randy, we need to have a talk." She led him away, and Brielle snickered.

"Randy's in love with her," said Brielle, "and she can't convince him she's not interested."

"He's like a puppy," said Jessica.

Corey and I stayed silent, watching and listening.

"I want some cookies before they're gone," said Paul. "Bree, you want anything?"

"Let's go." Brielle stood up, took his hand, and they walked to the crowd at the refreshment table. Jessica looked at Brooke and I—and Corey—uncomfortably, then slipped after them. Ingrid walked toward us.

"You realize what we have to do now," said Ingrid. "A neighborhood-watch program." She took a tiny bite of banana bread and wiped her mouth with a napkin. "It'll help us catch any suspicious activity, but it'll also help us control any accusations before they get out of hand." She looked at Corey. "Would your parents be interested in joining a neighborhood-watch program?"

"I don't see why not," said Corey. "I can go ask them." He looked at me one last time, a kind of noncommittal acknowledgment that was neither a smile nor a frown, and walked away.

"I haven't talked to Beth yet," said Ingrid, "but she goes along with everything. And I'm sure I can get Sara involved as well."

"We're in too," I said.

"You don't need to trouble yourselves," said Ingrid. "You're not even really a part of the neighborhood."

"It's the least we can do," said Brooke. "You've helped us, and we want to help you."

"That's wonderful," said Ingrid. "Say what you will about the youth of America, we raise them right in Dillon. And wherever you're from."

A neighborhood-watch program would give us the perfect excuse to wander through the town learning about people. Our plan was working out perfectly.

But Attina had a plan of his own, and Corey's behavior had convinced me that I had no idea what that plan was.

16

I took a bite of whatever I'd picked up from the refreshment table, not paying attention to what it was. "Talk to Corey," I said to Brooke.

She glanced at him across the crowded floor of the church. "I don't like him," she said.

"He's probably a Withered," I said, "and almost certainly a killer. I'd be disturbed if you did like him. But you don't have to like him, just . . . talk to him. We need to get to know him better, and he doesn't like me. Or at least he knows that something's up with me. You can go make friends."

"You want me to flirt with him?"

"I didn't say that."

"But that's what you meant," she said. "You want me to smile and blush and laugh at his jokes and make him like me."

"I'm just saying you're better at it than I am."

"Because I'm a girl."

"Because I'm a sociopath," I said. "We're not charming people."

"Yes you are," she said. "Ted Bundy was the most charming person his victims had ever met."

"I'm not Ted Bundy."

"But he might be," said Brooke. "And you want me to go and talk to him."

"Are you scared of him?" I asked. "How many Withered have we faced?"

"This is different," said Brooke. "He's a teenage boy—that calls for a very specific kind of interaction, and I can't do that. Maybe before, but not . . . like this."

"We have to get to know him," I said. "We won't be at this meeting together forever, which means we need to find out where he'll be next. He already introduced us to his social circle, so all we have to do is step into it."

"I don't know," she said, grimacing as she stared at their little group. "What do I say? I suck at this."

"You're great at talking to people," I said. "You were the one who asked me out on our first date."

"I'm not going to ask him on a date."

"That's not what I meant," I said, "I just mean that you are a social person—you know everything about everybody, because you talk to them. You talked to that girl in the car yesterday for hours."

"She wasn't a boy."

"What, are you . . . attracted to him?"

"Of course not," she snapped. Her hands were clenched in fists and she was practically bouncing on her toes. "It's a cultural thing—there are certain ways a girl talks to a boy and they're different in every era of history, sometimes in every year. And 99.99-whatever percent of my experience in this area is centuries out of date. I can't do it. I can't do it." She was gritting her teeth, and I recognized the signs too late: she was having another episode. I grabbed her hand and changed tactics immediately.

"It's okay," I said. "We can do it together."

"You asked me to do it for a reason," she said. "If it was something we could do together we'd have done it together."

"We *can* do it together."

She shook her head, still staring at him. "I screwed up. If I was Brooke I could do it, but I'm just a big pile of dead girls. I can't do anything."

I stepped in front of her, still holding her hand and now looking straight into her eyes. Talking to Corey's group could wait—saving Brooke was the most important thing in the world right now. "Look at me. Do you see me?"

Her breath was coming too quickly.

"Brooke," I said, "can you see me? What's my name?"

"I'm not Brooke."

"That's okay," I said. "You're you, and that's okay. Who am I?"

"You're trying to save me," she said, closing her eyes. Tears seeped from under her eyelids. "That means I'm having an attack, which I always do every time we have to do something important. We have to talk to them and I'm ruining this."

"Forget them," I said. "You're awesome and you're not ruining anything."

"Stop saying that!" she hissed, and I could see now that people around us were starting to look. "You think you're saying you want to help me, but all you're really saying is that I need help. That I can't do it on my own. I am broken—I'm a hundred thousand girls and every one of them is broken—"

"Marci," said Ingrid, stepping out of the crowd, "is everything okay?"

Brooke tugged on her hands, trying to pull free of my grip on her wrists, but her movements were stiff—not halfhearted, but as if she were physically fighting not just me, but herself. "You're okay," I whispered.

"Marci?" asked Ingrid.

"Yes I am," said Brooke. She straightened her back and looked me in the eye. I could tell just by the way she held herself that she was Marci now. "You want me to go charm somebody? That's what I'm here for."

She pulled on her wrists again, and I let her go. The depression had disappeared like a switch had been flicked, replaced by cool, brazen confidence. She walked to Corey and his friends and started chattering happily, smiling, laughing, even touching him lightly on the arm.

"None of my business," said Ingrid, and she walked away.

Marci didn't look desperate, or like she was trying to impress anyone, or even like she was trying to flirt. She just looked like she'd known the other teens for years and fit perfectly into their group.

I took another bite of whatever baked thing was in my hand. Zucchini bread, it turned out. I looked at it, then back up at Marci. All I'd asked Brooke to do was talk to him—we had to talk to him, so I'd asked her to do it. But it had hurt her so much that Brooke had run away, retreating into her own mind and calling out someone else who could do the job for her.

Was Marci helping Brooke deal with a situation she couldn't face? Or was she stealing her life away, second by second?

And which one did I want: the smart, capable girl I loved, or the screwed-up girl who wanted to die?

I set down the bread and watched them talk.

About ten minutes later Corey and Paul walked out, Jessica and

Brielle leaving with them. Marci walked back to me and wiggled her eyebrows dramatically—something Brooke had never done, but I'd seen Marci do it a hundred times. "Eating out of the palm of my hand," she said. She picked my zucchini bread and popped it into her mouth. "Turns out this town has an ice cream place by the delightful name of Kitten Caboodle. We're meeting those young ladies and gentlemen there tonight."

I nodded. "Suckin' on chili dogs outside the Tastee-Freez."

"What?"

"Classic rock," I said.

"Cool," said Marci. "But first, how about a little thanks? I'm, like, Brielle's best friend in the world, after ten friggin' minutes."

"Yes," I said, silently chastising myself. "You were awesome. If I could talk to people that easily, I . . . don't even know what I would do. Have a way happier life, for one thing."

"And you do things I can't do," she said. "We're a great team."

"Yeah," I said, looking at the open door. "Between the two of us, I figure we make just about one whole person."

We hung around a little longer at the church, meeting various community dignitaries and trying to seem as innocent and pious as possible. I even thought about quoting some of the scriptures I knew, but decided that the strong focus on death would make that seem creepy instead of faithful. Having Ingrid with us did wonders, as everyone in town seemed to know her and respect her. We rode her reflected goodwill for all it was worth. We even chatted with Corey's parents, Steven and Jennifer, though it was mostly just small talk to get them to like us. The real questions could come later. When it was all over we helped clean up and carry all the plates home—not just Ingrid's, but Beth's as well. She hobbled behind us with her cane, remarking on how much brighter the neighborhood seemed now that everyone had come out of hiding, and spinning out grand plans for the neighborhood watch.

At the house, we unpacked some of our things, hanging our clean clothes in the closet of the pink bedroom to help air them out a bit, giving them the chance to smell like a home instead of a highway. Later we washed all the dirty dishes from Ingrid's baking, then walked out to Main Street to look for a place to get a real haircut. We found a salon with one lone stylist, a woman named Cindy, who cut my hair short and trimmed Marci's short bob all the way down to a pixie cut. Two dollars and eleven cents left.

We stepped outside, where we'd left Boy Dog tied to a pole, and looked around. I brushed at the back of my neck, trying to dislodge the last of the itchy hair clippings. It was past dinnertime, but we'd filled up on bread and brownies at the community meeting, and were so accustomed to going hungry that we didn't feel any need for food. We strolled the two blocks toward Kitten Caboodle, which turned out to be a small stand with no interior seating—just a drive-thru window in the back and a walk-up window in front, next to an asphalt lot with five round tables. These were bright red, made of old, scratched fiberglass, and bolted to metal frames with semi-circular benches. The frames, in turn, were chained to the ground, and I wondered what high school prank had necessitated that measure. We asked the clerk for a paper dish full of water for Boy Dog, and sat in the late evening light and waited.

"What day is it?" asked Marci.

"Wednesday."

"I mean what day of the month?"

I thought for a minute. "July something," I said at last. "It was on the news show we saw the other day, so just add two and there you go. I don't remember what to add two to, though."

"July," said Marci. "Where were you for the fourth?"

"I don't know," I said. "On the road somewhere."

The girls showed up first and they immediately fell into a conversation about Marci's hair.

"I've always wanted to try mine that short," said Brielle, touching her own very long hair. "But I think my parents would blow a fuse. And Paul would hate it."

"Does Paul like you or your hair?" asked Marci.

"He likes her butt," said Jessica.

"Can you blame him?" asked Brielle with a grin.

"Seriously, though," said Marci. "If he likes you, he'll like you no matter what your hair looks like."

"People always say that," said Brielle. "But it always sounds so one-sided to me. I'm not the only one in this relationship."

"You're the only one wearing your hair," said Jessica.

"But there's something to be said for accommodating someone you like," said Brielle. "If it was a big deal, sure, I'd cut my hair off. But if I don't really care either way, and he cares a lot, why not keep it long?"

"What kind of accommodations does he make for you?" asked Marci.

Brielle pursed her lips and didn't answer. After a moment she looked at me. "What do you think, David? Guys like long hair, right?"

"I don't like having to tuck it behind my ears all the time," I said. It wasn't what she meant, but I was only half paying attention, and unhelpful sarcasm was apparently my default mode. I looked up the street. Where was Corey? Was waiting for him at a specific time and place a trap? Would he try to hurt us so publicly?

"I mean on girls," said Brielle. "Paul or no Paul, and I say this in all humility, this is man-catching hair."

I looked at her and admitted to myself that she did indeed have incredible hair. It had looked good at the church meeting, but she'd obviously done something to it since; it was wavy and full and caught the setting sun perfectly. I imagined myself combing it, flat on an embalming table, over and over until it shone like gold—

"It's not about bodies," I said. "It's about whoever's inside of them."

I looked at Marci. In Brooke's body. She looked back, saying nothing, then turned to Brielle. "If only it were that easy, huh?"

"I don't want a boyfriend 'til college," said Jessica. "All the boys are idiots."

Marci looked at me with a wicked grin. "Preach."

"Boys aren't that bad," said Brielle.

"I don't mean all the boys in the world," said Jessica. "I mean all the boys here. They're the same boys I've known since preschool. Braden Cole is the cutest boy in my grade, and he threw up on me on a kindergarten field trip."

"If you don't want boys who throw up on you, college is going to be a big surprise," said Marci. I looked at her, wondering at the comment—she'd died as a sophomore in high school. But I supposed she had plenty of memories mixed in with her own, memories belonging to girls Nobody had killed when they were older. Had she torn through a university once, thinking that the perfect life she wanted might be there? I wondered how long that had lasted, and what kind of life, if any, might finally satisfy her. And I wondered how much of Nobody's restlessness was still there, latent in Brooke's fragmented mind.

"I love your highlights," said Brielle, looking at Brooke's blond hair again. "Are they natural?"

"They are!" said Marci cheerfully. "And I love them. It's kind of fun being blond—"

She didn't look at me, but I could tell from her sudden pause that she was frozen in shock at the accidental slipup. Marci had had dark black hair all her life.

"Did you dye it?" asked Jessica.

"I had it black for a while," said Marci, touching Brooke's hair with her fingertips. "This is great, but . . . I kind of miss the old hair."

"You look great blond," said Brielle. "It suits you."

Corey came from behind the ice cream stand, stepping softly as if he was trying to sneak up on us, but I saw Boy Dog's head move. I turned my own head just enough to see Corey from the corner of my eye.

"Welcome to the Kitten Caboodle," I said, summoning all my will not to look at him directly—to allow him to sneak up behind me. I was, for a moment, terrified.

"We just call it Caboodle's," said Paul, walking behind Corey.

"Is that the owner's last name?" asked Marci. Her eyes lit up. "Does that mean his first name is Kitten?"

"Don't I wish," said Paul.

"It's just a cute name," said Brielle. "I don't think it means anything."

"It's a pun," said Jessica.

"Obviously it's a pun," said Paul. "We mean beside that."

"Five-oh," said Corey, looking past us toward the street. We turned and saw a man walking toward us, swaggering slightly in the brown uniform of the state police.

"Crap," said Brielle, muttering so softly I could barely hear her. "Officer Cuddles."

"Good evening to you fine young ladies," said the officer. "Are these boys bothering you?"

"No, Mr. Glassman," said Brielle.

"Officer Glassman," said the officer. I looked at his name tag and saw the vague outline of a name that might be Glassman; I looked at his face instead and saw clearly Sara's features reflected in him—the same nose, the same shape in the cheeks. He was definitely her brother. He looked at Jessica and Brielle, lingering just a little longer than he needed to on each one, then turned to look at Marci. "You're new in town."

And there was that old, familiar feeling again—not hate, but a sudden, almost crystalline clarity: I could kill this man without the tiniest bump in my heart rate.

No.

"Just passing through," said Marci. Her endless joviality was gone, replaced by a brusque dismissal. She acknowledged him, gave the barest minimum of an answer, then turned away. She looked at Corey—why at Corey, of all people?—and nodded her head toward the ice cream stand. "We gonna get anything?"

The dark, near-scowl on Officer Glassman's face showed that he didn't like being ignored and he had the authority to make sure we noticed him. "What's your name?" he asked. Almost as an afterthought he turned to me as well. "You too, kid. What's your name?"

"David," I said.

"Got any ID?"

"What flavors do they have?" asked Marci, still looking at Corey.

"I asked for your name," said Glassman again, louder this time.

"Marci," said Marci, looking at him again. "Are you from around here?"

It was obvious that Glassman was a jerk, and judging by the nickname Officer Cuddles, he had some kind of a reputation. Based on the way Corey and Paul looked uncomfortable, but Jessica and Brielle looked outright disgusted, it wasn't hard to guess where that nickname had come from. The look on his face oscillated between lechery and anger; he could barely keep his eyes off of Jessica's legs, easily visible in her jean shorts. And any time his look strayed elsewhere it was on one of the other girls, and well below their eyes. The local kids were all staying quiet, implying that this kind of thing happened often enough to be familiar, but never got bad enough to merit fighting back. I assumed he would pester us a little, maybe leer a bit, and then move on. He certainly wouldn't try anything in the middle of Main Street like this.

But he might still insist on seeing our ID. And he looked like the kind of guy who, when we couldn't show him any, would relish the opportunity to throw his weight around a little. We might lose everything we'd worked for, right here at Caboodle's.

"I grew up here," said Glassman. "Dillon's first settlers were Glassmans."

"Did they work in glass?" asked Marci. She didn't smile when she said it—she wasn't flirting—but she was definitely playing him a little. Feigning interest in his story to help him feel important, trying to defuse the initial burst of anger that had prompted him to ask for our IDs. Ignoring him had been her first gambit and it had backfired; now she was trying to keep him friendly.

"I . . . guess so," said Glassman. "I hadn't really thought about it."

"Maybe in England they did," said Marci. "And then when they came over here they started farming. Or ranching, I guess." She scrunched up her forehead and nose, twisting her lips in an adorable look of innocent confusion. I worried she was taking it too far. "Do they have a lot of ranches around here?"

"This is corn country," said Paul. "Well, corn now. A lot of it used to be wheat—"

"It was the government subsidies that changed the focus," said Glassman, stealing back the spotlight without even looking in Paul's direction. "Biofuels and whatnot. It doesn't pay to be in anything but corn these days."

"Being a cop's more interesting anyway," said Marci, but Jessica's face fell so fast when she said it that I knew Marci had made some kind of blunder, tripping over some invisible Dillon trip wire.

Officer Glassman's eyes darkened—his eyebrows knit together and his eyeballs appeared to get darker in their shadow. "You got a problem with the state police, missy?"

"Marci," said Marci, and Glassman and I both stared at her in shock—he was already getting angry and she'd corrected him, blunt as could be. But even as he was starting to snarl out a protest, she laughed out loud—high peals of laughter that seemed to shake her whole body. She covered her mouth with her hand and raised her eyebrows, trying to stifle the laughter, and then started spewing out a high-speed apology: "Oh, I'm so sorry I'm so sorry, I thought you were saying my name and so I was telling you it was Marci, I'm *such* an airhead, I'm so sorry, please, um, please—" She looked as apologetic as a person could look while trying not to laugh, and her laughter was so infectious that Glassman and Paul both started chuckling with her. None of the rest of us did, though I tried to smile to keep the general atmosphere going.

"No harm done, Marci," said Glassman. He hesitated a moment, thrown so thoroughly off his guard that he didn't know what to say next. "You, um, here for ice cream?"

"What flavor do you recommend?" asked Marci, recovering her composure just slowly enough to make the laughter look sincere. She wiped a tear from her eye to complete the effect.

"Raspberry," said Glassman. "Dillon's famous for its raspberries."

"Awesome," said Marci, and she jumped up from her seat on the scratched red table. "Thanks! Come on guys." She motioned to us with her head, sticking her fingers in the back pockets of her jeans, and turned her back on Glassman to walk to the ice cream counter.

The rest of us took our cue and followed Marci, while Glassman just stood dumbly and watched, completely outmatched in Marci's verbal chess game. He didn't try to stop us—the conversation had arrived at his own dismissal so naturally he couldn't protest it. I waited the longest, letting the rest bunch up in the line while I watched Glassman's face. The last one to go was Jessica. As she turned, she dropped her phone. She stopped to pick it up, grimacing in fear that she'd somehow broken the spell, but all Glassman could see was her butt, bent over and pointed right at him, perfectly displayed in her tight shorts. He stared at it, and I saw him swallow and clench his fists. I looked away, not wanting him to see that I had seen him. When Jessica walked past me I moved directly behind her, cutting off Glassman's view.

At the bar, we all made pointless small talk, not daring to look back. After a minute or two, I glanced back as discreetly as I could, hoping not to see him still standing in the same place. The truth was almost as bad—he was across the street, sitting in his squad car and staring.

I couldn't say for sure at that distance, but I'd have bet anything he was staring right at Jessica.

"Thanks for getting rid of him," said Brielle. "And please teach me how to do that."

"He's not gone yet," said Corey. I hadn't even seen him look. Jessica turned and looked at the squad car.

"Frickin' Cuddles," said Paul. "That guy gives me the creeps."

"You're not the one he was undressing with his eyes," said Brielle.

"I take it he does that a lot?" I asked.

"That's the rumor," said the kid behind the counter.

"He was always pretty touchy-feely," said Brielle. "But after he left Dillon to join the state police we heard about a girl in another town—"

"Crosby," said Paul.

"No," said the kid behind the counter, "it was Taylorsville."

"It was somewhere," said Brielle. "Nobody knows exactly what happened, but he's totally a skeeze."

"Sounds like an urban legend," I said.

"It definitely happened," said Paul. "I met a guy who knew the girl he attacked."

"If it definitely happened he wouldn't still be a cop," said Marci. Her father was a cop. "They hate pedophiles more than anything."

"Maybe," said Jessica. She didn't seem convinced.

"You saw the way he was looking at us," said Brielle. "Even if there wasn't a girl in Crosby or wherever, there's going to be one someday. Somewhere." Glassman started up his police cruiser and pulled out into the street, driving away. Brielle watched him go, her eyes cold. "If he comes after you, Jess, I'll kill him."

17

It started with a scream. Distant, it sounded like, but nothing in Dillon is all that distant. I learned later that it was only a few blocks away from our guest room in Ingrid's house, which isn't that far for a scream to carry. Pretty far to wake someone up, though. I was lying on the floor and opened my eyes, not even sure what had woken me. Brooke was asleep on the bed; I didn't let myself look, but I listened, and her breathing was soft and steady. Boy Dog was snoring on the floor. I was in front of the door, blocking Brooke from leaving, and anyone else from entering. The house was quiet, as was the town. The light of a pale quarter moon drifted through the slats in the window blinds.

And then someone screamed again.

You would think, after the kind of life I've lived, that I'd be some kind of expert on screaming—that I could tell from a single cry at least the gender of a screamer, if not the age and some other details. Maybe that happens eventually, but if all the screams I've heard aren't enough,

I certainly don't want to know how many it would take. Extreme pain and extreme terror have a way of blending all voices into one primal sound, as if there were only one scream, and we just tapped into it now and then.

I sat up straighter, listening, wondering what I should do. Run out and find them? And then what? I was useless in a direct confrontation; at best, I would give myself away to Attina, letting him know exactly who was hunting him and ruining all my future attempts to gather information. At worst, he'd kill me too.

And it had to be Attina causing the screaming, right? This town had gone for decades without a violent attack, and now they'd had two in less than a week. There was no way that was a coincidence. But Derek Stamper had been killed slowly and in private, and no one had known until the body was found more than an hour later. Did that mean this was a different killer? Or a different situation? What had changed in the circumstances to prompt such a marked changed in the Withered's methods?

I stood up, shucking the blankets I'd been wrapped in and walking to the window. The floor creaked under my feet, but only softly. I moved a slat in the blinds and looked outside; the world was empty and dark, colorless in the moonlight. I saw trees and houses and parked cars, all motionless in the silence. There wasn't even wind. I don't know what I was expecting to see, certainly not some transformed demon killing someone right in front of the—

Another scream, longer than the others. Was the pitch different? I couldn't tell.

What if it wasn't a Withered at all? What if it truly was a coincidence, two attacks in less than a week, and this one was just a mugging or an assault, and I could stop it and was too afraid to do so? But I had reason to be afraid, maybe more than anybody else in the town, because I knew what could happen if I was right. I'd seen

Withered kill. I'd seen the aftermath, and I'd seen it up close. Worse than the violence, I'd seen glimpses of the minds behind it, tortured by time and warped over ten thousand years. I'd seen them not just take lives but take them over, stepping into people's shapes and faces and living their lives for them.

Stopping them was what I did. It was my entire life. But running out headfirst was not how I did it.

I waited by the window, watching and listening, but the screams were done. Three short cries, and a life was over.

A few minutes later I heard an engine, then two, three, and who knows how many more. I could see red-and-blue reflections on the houses across the street, but not the lights themselves. Voices shouting. I couldn't hear what they were saying. A light came on in the house across the street, and then another in the house next to it. I looked at the round clock face on the bedroom wall, squinting to see it clearly in the dark. 1:30 in the morning. There'd be hours before we knew the truth.

Was it worth it to go out and look? Now that the police were there the danger—probably—was gone. And I knew I wouldn't be the only one stepping out in the middle of the night to rubberneck whatever grim cleanup the police were trying to do. It might even serve as an alibi, in case suspicion ever turned to us—*obviously I didn't do it, I was right there with you instead of running away.* Or it might just as easily create suspicion where none had existed, causing the police to remember me when they thought about the crime scene. Guilty parties showed up at their own investigations all the time—not enough to make it suspicious, but certainly enough to remove it as an alibi. More than anything, though, if I went I'd have to take Brooke with me, or risk her waking up in confusion and wandering away. She needed sleep, especially now that she had a real bed for the first time in a week, and she needed to not be traumatized by the sight of another dead body. Better to stay here and wait.

I waited by the window, watching for any new information.

All night long.

Brooke was still Marci when she woke up the next morning. I explained what had happened, as briefly as I could, and she said I'd made the right decision to stay inside. I don't know if she believed it or not, but it was kind of her to say. We got dressed, staring at opposite walls in the pink, fluffy room. When we got to the kitchen to help with breakfast, Ingrid was already there, in her bathrobe and curlers, holding the phone and crying.

"Mercy," she said. "Mercy, mercy."

"Is everything okay?" asked Marci. She glanced at me, both of us knowing what the phone call was probably about.

Ingrid shook her head.

I stepped closer, trying to sound helpful instead of curious. "Is there something we can do?"

Ingrid looked at the phone in her hand as if were a museum curiosity, a bizarre object that had somehow transported itself magically into her hand. I saw that the screen was blank and black; whatever call she'd gotten was long over, and she'd been too shocked to put it down.

Marci sat next to her at the kitchen table. "We heard something last night," she said. "Police cars, some kind of trouble. Did someone tell you what it was?"

I would have asked the same question by saying that I'd heard screaming, but I could see instantly that mentioning the police cars was the smarter move. Marci was filling Ingrid's mind with the most acceptable, approachable part of the story: someone trying to fix it.

Mentioning the screams would only have made the story more horrible.

What would I do without Marci?

Ingrid nodded slowly, still sobbing into her hands. She wiped her eyes and sniffed, trying to regain her composure. "You met them yesterday, right? The Butler girls?"

No, I thought, please no. "We did," I said, nodding slowly. "Are they okay?"

"Jessica," said Ingrid, and she broke down sobbing again. We could barely understand the next three words: "Just like Derek."

Marci put her hand on Ingrid's back, looked at me silently, then wrapped her arms around Ingrid, who hugged her back, and Boy Dog walked toward them, sitting down on Marci's feet in a gesture of fat, furry devotion. I watched them, thinking.

Why Jessica? Both victims were people we had talked to, the night after we'd talked to them. Was it a message to us? Or was someone actively hunting us, and kept missing? I didn't know what kind of tracking system might result in that kind of repeated mistake, but Withered powers were virtually impossible to understand without knowing exactly how they worked. The people they killed and their reasons and methods always had perfect internal consistency—even when you disagreed with what they did, you could understand how they got there. They made sense. All you had to do was find the thing that made them all make sense—that secret, supernatural decoder ring that made all the clues click into place. Without knowing how their powers worked, though . . .

We'd talked to several people while we were in Dillon. Why had the Withered killed these two, specifically? What set them apart? They were both teenagers. They were both people we'd talked to on the street. *They were both* . . . And then I felt a sudden rush of relief, realizing a key difference between the two victims: I'd wanted to kill Derek and felt a sense of guilty responsibility ever since I'd learned that he'd died, as if I'd somehow helped to cause it. But I'd never wanted to kill Jessica. Even better, I was actively *planning* to kill Corey, and he was fine. If my plans for violence had been the root of these attacks, Jessica would have been untouched. I was off the hook—

—well, at least in part. It was still my responsibility to stop this Withered before he killed again.

"I need to call Sara," said Ingrid, clutching Marci tightly for a few more seconds before pulling away and reaching for her phone again. "She'll be a wreck."

"Did she know Jessica well?" asked Marci.

"Oh dear," said Ingrid, taking Marci's hand. "I was so broken up I didn't even tell you about Luke."

"Her brother?" I asked.

"He tried to save her," said Ingrid. "He was a hero."

"Wait," I said, sitting at the table across from her. "What was Officer Glassman doing with fourteen-year-old Jessica at 1:30 in the morning?"

"He was a hero," Ingrid insisted, her voice turning hard and angry. "He got cut up too, trying to save her." She picked up the phone, and I caught Marci's eye and nodded toward the living room. I left the kitchen, and she followed me.

"What do you think?" I whispered.

"No way Jessica was out there with him willingly," said Marci.

I nodded. "Do you think . . .? I don't know. Can you remember any Withered who were pedophiles?"

She frowned. "You think it's Glassman, now?"

"I still think it's Corey," I said, shaking my head. "He's weird and creepy and that 'it begins' looks awfully suspicious. But. None of that is hard evidence, and both victims were teenagers, and

Officer Glassman was leering at Jessica like crazy just a few hours before she died. So it's at least worth a mention."

"But Glassman wasn't even here the night Derek died," said Marci. "Sara told us he'd left the day before."

"Maybe he faked leaving early to build himself an alibi."

"A person that careful wouldn't turn around and kill a girl five hours after all of Main Street saw him talking to her. And then be found at the scene with injuries."

I sighed and nodded. "You're right. But what if . . . I don't know. It's too obvious to ignore, even if some of the pieces don't fit yet."

"Yet?"

"They might fit better when we learn more."

Marci nodded. "For now, let's focus on what we know. Both victims died the night after we talked to them."

"Even better," I said, "both of those conversations happened in Corey's presence."

"He's still the best candidate," Marci agreed. "I just wish we had more evidence."

"Maybe he recognized us that first night," I said. "Or he recognized Nobody's presence or influence or something, and so when we left he killed Derek to try to lure us back. He didn't kill anyone the first night because he didn't have a plan yet. He was still thinking. And then the second night he put his plan into motion: It begins."

"So what's his plan?" asked Marci.

"I have no idea," I said, shrugging helplessly. "Maybe it's a message to us, or to someone else, or . . . well, it's definitely about us somehow. Two murders in a peaceful town coinciding perfectly with our arrival is not a coincidence. We need to talk to his parents today, and maybe Brielle."

"Seriously?" asked Marci. "Her sister was just murdered."

"Of course," I said. "You're right. Maybe Paul, then."

"It's going to be hard to talk to anyone if the whole town's in terrified mourning the whole time we're here," said Marci. She grimaced. "How many more do you think he's going to kill?"

"I don't know," I said. "Maybe. . . . Wait."

"What?"

"There's another correlation," I said. "We've been here three days, and we talked to people on three days, but people were only killed on two of them."

"Because he was still forming a plan on the first day," said Marci. "Like you said."

"Maybe," I said. "Or maybe there's another common factor we haven't considered. What did we do on the second and third days that we didn't do on the first?"

"We . . . were here during the daytime," said Marci. "We went to . . . oh crap." She looked me right in the eyes. "We went to church."

I nodded. "Both days."

"What does that mean?"

"I don't know."

"Maybe it doesn't mean anything," said Marci.

"Maybe not," I said. "Maybe it does."

"We have to deal with stuff we can understand," said Marci, frustrated. "Actual clues we can actually follow, instead of just guessing at shadows."

"What, then?"

"We should . . . go look at last night's crime scene," she said. "There might be soulstuff, or claw marks, or some other evidence that the police won't know is evidence because it's too weird to be part of a standard murder."

"That's a good idea," I said. "We'll see if we can get close; it might be taped off still. And either way, I think we need to visit the cops."

"You want to bring them in on this?" asked Marci. "I liked Officer Davis, but he won't believe a word we say if we try to tell him this was a supernatural monster."

I shook my head. "I just want to find out what they know—I can't look at the bodies anymore, like I used to back in Clayton, so we've got to get our info some other way."

"The cops won't tell you anything."

"Not on purpose," I said. "That's why we're going to tell them something—they asked everyone who knows something to talk to them, so we're going to go do it. We're going to offer ourselves as witnesses to yesterday's encounter between Jessica and Glassman. And while we're in the building, we're going to eavesdrop on every conversation we possibly can."

"You're crazy," said Brooke. "They'll ask for ID."

"And we won't have any to give them," I said. "That doesn't make us suspects, and whatever it does make us they'll be too busy with the killings to bother figuring out who we really are." I wavered back and forth, grimacing as I thought. "I'm 99 percent sure we won't be suspects."

Marci raised an eyebrow. "Are you willing to risk that 1 percent?"

"To kill a Withered?" I asked. "I'll risk a lot more than that."

"We can't be on camera, though," said Marci. "This is going to be national news, now more than ever, and we can't be seen."

"I know."

Marci folded her arms intently. "If we get to the station and they have a camera, we come right back. We can't risk anyone back home seeing us."

"Obviously," I said, then paused. "It's a smart plan, but . . . you seem more emotional about it as well."

"The sooner Brooke's body gets recognized," said Marci, "the sooner I might get evicted from it."

I didn't have anything to say to that.

We set out to look at the crime scene only to find it already swarmed with people pressed up against the line of police tape, craning their necks to catch a glimpse of anything they could. Marci and I worked our way to the front, but other than some plastic tarps that were almost certainly covering blood stains, we couldn't see anything. A handful of state police were on the scene, working more to keep people out than to actually examine the evidence, and I wondered if they were already done or if they were trying to keep the scene clean for an incoming forensics team. Two grisly child murders in half a week was national news; we might get FBI. I wondered if it would be anyone I knew.

Was that Attina's plan? To make this so high profile it became too risky for us to stay and hunt him?

We pushed our way gently out of the crowd, waved solemnly at Pastor Nash, who stood near the back of the crowd, and headed toward the police station. Marci started working on our story, conjuring something placating to tell the police if they demanded ID, while I put together the beginnings of a plan to kill Corey. Only the beginnings, though. Killing a Withered was just as delicate as tracking one; if you knew their powers you could do it fairly easily, but otherwise it was all but impossible. We'd have to start the way we always started: the speed-bump test. But how to arrange it? We couldn't just be in the truck when we hit him—we'd end up in jail or worse—and if he survived we would have exposed ourselves for nothing. It had to be more subtle. But how?

And did we dare to do it in the first place? What if Corey, despite all our suspicion, was innocent? What if he was just a weirdo with poor social skills, and his Facebook announcement was a pure coincidence? "It begins" might just as easily refer to . . . I didn't know, a garage band or something. Maybe his mustache was coming in. Maybe he was binge watching something online. I, of all people, couldn't condemn a guy just for being suspicious and not fitting in.

But how could I know for sure? Every moment I didn't act was another moment when someone could get hurt. Better to have the plan ready, so I could employ it when the target was confirmed.

Assuming I could get hold of a truck in the first place, how would I do it? Maybe if I aimed the truck just right and stacked a bunch of bricks on the gas pedal? If he was in a specific place, like the tables in front of Kitten Caboodle . . . but how could I keep him from seeing it coming, and getting out of the way? How could I limit the collateral damage? Maybe if I caught him at night, drunk at the drive-in theater, or walking home in the dark. The more I thought about it the more I wanted to do it, like a junkie sitting and staring at a hit of meth—just sitting there, waiting, filling up my entire mind. I looked at every truck we passed, wondering how to steal it, how to rig it, how to clean my own DNA off it.

We arrived at the police station only to find it almost as crowded as the crime scene—though most of the people here were in police uniforms. There were too many just for this department; they had local police, state police, and volunteers from all over the region. Most of them were milling around in the parking lot and by the front door as if they were waiting for something—an order or an announcement.

There was an ambulance in the parking lot. That was new, but I didn't know what it meant. There were no cameras or news crews.

One of the officers stopped us as we tried to walk to the front door.

"Do you have business here?"

"The officer at the church meeting told us to contact him if we knew anything," said Marci, putting on her most innocent voice. "We were with Jessica a lot yesterday."

"And that's it?" asked the cop. "You hung out with the victim? Do you have more than that?"

"Officer Glassman was there," said Marci, dropping her eyes. I couldn't tell if she was really embarrassed or still acting.

"Damn Cuddles," said another cop, walking up next to the first. "Send them through."

The second officer motioned for us to follow him. He led us past the crowd of police and into the station itself, where we could hear someone yelling in one of the offices. The cop pointed us to the waiting area: seven or eight plastic chairs, most of them already filled with what I assumed were other witnesses. Marci and I sat down, Boy Dog panting languidly at our feet, and I strained to hear the shouting.

". . . another one? How the hell am I supposed to explain this?"

The response was too muffled to make out. The first voice shouted again.

"You're not getting out of this with a transfer, Luke!"

Officer Davis, the one from the church meeting, was yelling at Officer Glassman. "Another one" didn't refer to the dead body, but to Glassman's history with underage girls. I glanced at Marci, and she shook her head.

"You want proof the Withered are evil?" she whispered. "It killed the girl instead of the child molester."

"Listen!" shouted Davis. "I don't care what excuses you have! I don't care that you risked your life or got a few cuts or whatever pathetic excuse you're trying to give me. This town's ready to explode, and instead of solving their problems now I've got to deal with some dirtbag officer and his dirtbag fantasies." He paused, while Glassman murmured something I couldn't hear. "Do you think that matters?" asked Davis when he was done. "Of course it was all just gossip—that's why you haven't been fired—but this is evidence. If you're so damn innocent this time can you explain what you were doing with her at 1:30 in the morning?"

"At least he's as mad about this as we are," said Marci.

"I'm trying to hear," I said, but stopped speaking abruptly when another officer walked briskly around the corner, headed straight for us. I looked up, rehearsing my story one last time, but he walked right past us toward Officer Davis's door. His face was grim, his teeth clenched.

"That's not good," said Marci.

The newcomer opened the door, and we caught the second half of Officer Glassman's muffled argument: " . . . even talking about this! How is it even an issue? So you don't believe in bigfoot, fine, neither do I, but then it was a bear, or the biggest wolf you've ever seen—the coroner's report is going to back up everything I've said, no matter what you think I was doing with that g—"

"Quiet!" said Officer Davis. I could just barely see him through the door, and he looked furious. I wanted Glassman to keep talking, to say more about the monster he'd seen, but Davis turned to the man who'd opened the door and snapped at him: "I said no interruptions."

"Unless there was another dead kid," said the cop at the door. Every head in the waiting room swiveled toward him in unison, and the entire police station seemed to be suddenly on edge, listening. "Now we have."

"No," said Davis.

The cop in the doorway shook his head. "A local boy named Corey Diamond just got hit by a truck, in his own bedroom. Dead on impact."

"Holy mother," whispered Marci.

"In his bedroom. . . . " Officer Davis spluttered, trying to find words. "That's . . . Dammit. Is it an accident or another murder?"

"That's the thing," said the cop. "We don't know." He swallowed, like he was nervous. "There wasn't anybody in it—the truck was completely empty when it hit."

18

"I think someone's reading my mind," I whispered.

"We've got to get out of here," said Marci.

I looked around the police station, as if expecting to see a clawed, hairy monster peeking out from around a corner. "It's the only explanation."

The entire police station was buzzing with noise, cops and civilians and even suspects in their interrogation rooms, shouting and whispering and arguing and praying. What was going on? Who was behind it? Why were they doing it? Even Boy Dog was barking, little yips and growls of agitation. I felt a pain in my hands and looked down, realizing that I was gripping the armrests so tightly that the skin of my knuckles, chapped from wind and sun, was splitting open across the bones. Someone was reading my mind.

"We need to get out of here," said Marci again, grabbing my arm.

I felt a sudden burst of anger—how dare she touch my arm!—and pulled away, feeling furious and terrified and guilty all at once. I shouldn't react like that; Marci was my girlfriend, I loved her, of course she could touch my arm. Then I remembered it wasn't even her fingers that had touched me but Brooke's, and I felt another surge of anger, followed just as quickly by another surge of guilt. I shouldn't feel like this. I couldn't allow myself to feel like this.

I needed to burn something.

"Close that door!" shouted Officer Davis. "Let's keep some semblance of propriety in this station!" The cop with the message stepped into Davis's office and closed the door behind him, and the noise from the waiting room only got louder.

Marci stood up and grabbed my hand with Brooke's fingers, trying to pull me out of my seat. I clenched my teeth and gripped the armrests tighter, willing my skin to split open, relishing the sharp, tearing pain of it. "John," she whispered, and I closed my eyes and tightened the muscles in my neck, flexing them so hard my head began to shake. *Get out of my head*, I thought, *get out of my head!* I took a deep breath and tried to calm myself. *Whoever you are*, I thought, *I'm going to find you and tear you apart with my bare hands. Do you hear me? I'm coming for you!*

Marci tugged on me again and I stood, feeling nauseated at the sudden change in position. Or the anger. Or the helplessness. How could we fight this thing? Whoever it was had pinned us as Withered hunters the moment we'd stepped into town, had been reading our minds and taunting us with body after body, death after death. What other explanation could there be? The people we met, the people I wanted to hurt, were killed in exactly the way I wanted to kill them. And now our only suspect was gone—

I stopped at the front desk. "What happened to the body?" I asked.

The cop at the desk looked up with a frown, both annoyed by my question and confused by it. "What?"

"Corey Diamond's body," I said, "what happened to it? Is it still there?"

"You can't see the body—"

"But can you?" I asked. "Can anybody? Does the body still exist?"

"The hell are you talking about?" asked the cop. "We're not going to hide the body, no matter how many pieces it's in. What are you trying to say about us?"

"It doesn't matter," said Marci, "come on."

I let her lead me toward the front door. "It didn't disappear," I said. "It's not a Withered."

"*He's* not a Withered," said Marci, though her voice had no passion.

"That's what I said."

She pushed the door half open, her wrist limp, and stared out through the glass at the crowd of police in the front of the building. They were buzzing like a hive, talking and arguing as much as the people inside were. Some were running toward their cars, others held back townspeople. Was one of them the killer? A cop or a civilian or the driver of that truck passing by? It had to be someone. What did they say the population was, nine hundred? Add in the state police and whatever other drifters and delivery drivers happened to be in town and we could round it off to an even thousand. How many had Attina killed? How many more would he kill if we didn't catch him? If we just burned the whole city to the ground and took all of them out, was it worth it if we killed the Withered with them? Was there some formula for acceptable collateral damage? Was there enough math in morality to sacrifice a whole town of people?

I needed to burn something. I needed to scream and cry and hack a piece of meat into hamburger.

Marci wasn't even pushing on the door anymore. "It doesn't matter," she said.

Don't say it.

"It's gonna kill us too," she said.

I screamed in my mind, a long, inaudible howl of frustration, and then I swallowed all my rage, all my tension, all my pent-up emotions, choking them down like an owl in reverse, a ragged little bundle of bones and claws and bile, forcing it back down my gullet and pasting a broad, fake smile across my face. Her problems were more important than mine. "You want some ice cream?"

"I just want it to stop," said Marci.

"It will," I said, not even knowing what "it" she was referring to. I put my hand next to hers and pushed the door open, hoping that she would push with me, drawing strength from mine, but instead she just let her hand drop to her side. The summer sun beat down like a furnace, and I pulled her gently out into it, one hand on her arm and the other in front of my face trying to shield my eyes from the brightness. Boy Dog shoved past our legs, barking at the sun and heat and noise and everything else, like a tiny personification of the whole town's restless anger. Marci resisted and I tugged again, whispering gently. "It's all going to be just fine," I said. "We're going to figure out what's going on—you and me. And we're going to solve it." Then, remembering her rage after we killed Yashodh, her indignant fury at the thought that being a good killer was something to be happy about, I changed my tactics. "We're going to save everybody," I said. "Three people are gone, but they're the only ones."

"You don't know that."

"I do, because we're amazing," I said, leading her down the steps. The cops weren't even paying attention to us; they were too occupied with other concerns. "I know it because we're good at this, we're the best at this; we're going to save the lives of every single person in this town. All 997 of them, including the cops and the drivers. Everyone. Do you hear me, Marci?"

She started crying.

"Marci, do you hear me? I need you to talk to me. We're going to save everyone, can you say that? Say it with me: We're going to save everyone."

"I'm not Marci," she sobbed, and she broke away from me and ran.

I bolted after her, forgetting the cops, forgetting Boy Dog, forgetting everything in the world but that one girl, skinny and dirty and afraid. My feet pounded on the pavement, leaping off the curb and onto the dusty asphalt, arms pumping at my sides. Just one girl. I didn't even know who she was—maybe Brooke, maybe Regina, maybe Lucinda or Kveta or a hundred thousand others I'd never even met. It didn't matter. She needed my help. She ran toward a car, trying to throw herself in front of it, but it passed too quickly; she ran toward the cinder block wall on the far side of the road, head down like a bull, and screamed a wordless cry as she plowed herself into it, skull first, my fingers just inches too far away to pull her back. She hit the wall with an audible smack and bounced off, reeling and falling. I only just managed to grab her shirt as she fell to the sidewalk, catching her before she hit her head again. She threw up, and I rolled her over to keep the vomit from choking her. Seconds later I was grabbed from behind, half a dozen rough hands yanking me away, pulling me back.

"Don't take her away!" I screamed.

"Get off her!" shouted one of the cops, and suddenly cops were everywhere, appearing like magic as they caught up to us and surrounded us, misinterpreting Brooke's sprint and my chase as some kind of abusive scenario.

"She's a suicide risk!" I shouted.

"Keep your mouth shut!"

"She just tried to kill herself," I said, grunting as they slammed me to the ground and cuffed me. "If you try to separate us she will kill herself, you have to trust me—I was trying to help her!"

Brooke's body was still rolling around on the sidewalk, twisting either in pain or a seizure, I couldn't tell which. She'd hit her head so hard I was amazed she was even conscious. The cops tried to help her, but weren't sure what to do. I heard one call for an ambulance, and others knelt next to her, speaking in calm, businesslike phrases:

"Are you okay?"

"Was this boy chasing you?"

"Did he hurt you?"

I took another deep breath, trying to calm myself as much as possible. "Please believe me," I said. I stuck with the name everyone in Dillon knew her by. "Her name is Marci, though she has some mental problems and doesn't always answer to it. I'm her friend and I was only trying to keep her safe. Part of her mental illness makes her highly prone to suicide."

I saw someone step out of the shop she'd crashed into, an old man in an apron, and I shouted out to him. "You—you from the store. You're my witness, okay? This girl is a severe suicide risk, and I have to stay with her, and you just heard me warn these cops, okay? If they separate us, and she kills herself, you can testify it was their fault, okay? Sir, did you hear me?"

"Shut up," said the cop holding me down.

"Is there anything I can do?" the old man asked the police.

"Just stay back," said the nearest officer, "we have an ambulance on the way."

"Bring her some water," I said, "And all the ice in your store; she probably has a concussion." The man nodded and went back inside.

The cop on my back shoved me against the ground again, frisking me with his free hand.

"He's got a weapon," said the cop, pulling Potash's combat knife from the sheath on my leg. Dammit. "You want to explain this, kid?"

"Officer," I said, talking to the cop who was trying to help Brooke. "You see her hand? Yes, you—you see her hand? It looks like it's flailing randomly, but she's reaching for your gun. Just—just step away, that's right, and try to hold her down."

"What's your name?" asked the cop I'd warned, glancing at me as he grabbed at Brooke's flailing arms.

"David," I said. "I'm only trying to help her, you have to believe me."

"Why's she trying to kill herself?"

"That's a very long story."

"You've got time," said the cop on my back. There were at least six other police officers swarming around us; if Brooke had gotten hold of a gun, she'd be dead. I tried to look her in the eyes, to see how lucid she was, but she was squeezing them shut.

"Just let me die," she whimpered. "Just please let me die. It'll all be over and I can start again."

The cop holding her arms looked at her in surprise, then back at me. "Start again?"

"She's mentally ill," I said. "Most of the time she's fine, but when she gets like this you just have to ride it out. She'll be okay again soon."

"She can ride it out in the hospital," said the cop. "And you in the station, explaining all this."

The store owner came back outside with a glass of water and a bowl of ice. "Did you hear that?" I asked him. "They're going to separate us. Remember this when she dies in their custody—you have to testify that I warned them first."

"Fine," said the cop, "we'll take you with us to the hospital."

It's sad, when you think about it, how precarious our lives are. Our ways of living. Everything I'd tried to accomplish over the last year, all the secrecy and the hiding and the coping strategies to try to keep Brooke healthy, it was pointless now, everything lost forever in ten seconds sprinting across an empty street. If we'd been somewhere else, the cops wouldn't have seen us; if I'd been able to grab her more quickly, she wouldn't have gotten hurt. If I'd had a better plan, or better reflexes, or been a better person.

Now we were in small, regional hospital, locked in a room with the cops keeping watch outside, waiting for the results of an MRI. I was surprised a hospital this small even had an MRI machine, but I wasn't complaining. Brooke's unconscious body lay in a bed, her head bandaged and hooked up to softly beeping monitors. Boy Dog was being held in a kennel in Dillon. And somewhere a state police officer was trying to figure out who we were, and then the FBI would come, and they'd take Brooke away, and I'd go to prison or worse. And Attina would keep killing.

Or maybe, as soon as I was gone, he'd stop. Maybe I was the reason he was killing at all.

The hospital was in Crosby, the next town over, larger than Dillon but still rural, still nowhere near big enough that you'd call it a city. The hospital was barely a clinic, with an emergency room and a maternity ward and a handful of other medical services, though it was new enough to have a tiny radiology department. Five or six rooms for patients. It was clean, though. And it was one story, so we could slip out the window and run if it came to that. Maybe it already had, and I was too stubborn to see it. Where could we even go? Dillon was crawling with cops, and everybody would recognize us, so we couldn't hide there. But I didn't want to abandon the town, either. If I was the only one who could stop Attina, then everyone he killed before I stopped him was my fault.

My only hope was to convince the FBI, when they finally showed up, to let me go back for another try. My one last wish before . . . whatever they did to me.

I spent the morning with the door closed. I lit a match, thrilling at the little spark of flame, but the smoke alarm went off almost immediately and the nurse came in to take my matchbook away. So even that was gone.

Somewhere in the afternoon—about six hours into our stay at the hospital—I heard a knock on the door. Whoever it was didn't wait for an answer, but opened it just a second later.

"Iowa," I said, recognizing him immediately.

The man who'd followed us through Dallas paused in the doorway, taken aback at the statement. "Iowa?"

"The plate on your car," I said. "That sneaky black SUV that didn't look remotely like an FBI vehicle."

"Technically it wasn't," he said, closing the door behind himself and sitting in the room's other chair. "It was a rental. But I'm stationed in Lincoln, Nebraska, so an Iowa plate isn't all that surprising."

"Wow," I said. "What do you have to do wrong to get stationed in Lincoln, Nebraska?"

"Specialize in serial killers, apparently," said Iowa. He stood up again and stepped toward me, holding out his hand. "Agent Mills. Big fan of your work."

I let his hand hang there, unshaken. "What kind of work are we talking about?"

He held his hand out another moment or two, then shrugged and went back to his seat. "John Wayne Cleaver, special advisor to Agent Linda Ostler, and a key member of Task Force Goshawk, charged with a mission so secret I'm not even allowed to state it out loud in this room—though I assure you I'm very familiar with its particulars."

"Goshawk?"

"Some kind of a bird," said Mills. "I didn't name it."

"It's better than Boy Dog," I said.

"Your record with Agent Ostler was sketchy but acceptable," said Mills. "You talked back to your superiors, you pushed every button and boundary and envelope you ever came across, and you actively antagonized some members of your team, including and most problematically the therapist assigned to your unit, but you always got the job done. You enabled more . . . how can I put this without spilling state secrets . . . more 'apprehensions of nonstandard targets' than the entire US government had managed to achieve in the several decades prior to your term of service. You were on track for a commendation and a hefty pay bump before Fort Bruce."

"How much of a pay bump?"

"You keep focusing on the least important part of every sentence I say."

"My therapist used to say the same thing."

"I'm beginning to understand a lot of the personnel reports I've read."

"Do I want to know why you're here?" I asked.

He shrugged again. "Probably. Your personnel reports suggest that you want to know everything."

"Do I get to?"

"How much time do you have?" asked Mills. "The reasons I'm here are a very long list."

"Well I'm not going anywhere, as far as I know," I said. "Start with where I'm going next."

"I'm afraid we have to start several months before that," said Mills. "Tell me about Fort Bruce."

"Nice place," I said. "Kind of big for my tastes, though. And pretty dangerous now that the entire police force has been slaughtered by a supernatural monster."

"Can we do this without the sass?" asked Mills.

"I guess so," I said. "But it's really the only part I enjoy."

"The last anyone heard of your team in Fort Bruce was Dr. Trujillo calling to say that a combined operation with local police had gone wrong, and a Withered army was running wild through the city. When we arrived on the scene ten hours later there were more than thirty dead humans and what we surmised to be the remains of two dead Withered. You and Brooke were the only survivors."

"How did you know we'd survived?" I asked. "Maybe we'd just been eaten by the monsters."

"Most of the team assumed as much," said Mills. "I was the one who noticed that one of the human bodies had received a makeshift 'embalming' with eighty-seven-octane gasoline. That didn't prove anything, but it sure suggested a lot of really wild possibilities."

"The most lurid of which," I said, extrapolating the likely story, "was that I had gone full psycho, betrayed my team, and left a gruesome calling card to announce the beginning of my serial-killer career."

"Now it sounds like you've been reading *my* personnel reports."

"How true do you think that version is?" I asked. "Measured

in the number of armed marines waiting in the hall to 'apprehend' me?"

"Three," said Mills simply. "Plus two more outside. Which is not nearly as many as there could have been."

Brooke groaned, and we looked at her in unison. She moved her hand—more of a twitch than a conscious movement—and moments later the nurse bustled into the room.

"The MRI results are looking really clean," he said, studying the monitors and tapping a pen against his cheek. "It's practically a miracle. Now it looks like your girl is waking up."

"Woman," I said. Mostly just to bug him.

Brooke took her time regaining consciousness, and with the nurse in the room Mills and I couldn't talk freely. Mills caught my eye at one point, nodding toward the door, but I ignored him and looked back at Brooke. If they were going to separate us, they were going to have to do it by force.

"Hey there," said the nurse, shining a small penlight in Brooke's eyes. "Are you waking up now? Can you hear me?"

"Where am I?" asked Brooke. Her voice was raw and ragged.

"You're in a hospital," said the nurse. "You hit your head pretty hard. Do you remember that?"

"My head," said Brooke, and she tried to touch her bandage with her palm. A thick leather restraint stopped her hand just a few inches above the bed railing, and she rolled her head to the side to look at it, squinting her eyes in the bright light. She tugged on the restraint again, as if not comprehending its purpose, then tested her other arm and found it was restrained as well. She sighed and closed her eyes again. "Severe suicide risk," she said. "Yeah, I remember."

"I'm right here with you," I said, raising my voice a bit to make sure she could hear me.

She smiled. "John."

"His name is David," said the nurse. "Do you remember Da—"

"She's always called me John," I said. "It's okay."

The nurse nodded, glancing at Agent Mills as if he was trying to put us all together, like a puzzle. He looked back at Brooke. "Okay, sweetie, we're going to do a few more quick memory tests if that's all right. You hit your head pretty hard and we want to make sure you didn't scramble your noodles. You recognized John's voice and that's great—can you tell me your name?"

"No."

"Your name is . . . " the nurse began, but he stopped talking as a wide, wicked grin spread across Brooke's face. Her eyes were still closed. The nurse nodded. "I get it, sweetie, you're just playing with me. Let me rephrase the question: do you know your name?"

"Some of them."

"Start with the first one."

"Uh uh uh," said Brooke, her voice somewhere between playful and taunting. "That's a secret."

"You can tell me, honey, I'm a nurse."

"You're not going to get anywhere with this," I said. I'd seen this side of Brooke before, and it wasn't Brooke at all.

The nurse shot me a glance. "I have to test for brain damage."

"Physical damage is not her problem," said Mills. "Put in terms you're familiar with, she has dissociative identity disorder. Ask her name, her age, where she's from, any of the standard questions, and you'll get a dozen different answers. Sometimes more." He pulled out his badge and held it up, establishing his absolute authority over the situation. "You're going to go out in the hall and mark this test as done, and you're going to mark the results as positive."

"Negative," I said.

Mills frowned. "Whichever one means she's healthy and doesn't have any memory loss."

"So, negative," said the nurse.

"This is why I didn't go into medicine," said Mills. "You make no sense at all." He opened the door. "Thanks for your service to the United States government." The nurse left, and Mills closed the door.

"Would my pay bump have included a badge?" I asked. "Because what you just did looks super fun."

He slipped his badge back into his suit coat and walked to the side of Brooke's bed. "So," he said. "Are you going to tell us who you really are?"

"I'm an innocent little girl," said Brooke.

"He knows everything," I said softly. "You don't have to hide."

"In that case," said Brooke, opening her eyes and flashing another toothy grin, "he knows exactly who I am."

Mills stared at her, trying to think, and then stepped back in shock as the realization hit him.

Nobody laughed.

"You're . . . " said Mills. "I . . . didn't think I'd ever get to meet one."

"I can't hurt you," said Nobody, and her grin faded slowly away. "I've been dead for two years."

Mills shuffled backward another half step, and I couldn't help but feel a twinge of satisfaction at his discomfort.

"You wanted to know what happened in Fort Bruce," I said. "Now that you've met Nobody, you might actually be ready to hear it: the cannibal we were chasing turned out to be a sort of Withered king named Rack. He didn't have a face or a chest or a heart, but he could use hearts to talk to us the same way Nobody used bodies to get around. They're like parasites on the rest of the world, using humans as food and tools and even hiding places. He recruited one of our team to his side with the promise of money and power, but I was able to kill him by stabbing that teammate in the chest, filling his heart with gasoline, and then poisoning Rack with it when he tried to recruit me."

"That's . . . " said Mills. He seemed too squeamish to finish his sentence, so I continued.

"We left without telling anyone where we were going because we didn't want anything like Fort Bruce to ever happen again. We lost that many people because our methods were too obvious: you can't wage a war against someone without that someone noticing. The Withered noticed us and they fought back. I'd been telling Ostler since the beginning that I needed to do this alone, my way, and then all of a sudden I was the only one left alive so I took my chance and ran with it. Nobody and I have killed just as many without the help of Task Force Goshawk as we ever killed with it, and we've done it without anything like another Fort Bruce. You have to see that this is the best way to do it."

"That's not the way our government does things," said Mills.

"Effectively?"

"Unsupervised," said Mills. "We can't just have you running around killing people."

Nobody snorted. "So you'd rather have the Withered running around killing people?"

"A trained agent with decades of experience *might* earn the kind of autonomy you're asking for," said Mills. "Agent Potash might have gotten it. But you're an eighteen-year-old serial killer and his dead demon girlfriend. Are you crazy?"

"Technically," I said.

"You light fires everywhere you go," said Mills. "How do you think we've been tracking you? And even if you don't cause anything on the scale of Fort Bruce, you still cause problems and you still cause deaths. What are we supposed to tell the people of

Dillon? 'It's okay, don't worry about the deaths and the arson, our best teenage sociopath is on the job.'"

"Wait," I said. "What arson?" I'd been desperate to light a fire all day, but hadn't lit so much as a match my entire time in Dillon. *Oh no.*

"What do you mean, 'what arson?'" asked Mills. "The fire you lit this morning. The one that helped me find you so fast—I was already halfway from Dallas when the state police called me."

"I didn't light any fires," I said. "It has to be Attina."

"Who?"

"The Withered we're hunting," I said. "He's reading my mind somehow."

"What did he burn?" asked Nobody.

"The church," said Mills. "Burned it right down to the ground."

19

Agent Mills kept us in the hospital overnight, locked in the room. The nurse came to visit us every now and then, though he was always accompanied by a cop from the hall, and they never took off Brooke's restraints. I don't know how much the nurse knew, but the cops were on edge and that put him on edge. I sat in the corner and ignored them, focusing on the bigger problems: we still didn't know what Mills was planning to do with us, and meanwhile Attina was only getting more dangerous.

We had to stop him.

"It doesn't make sense," I said.

"He's reading your mind," said Nobody.

"Probably," I said. "Can he do that?"

"I don't know what he can do," said Nobody. "I don't have any memories of him at all, just the notes from Forman's book."

"What did the notes say?"

Nobody shrugged. "'Last seen in Dillon, Oklahoma,'" she said. "'Probably useless.'"

"So far he's shredded two kids, turned into bigfoot, crashed a truck with his mind, and burned down a church," I said. "That doesn't sound useless to me."

"Because you have no ambition," said Nobody. "All you want to do is kill loners in dead-end towns, and Attina apparently excels at that. But Forman was working with Rack, and they wanted to raise an army."

I bristled at her comment but kept my response impersonal. "And you think a telepathic bigfoot wouldn't be useful to an army?"

"Apparently they thought so," said Nobody. "We just have to figure out why."

"Great," I said. I rubbed my face and eyes, still on edge from last night and this morning, and everything bad that could possibly happen all happening at once. I needed to burn something, or break something, or scream, or cry, or jump up and down. I felt like a soda can that'd been shaken and shaken, relentlessly, for hours. The pressure was building and building and had nowhere to go. I had to let it out somehow.

Except I had to keep it under control, especially now that Mills was here, or the FBI would lock me up and take Brooke away forever.

I stood up to walk around. "Okay then, let's figure this out. Why does he do it?"

"Kill?" asked Nobody. "Burn things? Read your mind? You've got to be more specific."

"Why does he . . . " I shook my head. "Let's go back to basics. What does he do that he doesn't have to do?"

"You always ask that."

"Because it's always important," I said. "You want to get in somebody's head, you figure out what he's choosing to do."

"That's why I love you," said Nobody. "You always know exactly what to do."

"You don't love me," I said. "You're a fragmented memory trapped in a broken mind."

"Is that all Marci is, too?"

I clenched my hands into fists. "Don't talk about her."

"Or what, you'll hurt me?"

I gritted my teeth, hating every second of this conversation. "No."

"Then stop making idle threats," she said. "It's the sign of a weak mind. Now start solving this problem."

"Attina is choosing to murder people that we talk to," I said. "In exactly the ways I want to do it."

"And he's lighting fires you want to light, too," said Nobody.

"Everything he's done . . . " I said. "No, wait. It's not everything." I looked over at her. "I didn't want to kill Jessica."

"Are you sure? You want to kill a lot of people."

"I didn't think anything bad about Jessica," I said. "Officer Glassman, sure, but he's not the one that got killed."

Nobody sat up straighter in her bed, as much as her wrist restraints would allow. "What if he was the target, and she just got caught in the crossfire?"

"So we're looking at a Withered who can fail," I said, nodding. This was finally getting us somewhere. "Attina attacks teenagers because he can't take down a full adult."

"Maybe he's small," said Nobody.

I shook my head. "Officer Glassman said he was bigfoot," I said. "So he's either lying to make himself look better, or Attina's somehow huge and weak at the same time."

"Maybe he has a weakness that isn't physical," said Nobody. "Maybe he's . . . I don't know, afraid of people, or afraid of authority. Or he's afraid of loud noises—did Glassman get any shots off with his weapon?"

"No guns were fired," I said, remembering the sounds of the attack. "Just three screams. I . . . don't know why."

"Maybe he can incapacitate his victims," said Nobody, "which is how he was able to kill Derek so quietly."

I shook my head again. "Corey wasn't incapacitated, just surprised. In fact, all three victims were killed in completely different ways—and if the methods aren't consistent, they aren't important. He kills however he can, in whatever method gets the job done. Or, I suppose, whatever methods he gleans from my head. But the point is, we shouldn't be looking at *how* he kills, we should be looking at how he chooses *who* to kill. Why go after people I've thought about hurting?"

"To help you?" asked Nobody. "This is a demon who didn't do anything for decades, at least, and then started killing almost immediately when we showed up in town. You have a very attractive mind, with a strong sense of purpose, and maybe that got his attention. Look at me: I threw away everything I had to be with you—I changed everything I did—"

"You didn't change anything," I said. "Your obsession with me was just one more link in a very old chain. You saw something you wanted and you tried to take it, just like you did with Marci and Brooke and all the others. This is different."

"Don't brush me off like that," Nobody growled.

"You're not real," I said, pointing at her harshly. "I'll tiptoe around the other personalities but not you. You're horrible. And you're in wrist restraints so you couldn't kill yourself if you tried."

"I can break this body, though," she threatened. "No matter how they try to bind it."

I stared at her a moment, furious at what she'd done to Brooke, at what she was threatening to do, almost daring her to try something but knowing that anything she did, or that I did to her, would only hurt Brooke worse. Finally I turned away. "We need to talk to Officer Glassman."

"Why?"

"To find out what really happened. To see if he's lying about bigfoot. Too much of our knowledge about this case depends on the shouted testimony of a man trying to defend himself from a pedophilia charge."

"I wish Attina had killed him," said Nobody.

"Be careful what you wish for," I said. "Wishes are coming true a lot more often than they should."

Agent Mills knocked on our door the next morning and let himself in as I squinted and straightened in my chair. I'd fallen asleep and dreamed about nothing.

It was the best dream I'd had in ages.

"Rise and shine," said Mills. "Time to get on the road."

"Where are we going?" asked Nobody.

"Iowa," said Mills. "Just kidding, we're going to DC. You're both going to be debriefed by some very important people before we decide what to do with you."

"We need to go to Dillon," I said.

"To interrogate witnesses?" asked Mills. "To solve an unsolvable crime?"

"We just want to get our dog," I said, "but sure—we can interrogate people while we're there, if you want to. Let's start with Officer Glassman."

"He's already been questioned," said Mills.

"Not by anyone who knows what they're doing," said Nobody.

"I'm offended," said Mills.

"Did you ask him about the bigfoot reference?" I asked.

Mills put his hand on his chest. "I might be the only law enforcement representative who will ever take him seriously about that," said Mills. "So yes, I thought asking about bigfoot was the least I could do. And I believe him, too; whatever attacked him was huge and inhuman. Despite what the dead girl says, I do know how to question somebody effectively, and I know how to interpret their answers."

"Good," I said. "So did you ask him how he survived?"

Mills frowned. "What do you mean? His harrowing tale of violence and bravery is all he wants to talk about. He doesn't have a great answer about whatever he was doing there in the first place, but when the monster came for the girl he fought with it, sustaining multiple injuries to his arms before it knocked him aside and killed her."

"But does that add up for you?" I asked. "Why did the Withered target Jessica and not Glassman? Every other victim was male. Every other victim was in his room alone. Every other victim was someone I wanted to kill."

"You're admitting that pretty freely," said Mills.

"Something's wrong," I said. "You said serial killers are your specialty, right? So you've been trying just as hard as we have to put together a psychological profile that explains all three murders and the arson, but you can't. We don't have enough data yet. Jessica's death doesn't fit."

Mills stared at me a while, then looked at Nobody. "He's very intense."

"And he's taken," said Nobody. "Hands off."

Mills looked back at me, sucking on his teeth. He sighed. "I've been studying you too long to deny that you're good at this job. If I can buy you two days, can you figure something out?"

"Sometimes it takes months," I said.

Mills shook his head. "Two days."

"Three," I said. "Keep us here through Sunday at least."

"Why Sunday?"

"Because nobody started dying until we went to church," I said. "And now the church burned down."

"As I told him last night," said Nobody, "he has a very attractive mind."

Mills brought in a female police officer to watch Nobody while she changed; he and I waited outside, and he bought me some peanuts from the vending machine for protein. A few minutes later the officer emerged with Nobody, Brooke's wrists handcuffed behind her back, and we walked outside to Mills's black SUV, which was dinged up from the accident in Dallas.

"No armed marines?" I asked.

"Your psychological profile suggests that you'll avoid a physical confrontation at any cost," said Mills, opening the back door of his car. "It also suggests that you distrust authority figures enough to believe any unfair thing they tell you. Made you pretty easy to keep in line."

Was I really that easy to fool? I glanced at the familiar license plate: 187 RCR, Mills County. My head snapped up to look at him, cheerfully helping Brooke into the car: Agent Mills. I considered him with new wariness and got in the backseat without speaking.

Mills put Nobody in the passenger seat, where he could keep an eye on her, and cuffed her to the door handle. He chatted idly as we drove, asking my theories about the church and its relationship to the killings, but I didn't answer. I didn't think the church itself was a part of this at all, aside from the simple fact that it was the one thing, in all of Dillon, Attina had decided to burn. That meant it was important to him somehow, but I didn't believe there was anything beyond that. I'd only mentioned it to Mills because I knew it would pique his interest, and I wanted to stay in town as long as I could.

Put that in your psychological profile, smart guy.

We arrived in Dillon about two hours later and Mills took us for a spin past the burned-out hulk of the church before doubling back to the police station. The whole church lot was blocked off with wooden barriers and police tape, and the singed grass was covered with stacks of recovered hymnals and chairs and anything else that hadn't burned. I recognized several people from the town picking through the wreckage: Sara, Ingrid, Paul, and even Beth, though she was too frail to walk through the debris and had been relegated to sitting on the sidelines, pointing at things with her cane. She participated in everything, in spite of her age. I wondered about Paul: what had brought him to the church to help, without Brielle? Presumably she was still mourning for her sister somewhere, but if Paul was her boyfriend, why wasn't he with her? And why wasn't he in mourning for Corey?

"What do you do when a friend dies?" I asked out loud.

Mills looked over his shoulder at me, curious. "You . . . cry, I guess. Give your condolences to the family. I don't know, why do you ask?"

"Because I don't react the way other people do," I said, "so I don't know if what I'm seeing is strange behavior or not."

"What are you seeing?"

"Paul was back there at the church," I said. "Corey and Derek were his best friends, and yet he's right there, plugging away."

"That's not . . . automatically weird," said Mills. "A lot of people deal with grief by throwing themselves into manual labor. Or helping others. Paul's doing both, that's . . . probably healthy."

"So where's Brielle?" I asked.

"Some people *don't* do service and labor," he said. "I don't think you can catch a murderer just by looking at who turns up for a recovery project."

"Are you sure?" asked Nobody. "How many murderers have *you* caught?"

Mills didn't talk for the rest of the trip.

20

Agent Mills walked us straight to the front desk of the Dillon police station. "Hi," he said, flashing his badge, "I'm Agent Peter Mills with the FBI. I need to speak with Officer Glassman."

The receptionist looked at him, then at Nobody and me—me looking completely disheveled, and Nobody in handcuffs. She looked back at Mills. "What is this about?"

"Just some follow-up questions to Jessica Butler's murder," said Mills. He waved at us dismissively. "Don't worry about them, just give Glassman a call or . . . whatever you do to summon him." He wiggled his badge again, as if to underline his authority.

The receptionist sighed in relief. "It's about time we got some help around here. Are there more of you coming?"

"Soon, I hope."

"Best news I've heard all week." She dialed, and we waited.

She cocked her head, listening, then hung up the

phone again. Her voice was painfully apologetic. "I'm afraid he's not answering, and that's the only number I have for him. Do you want me try . . . I don't know, anything else? Just say the word and you've got it."

The cops in Fort Bruce had hated working with our team, feeling like we were stepping on their toes and throwing our weight around, but this station seemed practically overjoyed to have Mills.

Mills smiled. "Was that his home phone or his mobile?"

"Mobile," said the receptionist. "His home is in Tulsa. He's staying with his sister while he's in Dillon—ooh, let me call her."

"Thanks," said Mills. We waited, but after a while she shook her head again.

"No answer there, either."

"We know his sister," I said. "Let's go look in person."

Mills smiled at the receptionist a final time, thanked her for her help, and led us back outside. "Is it close?" he asked. "We could just walk."

"You've got my best friend in handcuffs," I said. "You don't get to parade her around like a freak show."

"Your best friend is a demon?" he asked.

"Well look who's Judgy Judgerson all of a sudden."

"I don't mind the cuffs," said Nobody.

"I do," I said, shooting her a quick, worried glance before looking back at Mills. Was she getting depressed again? "You take them off, or we go in a car."

"Car," said Mills, and prodded us back toward his SUV. "The demon and I aren't best friends yet."

We drove the four blocks to Sara Glassman's house, and I was surprised to see two cars in the driveway: Sara's little sedan, and a police car. I glanced at the clock on the SUV's dashboard. "10:27," I said.

"Does that mean something?" he asked.

I looked at the cars again, and then at the house. "It means they're not asleep—maybe one, maybe, but not both. And we didn't see them at the church cleanup project."

"They could have walked somewhere," said Nobody.

"And if we'd walked we could have walked past them," said Mills.

"Coulda shoulda woulda," I said, stepping out onto the sidewalk. The house looked quiet, the windows were closed, leaves on surrounding trees rippled softly in the wind. I walked up to the porch, not waiting for Mills to uncuff Nobody from the car door; if I was quick, I might have a chance to talk to the Glassmans before Mills caught up. I knocked loudly and listened for footsteps. No one came. Mills and Nobody walked up the front walk, and I knocked again. They climbed the stairs and stood beside me, and Nobody held up Brooke's cuffed wrists.

"At least they're in front," she said. "I can catch myself if I trip."

"I can change that if I need to," said Mills.

No one came to the door.

Nobody leaned forward and tried the door handle; it pushed right open. "That's lucky," she said.

"Is it?" I asked, and I stepped inside. The whole situation was looking more and more ominous.

"We're with the FBI now," said Nobody. "Can we go in there without a warrant?"

"*He* can't," I said, scanning the room quickly. "You and I are not currently employed by a law-enforcement agency." The living room was mostly how I remembered it—not messy, but full of organized clutter.

"Ms. Glassman?" called Nobody, stepping in behind me.

Mills stepped in as well. "Seriously, guys. I'm pursuing two teenage fugitives through a town where three people have been murdered—I have enough probable cause to start breaking down walls if I want to, let alone come inside and look around." He picked up a newspaper. "Yesterday's date."

"I didn't see a new one on the porch," said Nobody. "They must have already—" Something soft and small thudded into the porch, and she glanced outside. "There it is. Paper boy's passing on his bike."

"They wouldn't leave their door open overnight," said Mills, "so obviously they opened it up this morning and went for a walk."

"Through the close-knit neighborhood that thinks he's a pedophile," I said, moving into the hall. "Somehow that doesn't seem high on the list of possibilities."

"Neither is a twisted double murder," said Mills. "You jump to your conclusions, I'll jump to mine."

I turned the corner into the kitchen, and there they were: him in his uniform, her in a blouse and skirt, seated at the kitchen table—face down in their plates of food. Their hands hung limply at their sides. I stepped closer and looked at the dish on the table: some kind of casserole, brown and dried out. They'd been here since dinner last night, at least.

"Holy mother," said Nobody, rounding the corner behind me.

"What did you find?" asked Mills as he stepped into the doorway behind her. "Oh, eff this whole thing."

"Eff?" I asked, and I touched Sara's arm, testing the movement in the joints; she bent easily at the elbow and shoulder.

"We don't all talk like we're on *The Wire*," he said. "Stop touching them, this is a crime scene."

"That's why I'm touching them," I said, letting go of the arm. "Rigor mortis has already come and gone; they've been here fourteen, maybe only twelve hours."

"Rigor mortis takes longer than that," said Mills.

"Not in this heat," I said. "Trust a mortician." I bent down to look at their heads, but straightened immediately when I saw Mills pull out his phone. "Don't call it in yet."

"Of course I'm going to call it in."

"This is our only chance to examine the bodies," I said. "And no, don't say that the police have a forensics team to do that for us, because you know they won't find everything we will. They don't know about the Withered, or anything supernatural—they might skip over a dozen vital clues because they don't know what they're looking for."

Mills held the phone in front of him, then sighed and put it away. "Fine," he said. "You've got twenty minutes."

"You can give me way more than that," I said.

"Every house on this street saw us park and come inside," he said. "If there's more than twenty minutes between us entering and us calling the police, it's going to look suspicious as hell."

"Easy," said Nobody. "This isn't *The Wire*."

Mills sneered at her, and I looked back at the bodies. Twenty minutes.

Come on, bodies. Talk to me.

I was never more comfortable than when I was around dead bodies. They were calm, they were predictable, they were everything that put my mind at ease. Trying to decipher the vagaries and intricacies of human interaction was exhausting, like running a marathon with your mind. But puzzling over a dead body was relaxing, like a crossword or Sudoku. What were these bodies telling me?

They were face down in their plates—not just head down, but literally face down, as if they were looking at their plates when their heads lowered. Sara's plate was covered with the cascade of her hair, black streaked with gray; I lifted some strands of it and saw that her head and plate seemed the same as her brother's. There didn't seem to be any force of impact on the food, which you might have seen if their heads slammed down. So they lowered their heads slowly, and straight forward. . . . I repeated the motion with my own head, seeing how it felt. "They fell asleep," I said.

"Why?" asked Mills.

"I'm working on that."

Nobody lifted Officer Glassman's arm. "Why are their arms hanging straight down?"

"Because they're . . . ah—" I almost said *because they're asleep*, but that only described the current position, not how they got in that position. What had their hands been doing when they fell asleep? No one eats with their hands straight down at their sides; they'd be up on the table, or maybe resting in their lap. I looked at the silverware—it was scattered across the table, like it had been dropped haphazardly. Two knives, two spoons, and a fork. "Where's the other fork?" I lifted the other side of Sara's hair, but it wasn't under there.

"Here," said Nobody, stopping to pick it up from the floor under Sara's chair. She handed it to me with her cuffed hands and scrunched her nose into a sniffing scowl. "It smells."

I held it close to my nose; it smelled strongly of chemicals, like maybe a cleaning solution. "It's not bleach, but it's something like that."

"Poison in the food?" asked Mills.

"The smell's too strong," I said. "They'd have known it was there."

"Unless the food was smellier than the chemicals," she said. She leaned in over the table, looking closer at the casserole. "Fish? And curry powder." She sniffed again. "Pakistani."

"How can you possibly know that?" asked Mills.

"I've been Pakistani a couple hundred times," said Nobody.

"Whoever used the curry didn't know how, though. It smells awful."

"That happens when you lace your curry with detergent," I said. I grabbed Officer Glassman's head and raised it, revealing his face covered with flecks of rice and herbs and his mouth full of a thick, white froth.

"Drain cleaner," said Mills. "I've seen that effect before. There's no way they would have just dozed off like this, though—swallowing drain cleaner is horrifically painful. It eats you apart from the inside."

"Then there's probably a sedative in there as well," I said. "One drug to knock them out, another to kill them, and strong, smelly food to cover it all up."

"Why would a Withered kill with poison?" asked Nobody. "Doesn't he have claws or . . . maybe teeth? Jessica and Derek were cut to ribbons."

"But Corey was hit with a truck," said Mills. "It's different every time."

"More to the point," I said, "why would he use poison when *I* never would?"

"Not everything is about you," said Nobody.

"But almost everything here has been," I said. "Jessica's death stood out because it was the one idea that didn't come from me. Now neither does this. I think we have to consider the possibility that we're looking at two unrelated cases."

"A Withered that's reading your mind," said Mills, "and a pedophile hunting little girls. Which makes this a revenge killing."

"Murder-suicide?" asked Nobody. She looked at the scene, frowning. "Sara gets fed up with his crap and decides to take them both out, out of guilt for not stopping him earlier?"

"You have a one-track mind," I said. "There's no way this is suicide."

"Why not?"

"You saw this kitchen when we ate here on Sunday—it was covered with dirty dishes she'd used in cooking. The same when we helped bring back pans and plates from the town meeting. Sara leaves the dishes until after she eats, habitually. So if she'd cooked this meal the kitchen would still be messy. Somebody else cooked it."

"Or the killer cleaned the kitchen," said Mills. I glared at him, and he held up his hands. "I'm just saying. Weirder things have happened."

"Sara loves cooking," said Nobody. "Why would anyone have to cook for her?"

"Because there's a meal-share program for the out-of-town police," said Mills, snapping his fingers. "I saw the sign-up sheet on the wall at the station. Hang on." He dialed his phone and held it to his ear, waiting while it rang. "Hi! This is Agent Mills again, I believe we spoke earlier today? That's right. Absolutely charming. Listen, I have one more question about Officer Glassman, if you don't mind. Who was on the list to feed him last night? Yeah, I can wait." He looked at us. "She's checking the chart. Set that down really carefully so they can't tell we moved it." I set Officer Glassman's face back into his plate, trying to match the impression in the food exactly. "Whoa," said Mills suddenly. "Are you kidding me? What idiot set that up?" Nobody and I looked at each other, then back at him. "Okay, well, my apologies first of all, and second, you're going to want to send some black-and-whites to pick her up immediately, and then send some more on over to the Glassman residence. That's right. As soon as you can. And then pack up your desk, because you're fired—I know I don't have the authority, and I'm sorry, but the writing's on the wall after that food chart you put together. Thanks, bye-bye."

He looked at us, shaking his head. "This casserole came from Brielle Butler, Jessica's sister." He shoved his phone into his pocket and walked back out toward the porch. "Effing eff."

21

Brielle was at home when the police arrived, planning Jessica's funeral with her parents and little brother. We weren't there for the arrest, obviously, but we were back in the station by the time they brought her in. They were surprisingly gentle with her. I'd always heard that cops got really rough with people who kill other cops, but I guess they hated traitorous cop pedophiles more, just like Marci had said. They practically treated her like royalty.

Not that this made Brielle any less arrested.

"She looks sad," said Nobody. I glanced at her warily, studying her face; those kind of dreamy, semilucid statements often marked a change in personality. Had the sight of Brielle brought this one on? Did the nature of the trigger affect which new girl would take over? I looked back at the closed door of the interrogation room, wondering who would be sitting beside me in a moment. Marci again? One of the others? Or someone completely new?

Agent Mills sat down beside us. "The chief's assistant swears she changed the food rotation at the last minute, precisely because she didn't want the Butler family making food for the Glassmans—not that she thought they were capable of poisoning anyone, obviously, but because she didn't want to torture them with the association. Swears up and down she canceled the meal completely. Brielle and her parents insist the same thing."

I glanced at Nobody again. She was staring intently at her hands. "So who made the food last night?"

"The community volunteer in charge of the food rotation was, you guessed it, Sara Glassman. So we don't know who she picked in the last-minute switch. We can search her house for a written record as soon as the forensics team is done with it, but barring that, our only chance of tracing the food is if someone can identify the casserole dish." He leaned back in his chair, rubbing the heels of his hands into his eye sockets. "I miss the days of BTK."

"You look too young to have worked BTK," I said. "He was caught years ago."

"True," said Mills, "and thank you. But I was in college during that whole final thing, when he came out of retirement and sent new letters and all that stuff with the floppy disk and the DNA. That's why I went into serial killers in the first place—because that investigation was brilliant. Start to finish. The people involved, the procedures they used, the combination of new technology and old school legwork; that's what I wanted to do. And so I studied and I graduated and I joined the FBI—and it's gross and full of dead bodies and sick minds, but it's awesome, you know? I've read your file, I know that's what got you hooked, too. Looking at a crime and using all those pieces to crawl into someone's head. Like you did with the Glassmans."

"And then they saddled you with me," I said.

Mills smiled thinly. "And nothing ever made sense again." He pointed at the closed interrogation room, where Brielle was waiting in hopeless terror. "She would have made sense: angry sister wreaks horrible vengeance. The narrative works. You know what they found when they picked her up? That cop with the mustache, right there by the desk, he told me the whole story. She kept saying 'How did you read my journal? How did you read my journal?' So they found the journal, and there was the whole plan: she hated Glassman and she wanted to kill him. She even laid out the poisoning thing, all right there in ink on paper. And yet the chief's assistant canceled the meal, and the family spent the entire afternoon and evening at the church cleanup with dozens of witnesses. She has the perfect motive but the perfect alibi." He sighed. "And not a speck of curry powder in the kitchen. We have a tiny town with five murders in under a week, and none of them make sense, and the best suspects end up as victims, and *nothing makes sense*. I'm literally starting to wonder if there's a gas leak in town, because everyone's crazy."

"No, I'm not," said Brooke's body. She looked mostly asleep.

"Everybody move," said a voice, and we looked up at the crowd of cops and detectives and secretaries, which were no longer milling or arguing, but moving in a single direction. Mills and I stood up.

"What's going on?" asked Mills.

"Town meeting," said the cop with the mustache. "Davis wants to talk to everyone again, tell 'em to stop taking matters into their own hands and let us work."

I pointed at the interrogation room. "What about Brielle?"

"Released to her home," said the cop. "Too much evidence in her favor."

I watched him turn and walk out the door, then looked back at Brooke. "You awake?"

"Huh?" she looked up.

I took one of her cuffed hands, both to help her to her feet and to help her feel at ease for my next question. "Who are you?"

"The one and only," she smiled. "Original flavor."

"Welcome back," I said, pulling her up. I was relieved to have Brooke again, but couldn't help but feel a pang of loss that she wasn't Marci. Would Marci ever come back? Or had I finally lost her for good? The thought made me feel awful, like I'd just killed a puppy. It was Brooke's body, and it should be Brooke in charge of it. I was a horrible person for even thinking about anything else, let alone wishing for it. I kept my voice even and changed the subject. "Do you remember Agent Mills?"

Brooke looked at him, pursing her lips. "Iowa?"

"One license plate," said Mills. "Come on, I'll drive us to the meeting."

"Take off her cuffs first," I said. "No more demon, no more cuffs."

Mills stared at us a moment, then sighed and pulled out his little silver key. "Just three days, you said. Just give us three days." He pulled the cuffs away and slipped them in his pocket. "Now I'm screwing with crime scenes and untying a demon."

"I'm not a demon," said Brooke, rubbing her wrists. She stopped suddenly, cocking her head to the side. "Was I Nobody again?"

"You're always yourself," I said calmly, leading her to the door. "Deep inside, you're always you."

22

With the church burned down the meeting was held in the local school, which had a large gym for basketball games but no efficient way to cool it in the summer. Brooke and Mills and I pitched in pulling out bleachers and setting up chairs as the townspeople slowly heard the news and started trickling in. None of them were happy, and many of them were terrified. A lot of the people I'd seen with families last time were now here alone, having left their kids and spouses at home. No one wanted to be outside. Ingrid had to drag Beth practically kicking and screaming. Almost a full hour after we arrived the meeting began, and Officer Davis stood in the center of the basketball court to speak.

"Thank you all for coming to another meeting," he said. "I assume most of you have heard the news about the latest deaths, but I wanted to make sure you heard it from me, as an official, credible source. No gossip and no backbiting. At approximately 10:30 this morning the Glassman family, Sara and her brother Luke, were found dead in Sara's home. They appear to have died sometime last night. Some form of poison appears to be involved, but I want to stress that it is too early for me to speculate on exactly what happened, or how, or why. I urge you to show the same restraint."

"You're supposed to be keeping us safe!" shouted a man in the front row. The crowd was restless, some muttering, some shaking their heads. Their terror was quickly turning to anger, now that Officer Davis was making himself a focal point.

"That's what I want to talk about next," said Davis, shouting over the low rumble of voices. "Just stay calm, stay calm. Let me talk." The room quieted. "That's exactly what I want to talk about next."

"I'm sweltering," Brooke whispered, fanning herself.

"Just listen." I wiped the sweat from my forehead and watched Officer Davis carefully.

"As you know," he said, "this town has had five deaths in less than a week. We have no clear evidence linking any of them to each other, and one of them might even have been an accident, but the fact remains that this volume of deaths has very few precedents. The nature of those precedents suggests two courses of action, and I'm afraid you're not going to like either of them."

"It's too damn hot in here!" shouted a frail voice behind me. The crowd looked over, and I turned to see Beth standing in the back row, shaking her cane. Ingrid tried to pull her back into her seat.

"Well," said Ingrid, laughing drily, "everyone's thinking it."

The crowd laughed with her, some of the tension broken, and Beth eventually started laughing too. I looked back at Davis and hoped the laughter would ease the blow of whatever he said next.

"Number one," said Officer Davis. "The presence of a possible spree killer, or even a mass murderer, has garnered national attention. This is good because it means the cavalry is coming: within the next twenty-four hours we will have national guard, active army, and the police SWAT team in from Oklahoma City. Do any of you remember the manhunt for the Boston bombers? That's the kind of protection we're talking about—dozens, if not hundreds, of boots on the ground, patrolling your city and rooting out this killer. You'll be as safe as we can make you."

"Dammit," I whispered. "We're going to get another Fort Bruce."

"Boston was a lockdown," said a woman in the crowd. "Are you going to trap us all in our homes?"

"That's the bad news," said Officer Davis. "There are only two ways to keep you safe in a situation like this, and if we evacuate you, we'd just be letting the killer slip out with you. We have to keep you here and, for your own safety, we have to keep you under lockdown."

"No one's told me about this yet," whispered Mills, pulling out his phone. "Excuse me." He got up and walked to the door, holding the phone to his ear.

"This is going to get ugly," said Brooke. By the murmurs in the crowd I could tell they had similar thoughts. Even Beth was cursing under her breath, more harshly than I'd have expected.

"I know you're not happy about this," said Officer Davis, "but please remain calm. We will be bringing in food and water and other emergency services. While you remain—"

"What about our jobs?" a man asked.

"You get a day off," said Davis.

"You can't call in sick to a farm," growled another man.

"I understand that this is difficult," said Officer Davis. "But what do you want us to do? Martial law will give us the breathing room to catch this killer before any more of you die. We're doing this to protect you."

"You're doing this to control us!" shouted Beth, and the crowd shouted in agreement. A mob was forming, and she was their voice.

OVER YOUR DEAD BODY

"We have leads we are following as we speak," shouted Officer Davis. "Chemical samples from the Glassman's house. Footprints and weapon marks from the attack on Jessica Butler. Forensic data from the truck that crashed into Corey Diamond's bedroom."

"What's to stop another truck from crashing through my window?" shouted a man in the back. "You can't even keep us safe in our homes!"

"If anyone is on the street they will be seen," Davis shouted. "If anyone starts a truck or walks through an alley or even picks up a weapon, *they will be seen*." He pounded his fist as he talked. "Do what we tell you and no one will get hurt. And for the love of God, do not take the law into your own hands. Don't open your doors for anyone but my men, but don't shoot anyone, either. I know you all have guns and I want you to be able to protect yourselves, but if people start shooting each other through their windows I will come down on you like the hammer of heaven. Stay in your homes, enjoy your vacation—mandatory as it may be—and let us do your jobs. The army gets here tomorrow, but martial law begins in one hour. Meeting adjourned."

"This is terrible," said Ingrid.

"It's a necessary evil," I said. "Go home and get Beth home and just do what they say."

"Are you coming?" asked Ingrid.

"Maybe just to stop by for our clothes," I said. "I'm sorry I don't have time to explain."

"Marci?" asked Ingrid, looking at Brooke.

"Not anymore," said Brooke.

Ingrid frowned, confused by the response, but took Beth's hand and joined the crowd walking slowly toward the door.

"This is our chance," said Brooke. "Mills is gone, so we can hide and get away from him."

DAN WELLS

"We need him," I said. "He's our only way out of this town."

"You want to leave?"

"I want to kill Attina," I said. "But first I want to get you out of here."

"No," said Brooke.

"No arguments," I said. "Getting you out is the number-one priority. There he is." I grabbed Brooke's wrist and pulled her toward Mills, who was talking to one of the local men.

" . . . don't take the law into their own hands," the man muttered as we came up behind him. I recognized him from somewhere. The church, maybe? Of course: it was Randy, the man in love with Sara. He seemed practically red with rage. "What do you think that Butler girl was doing?" he demanded. "Someone oughta pour some Drano down her throat, see how she likes it."

"Agent Mills," I said, "can we speak to you in private?"

Mills gratefully excused himself from the conversation, leaving Randy to rant at the next person who came by, and walked with us toward the nearest door. "Do you have something?"

"You were right," I said. "Everyone in Dillon is crazy."

"What?" asked Brooke.

"Not real crazy," I said. "Gas-leak crazy." I glanced at the other people and police still filling the room, too close for me to say my true suspicions out loud. "In a manner of speaking."

Mills hesitated a moment, then leaned in as well. "You think the Withered is making people crazy?"

"The one we're hunting is named Attina," I said. "Brooke doesn't remember his powers, and we've been wracking our brains trying to figure them out based on the killings, but what if Attina's not doing any of it personally? What if he's making other people do it?"

Mills nodded. "So we can't find a unifying theory that ties together all five deaths, plus the arson, and you think maybe that's because there are multiple killers and thus no consistent reason or method. Or, I suppose, the alleged craziness *is* the consistent reason."

"It makes everything work."

"Only in the barest sense," said Mills. "You tell any cop in the country that their murder case is caused by 'everyone just going crazy all at once,' and they'll laugh in your face. It's not evidence. It's not even circumstantial evidence."

"A gas leak would be evidence," I said, "if you could find one. Maybe Attina is a supernatural gas leak. He sits here in the town, minding his own business, but then something sets him off and he starts . . . leaking 'crazy.' He starts emitting violent tendencies into the air, like a psychic broadcasting station, and people just start hurting each other."

"And Glassman's bigfoot?"

"A lie to cover himself," I said. "He's probably the one that killed Jessica, overcome by Attina's influence, and when he snapped out of it he made up that story to explain it."

"Maybe he was hallucinating while he did it," said Brooke. "Maybe he thought Jessica was a monster and that's why he killed her."

Mills looked around the room. "So who is it?"

"If it works the way I'm thinking," I whispered, "it may as well be all of them."

Mills clenched his teeth, looking around the room, then looking back at the closed interrogation room. "It's not enough."

"You have to get Brooke out of here," I said.

"No," said Brooke again.

Mills looked at me through narrowed eyes. "You want to leave? I thought you were going to posit some brilliant method of catching the Withered."

"We're in a town where random people are killing each other for random reasons," I said. "This is not a town we want to be in."

"But you're supposed to be the idiot who runs into the mouth of hell every time it opens," said Mills. "Your psych profile's pretty clear about that: you don't abandon people while a Withered picks them off."

"Why else are we even here?" demanded Brooke.

"I'm staying," I said. "But Brooke is . . . Listen. I have been alone my entire life." I don't know why I was telling him this, but it just came spilling out. "Even when I had people looking out for me, caring for me, doing everything they could to help me, I was alone because I thought I was alone. I acted like I was alone. I hated my life and myself and everything else, but now . . . somewhere . . . " I couldn't say it in front Brooke—that somewhere inside of her was the only person I'd ever loved. That I was saving Brooke because of Marci. "Listen," I said again. "When I'm with her I'm myself, for the first time in my entire life. She makes me, me. And I'm not going to lose her again." I looked Mills right in the eyes. "Not to some lunatic town full of human booby traps just waiting to go off and kill someone. We can't predict how it's going to happen, or where, or by whom, so we get her out, we get her safe, and then I find this Withered and I make it stop."

"Do you have a plan?" asked Brooke. Her voice was thin, but determined.

"I'll make one when you're safe," I said firmly.

Mills shook his head, biting his upper lip as he looked around. "The cavalry are coming," he said. "I just talked to DC—everything Davis said is true and it's already in motion. This town is about to become the safest place on the whole frigging continent."

"Are you not listening to me?" I asked. "You're going to bring a bunch of men with guns to a place where people are randomly turning into murderbots? And you think that's safe?"

"We can't prove that's what's actually happening," said Mills.

"You want to risk another Fort Bruce on me being wrong?" I asked.

Mills shook his head again. "Nuke it from orbit," he muttered. "That's the only way to be sure."

"I was in that movie," said Brooke.

Mills looked at her, blinking, then back at me. "Do you need to get anything first?"

"Her clothes," I said. "And Boy Dog."

His eyebrows rose in disbelief. "Does he make you, you, too?"

"I will kill you with my bare hands," I said. "I don't hurt animals or allow them to be hurt by inaction. I have rules that keep me controlled and you safe. Get my dog out of this town, or I cannot describe to you the cataclysmic ways I will make you regret it."

Mills stared at me, then shook his head and walked toward the door. "Come on, then. And next time you see Nobody, tell her I put the cuffs on the wrong psychopath."

We gave him directions to Ingrid's house, and he drove in silence, presumably second-guessing this entire plan. Was he really going to just let me go? Could he possibly explain it to his superiors? Or was he going to go back on the whole thing at the last minute?

"You have to stay with her the entire time," I said. I was in the front seat, Brooke was alone in the back. "Leave her alone for two seconds and that might be the two seconds a different personality takes over."

"I'll keep her safe," said Mills. "And you have my rock solid guarantee on that because I know it's the only way I'm getting you back again."

"He'll hold me hostage for your return," said Brooke softly.

She sounded betrayed, but worse, she sounded resigned. Something horrible had happened, and she didn't have the will to fight it. I didn't how to respond to her, so I turned back to Mills. "Keep her away from anything that can be used as a weapon. She tried to slit her wrists with a screw from a table leg once."

"I don't want you to leave me," said Brooke.

"I won't," I said. "I'm not. This is just like the shower at the truck stop, okay? You do one thing while I do another."

She smiled wistfully. "I knew we missed our chance back there."

"We'll get another," I said, feeling a wave of heat pass through my body. I wondered if I was blushing and what Mills was thinking, but I pushed that away and focused on Brooke. "I'm the one who walks into hell, remember? They can't take you anywhere I won't come to find you. I will always protect you, no matter what."

At that moment, something massive hit the car, blocking out the light in my side window, and before I could see what it was the car was spinning out of control, swerving to the side. Mills yelled something incoherent, scrambling at the wheel, and then we slammed into something else and the airbags exploded, punching me in the face and knocking all the air from my lungs.

I blinked, stunned and deafened and trying to remember where I was. My seat moved, jostled by something, and then my window went dark again. The air was full of powder from the airbags, drifting and swirling in front me. Sounds returned slowly. A scream. A metallic rip. Another scream.

Brooke.

I tried to turn around to see her, but my seatbelt had locked itself tight. I swatted at the deflating airbags, trying to reach the buckle. When I finally released it I twisted in my seat, looking behind me. Brooke's legs were leaving the car, almost as if she were flying. Or being pulled. Something huge was still blocking my window, I couldn't tell what it was. I fumbled with the door handle and lock, desperate to get outside, screaming Brooke's name. The door opened suddenly and I spilled out onto the road. I looked up.

A massive beast towered over the car, Brooke held tight in its powerful claws. It wasn't hairy or scaly, but it had thick, rough skin, like a rhinoceros or a . . . a dried lake bed. I couldn't even tell if it was flesh or mud. It roared when it saw me, clutched Brooke close to its chest, and ran.

And disappeared.

23

We were wrong.

I looked around the street; our car had hit a tree just a block from Ingrid's house, and the street was full of people and other cars, all on their way home from the town meeting, all of them frozen in shock. I jogged a few steps in the direction the monster had gone, still reeling from the accident, and saw that people in that direction were still screaming and shying away from something I couldn't see. The monster was still there, it was just . . . invisible, somehow, to people who were too far away from it. I sprinted after it as fast as I could, desperate to catch up, but the town was small, and I reached the end of it in just a few blocks. The monster was gone. With no people left to see it, I had no way to track it.

And I had no idea how to find it because everything I'd thought I knew about it was wrong.

Jessica's death had seemed so different from the others, and I'd been certain that Officer Glassman was lying about the "bigfoot," and yet here it was. There was no supernatural gas leak, there was an actual monster with actual claws. Glassman's apparent lie was in fact the only useful testimony we'd gotten the entire time. And now he was dead.

I turned and walked slowly back into the center of town, my mind racing through the facts, trying madly to reorganize them into something I could use. Why had it taken Brooke? Why had it run from me? Did it think she was still Nobody and want to talk? Did it know I was hunting it and want to get away? But why not just kill me? Unless it really couldn't. That had been our first theory with Jessica and Glassman—that the monster had come for him and killed her as collateral damage when he fought back. Maybe his death two days later was the work of the same monster coming back to finish the job—and maybe that's why it had used poison, since the physical attack had failed the first time. But who would want to kill Glassman? If the stories about him were true, there might be plenty of people in town who wanted to kill him . . . but why would a Withered want to kill him? What did it gain? Especially since most of the rumors about him were apparently just rumors. He visited his sister all the time, and no one had ever tried to kill him before. What had changed?

The answer was obvious: Jessica had changed. Six years ago she'd been eight, now she was a pubescent fourteen. And while she wasn't the only fourteen-year-old in Dillon, she was the only one he'd leered at. The only one he'd confronted directly. The only one with an older sister who swore to kill him.

Brielle had a motive for both attacks and had threatened to carry them out. Was it her? If she'd attacked Glassman and ended up killing her own sister accidentally, it would make her even more likely to come after him a second time, and screw the collateral damage like Glassman's innocent sister. It made sense. Brielle's boyfriend, Paul, was the only one of the group who hadn't been killed, so that strengthened the theory a little more. She'd had an alibi for yesterday's attack, but if she was a Withered who could change shape and turn invisible, who knew what else she could do? She was my best lead, and I had to follow it.

I was still a few blocks from Mills's car. A group of people were gathered around it, but at that distance I could barely even count them, let alone see what they were doing. Was he dead? Injured? Had they called an ambulance? I turned sharply to the side, taking another street. This would be easier without him looking over my shoulder. I could do it my way. I stopped the first person I passed on the sidewalk, a middle-aged woman who was clutching her hands to her chest as she walked quickly toward her home, her eyes wide and darting around for danger.

"Excuse me," I said. I kept my voice calm and nonthreatening. "Do you know where the Butler family lives?" Brielle wouldn't be there if she was the monster, but her family would, and I had to find out what they knew if I had any chance of killing this Withered.

"They're 30, um, 32 Willow."

"Thank you."

She kept walking, and I hurried on my path. We only had about thirty minutes left before Officer Davis started his lockdown. If I was going to do anything with the information I hoped to collect, I had to work fast. Willow Street was just a few blocks over, on the far side of Main, and I found number 32 just a couple of blocks later. It was a single-story home with a narrow front but stretching back into a long yard. The street was empty, the doors were closed, and the curtains were drawn. No one would see what I was about to do.

I needed to get information fast if I was going to save Brooke's life. I didn't have time for finesse or subterfuge or a drawn-out investigation. The monster holding Brooke might kill her at any moment. If the Butler family had any clues that might help me, I was going to get it out of them as quickly and efficiently as I could. It was not going to be pretty.

The cops had taken my knife when they'd taken Brooke to the hospital, so I walked down the road a bit, looking in the windows of trucks. Sure enough, the second one had a gun rack with a pair of hunting rifles. *God bless these rednecks.* I tried the door, but it was locked; I walked around to the passenger side, hoping I wouldn't have to break a window, and sighed in relief when the handle turned. I unsnapped the straps on the nearest rifle, a long hunting model like the one Derek had held. I pulled a pack of ammo from the glove compartment and loaded it quietly as I walked to the door of the house. I hated guns. They were messy and loud and impersonal. But they were scary as hell.

Ding-dong.

I listened for footsteps and rang again.

Ding-dong.

I heard a voice and hid the rifle just out of view behind the door jamb. A man opened the door partway, stopped after a few short inches by a metal chain.

"What do you want?"

"Hi, sir, my name's David, and I'm a friend of Brielle's. Is she home?"

"We're not interested in visitors right now."

"I know, sir, and I know Officer Davis told everyone not to let people in their homes, but the lockdown hasn't started yet and this will only take a minute. I know you've gone through a lot lately, and I know it's hit Brielle really hard, so I brought her a little something to cheer her up. It'll only take a minute."

Mr. Butler stared at me moment before speaking. "You're that new guy just passing through town, right? With the girl?"

"That's right, sir. I met Brielle at church." *Thank you, Marci, for insisting we go to church.*

"Yeah," said Butler, "I remember. You had that great dog. Basset hound?"

"That's right," I said.

"I love those dogs. And I do remember Brielle saying she liked you. Where's your girlfriend?"

"She's with Ingrid."

"All right then," he said. "I guess if it'll only take a minute." Apparently he thought Brielle was home, which fit with my theory that she could fake her own alibis—an invisible Withered could slip in and out with no problems. Or maybe she really was home, and the Withered that had Brooke was someone else, and I was terrorizing this family for nothing. *No*, I thought, *not for nothing. For information.* He closed the door, and I picked up my rifle, and when he opened it again without the chain I smashed him in the face with the butt of it, breaking his nose and pushing him back inside. He cried out, clutching at his face, and I hit him again, in the knee this time, knocking him to the floor. I closed the door.

"What the—?" He writhed in pain, trying to get up, and I leveled the rifle at his face.

"Quiet."

He shut up instantly.

"Call your wife," I said. "Keep your voice as calm and easy as possible or I will shoot you in the face and get her myself. Do you understand me?"

"Are you going to kill us?"

"No," I said. "But I'm going to bind you, and possibly torture you. No pun intended."

"Pun? What's wrong with you?"

I paused, thinking. What was wrong with me? I never acted like this. Or at least I hadn't since . . .

. . . since I'd been with Brooke. She kept me sane, and she was gone. I'd snapped more quickly and completely than I'd thought possible.

And I'd do a lot more before I was done.

"I promised a friend I'd walk through hell to get her back," I said. "Don't make me bring you with me."

He nodded. I prompted him with the rifle, and he called out in the calmest voice he could muster: "Honey? Can you come into the living room for a minute?"

We waited in silence, and when Mrs. Butler walked into the room she yelped in shock.

"Stay quiet," I said. "Do exactly what I say or I will kill him. Do you understand me?"

"Why are you doing this?"

"Answer my question or I will demonstrate my seriousness."

"Yes," she said. "Yes, I understand you."

"Who else is in the house?"

"Just the kids," she said. "All three—" she broke down, sobbing. "Both of them."

"Call your son," I said. "Don't let him think that anything is wrong."

She hesitated a moment, then said, "Noah!" Her voice quavered, and I raised the rifle—just a millimeter, to get her attention—and she called out again. "Noah, honey, can you come into the living room?"

This is where it got tricky. If Brielle was home, and if she was a Withered, she could walk in at any moment and kill me. I had a gun, but that was all posturing; I was a horrible shot. Glassman had fought off the demon, but I didn't have the physical or combat training he did. I had to work quickly and hope I could learn something valuable before the Withered came back.

A short kid, maybe eleven years old, ran into the room, freezing when he saw his bloody father, and me with the rifle. "What?"

"Don't shout, talk, or do anything stupid," I said to the boy. "Get down on the floor, face down, and put your hands behind your head. Mrs. Butler, tie him up."

"Why are you doing this?" asked Mr. Butler.

"Because I need information," I said, "and I don't have time to deal with you trying to fight back while I get it. Ma'am, tie him up. Use your husband's dress shirt—those tear into strips really well."

"You want me to take my clothes off?" he growled.

I pushed the rifle toward his face, and he stopped talking. "I want you to tie each other up before I just get fed up with how slow you are and shoot you instead."

"Okay, okay," said Mrs. Butler, walking quickly toward her husband. "I'll do it, just don't shoot anyone." She pulled off Mr. Butler's shirt and started tearing it into strips. Noah was crying on the floor.

What was I doing? This isn't who I am. This isn't who I wanted to be. I was doing this to help them, to kill a Withered who was murdering this town faster than we could even process the evidence. Derek Stamper wasn't even in the ground yet, and already the morgue was overflowing. What I was doing was right and good, but . . . was this really the only way? Was it even the best way? That boy on the floor would remember this for the rest of his life. He'd have counseling and flashbacks and who knew what other trauma symptoms. Childhood victims of violent assault showed a tendency toward violence themselves—not all of them, but enough for me to wonder: was stopping one monster really worth it, if all I did was make another?

It's not the same, I told myself. *I can't think like that.* Giving one kid some bad nightmares and a short temper was nothing compared to the horror that was stalking this town. That was holding my best friend, my only friend, my only hope of ever finding the rest of the Withered and stopping them once and for all. Surely her life, in those terms, was worth at least three others. Surely it was worth far more. Was there an exact number somewhere? How many people would I bind or torture or kill before it became too many, and I had to let Brooke die? I was stymied, as always, by the math of morality. I couldn't murder my way to peace.

"Done," she said.

"Now tie up your husband," I told her. "And make the knots tight. Killing you would break my heart, but it's not like I'm using it for anything."

She tied up her husband, binding his ankles, then tying his hands tightly behind his back, before propping him in a corner with their son. I used the last few strips of cloth to tie her hands and ankles as well, and then stepped into the kitchen to look for a knife. They always felt better than guns. There was a knife block on the counter. I pulled out a large, broad-bladed chopping knife and tested the edge. They kept their knives sharp. I took it back into the living room and held it up. "It's a cleaver," I said. "You don't know why that's funny, but trust me."

"You said you wanted information," said the father. "Just ask your questions and leave us alone."

"Has your daughter been acting strange lately?"

"She's heartbroken," said the mother. "All of us are."

"Does she act guilty at all?"

"Why would she act guilty?" asked the father.

"Yes or no?" I asked.

"No," said the mother. "Nothing that happened to Jessica, or to that bastard Glassman, was her fault."

"What about before that?" I asked. Attina hadn't been born as Brielle—she'd taken her over at some point, killing the real girl and assuming her shape and identity. "Think back months," I said. "Three, four, maybe as many as seven years. Was there a moment when her behavior changed suddenly?" I thought about Marci and Brooke and the adjustment period each had gone through when Nobody took over their bodies. "Did she go through a few days of complete isolation, cutting herself off from the rest of the world? It would have been followed by markedly different behavior. Has Brielle done anything like that?"

"You mean . . . puberty?" asked the mother. "I don't understand what you're looking for. What are you going to do to my baby?"

"If she's still your baby," I said, "nothing at all. Can you think of a sudden shift in her behavior or attitude or even her food preferences, something you can't attribute to puberty? Like one day she suddenly stopped listening to the same music she used to love, or she changed all her friends at school?"

"Every teen goes through that," said the father. "I did it, you probably did it as well. I don't know what you're getting at, or what you want from our family, but there's nothing wrong with Brielle. She's a wonderful person."

Just like I feared—puberty was so volatile anyway, it was the perfect time to jump in and take over a life. They couldn't prove that she was or wasn't a Withered; I needed more information.

"I can see this is getting us nowhere," I said. "I'm going to gag you now and go take a look at her room. Mrs. Butler will come with me, so you two stay completely still or she will not be coming back.

No moving, no talking, no calling for help, no crawling for the door. Do you understand me?"

"Yes," said the father, and the boy echoed him softly. I ripped strips from a throw pillow and gagged the two males, then sliced away the ties from around the mother's ankles. The blade carved through the shirt with a smooth, delicious, ripping sound, and I had to hold myself back from cutting anything else. *One, one, two, three, five, eight, thirteen—* That only made me think of Brooke, lying unconscious in a bad motel. *Focus!* I backed away, breathing deeply. When I had myself under control again I gestured with the knife for the mother to stand up. "Lead the way and don't do anything stupid." She led me through the kitchen and down the hall; I grabbed the rifle as we walked past it.

"It's here," she whispered, stopping at the end of the hallway. "She shares it—shared it—with Jessica."

"Open it." I kept my voice quiet as well, just in case she was home already—crawled back through the window after kidnapping and killing Brooke.

If Brooke was already dead, I didn't even know what I would do. . . .

Mrs. Butler opened the door softly, pushing it slowly and stepping inside. I followed her closely, keeping the knife by her back and the rifle ready in my other hand, bracing myself for another attack by that towering, inhuman Withered—

And then Mrs. Butler screamed, a long, horrible wail of abject despair. I pushed her forward so I could come in past her, and she dropped to her knees shouting "*No no no!*" at the top of her lungs. Brielle was sprawled haphazardly on the floor, limbs limp and lifeless. I walked toward her, not believing my own eyes: she was Attina. She had to be. All the clues made sense. And yet here she was, as dead as the others. No ashy sludge anywhere. The window was broken, the sill gouged with claw marks. A Withered had definitely been here, even if it wasn't Brielle. I saw something white by her lips, and bent down to look. The smell of drain cleaner was so strong it made me gag. Foamy bubbles mixed with blood dribbled from her mouth, eating away at the carpet beneath. Her eyes were open, wide and terrified.

"Call the police," I said.

"What?"

"It's a revenge killing," I said. "Whoever killed her did it the same way Glassman died. I heard someone talking about it at the meeting: 'Pour some Drano down her throat and see how she likes it.'" I stared at the body, too stunned to move. "Word for word."

"You tortured my family!" she screamed.

I looked down at the knife and the rifle in my hands, at the makeshift bindings so tight around her wrists they were rubbing her raw. "I'm . . . sorry."

"Get out of my house!"

I looked back at Brielle's body. Someone had filled her with drain cleaner that was eating her away from the inside. Enough to kill her where she stood. Randy was the man's name—he was in love with Sara and he'd told Agent Mills he wanted someone to hurt Brielle in the same way. And now someone had. Why? That's the part that never made sense: why? The monster I'd seen had teeth and claws—why did it use drain cleaner? Why did it use chemicals on Brielle and knives on Derek and a truck on Corey? And why avenge a death Brielle hadn't even caused? What could the Withered possibly gain from killing people *other people* wanted dead?

Oh.

Oh no.

"We were so close," I murmured. So close. But it wasn't the Withered making the rest of the town kill, it was the other way around.

The town was making the Withered kill. Randy wanted vengeance for his lost love, wanted Brielle to suffer the same way Sara had, and so Attina had done it. Brielle wanted Glassman to die for attacking her sister, fantasized about poisoning him for revenge, even went so far as to write the whole thing out in her journal, step by step . . . and so Attina had done it. I'd wanted to light a fire and Attina had lit one. I'd wanted to hit Corey with a truck so Attina hit him with a truck. Officer Glassman had leered at underage girls for years, trapped by a desire he didn't dare to act on, but he'd wanted it so bad, wanted to dominate Jessica so completely, that as he watched outside her window Attina had leapt up and done the job more horribly and completely than he'd ever intended. And all of it, every death, every attack, every last catastrophe this town had seen, had started when I wanted to cut Derek into pieces. We never would have done it on our own, but Attina did. Attina had sensed it or felt it or known it, through whatever awful mechanism that lurked inside his mind, and he had done everything. Attina was a mirror, a perfect reflection of the community's unspoken desires. It had been dormant for decades, maybe since the beginning of the town, hurting no one because no one in Dillon wanted to hurt. And then I arrived.

And unleashed hell.

"Get out of my house," Mrs. Butler growled.

I moved the knife less than an inch from her face, still staring at Brielle's corpse. "The Withered are defined by what they lack," I said, thinking out loud. I could figure this out. Every Withered made perfect sense within its own reality, and now that I knew what that reality was, all I had to do was follow the logic. "Nobody didn't have a body, so she stole them from other people."

"What?"

"Elijah didn't have memories. Rack didn't have a heart. Forman didn't have his own emotions, so he felt everyone else's. Attina uses other people's will, their ability to choose and act, which means he doesn't have his own. It's an empty vessel, a hollow shell, a spineless nothing who has no desires, no wants, no self-interest. Someone who fits perfectly into this town because it always wants exactly what everyone else does. A pushover—no . . . a mascot. Attina is the most representative example of Dillon life. It goes to church. It participates in community events. If you want food it makes food; if you freak out in a town meeting, it freaks out. If you want to hide or cry or complain, it—of course. Beth."

"Beth?" whispered Mrs. Butler. She was trembling in terror. "Beth Gleason?"

" 'It's too damn hot,' " I said, repeating her words from the gym. " 'Everyone was thinking it anyway.' " I pulled the knife away from Mrs. Butler's face. "I wanted to get Brooke out of Dillon, so she took Brooke out of Dillon. That's why she ran—she wasn't afraid, she was protecting the person I wanted to protect. Ingrid came right out and told us: Beth will go along with anything." I looked at Mrs. Butler. "Where would Beth go outside of town? If she needed to get away?"

"I . . . " Mrs. Butler swallowed, looking at the knife still inches from her face, too emotionally battered to think straight. "I don't know. Maybe one of the old farms?"

"There's a lot of them," I said, remembering our ride into town the first night. We'd passed a dozen or more farms, all spread out in the flat land around the town. "Do you know which one specifically? Somewhere she'd feel familiar and safe."

"Are you saying she . . . that she did this? That Beth killed my girls?"

I looked at the clock on the wall: time was up, and the lockdown was in place. I'd have to be as stealthy as possible. "I know you think

I'm crazy and evil and you have no reason to trust me." I opened the window to slip out that way. "But yes. Beth killed your girls, and I'm going to go kill her."

"She has an old farm," said Butler, wiping her eyes and fixing me with a grim expression. "She hasn't lived there in thirty years, not since her husband died, and she sold all the surrounding land but kept the house. Uses it for barbecues and church parties." She pointed north with a trembling finger. "Take Main Street about two miles, then turn on Barkwood Road and look for the mailbox with a rooster on it. It's about another two miles." She gritted her teeth, her fear coalescing into sudden, fierce anger. "Make it hurt."

24

Beth Gleason. She stayed in the background, she did what she was told. She went to church because everyone went to church, and when Marci and I had talked during the sermon she'd shushed us, not because she wanted to but because everyone else wanted to. They were all looking at us, but Beth was the one who said it. In today's town meeting everyone had been angry, but it was Beth who'd said it. She was the personification of the community as a whole—and ever since Brook and I had arrived, that community had been tearing itself apart.

Everyone thinks dark thoughts sometimes. Did mine finally set her off because . . . they were more intense? More single-minded? Other people thought about hurting each other, but Attina didn't absorb thoughts, she absorbed intentions. The will to act. I was the only one in town with the true, unmitigated desire to kill someone, and the clarity of purpose to actually go through with it. Brooke or Marci or whoever it was at the time would always calm me down, but Attina didn't have that. She had all my rage and nothing to hold her back.

I had to hurry.

The town was quiet, already on lockdown, but without the large influx of troops coming the next day, it was still relatively empty. They couldn't be everywhere at once. I walked softly down the side of the Butler house, just far enough to peek out at the street. A cop car drove by, and I ducked behind the Butler's garbage can. The car was moving south, away from where I wanted to go, but I couldn't risk going right out in the road. I slinked back into the yard and started hopping fences.

The yard north of the Butler house was well-groomed, the lawn cut short and clear of any toys or benches or trees. With no cover to hide in I ran to the next fence without stopping, dumped my knife and rifle over the top and hauled myself over after them. This yard offered more concealment and I was able to crouch behind a small garden shed to get my bearings. Most of the people, I hoped, would be looking out their front doors rather than the back—this made it easy to jump from yard to yard, but my next fence vault would take me to a north-facing home and I would have to run out the driveway and across the street directly toward another row of houses. Anyone looking out would be certain to see me. But what would they do about it?

Most of the people in the town were armed—the unlocked truck with the gun rack I'd found was proof enough of that. If someone saw me running toward his house with a butcher knife and a rifle, would he see me as a threat or as another concerned, armed citizen? My best chance at avoiding trouble was to act like the latter, and walk slowly across the street as if I belonged there. It was a strategy that had always worked in the hallways at school: look like you have a hall pass and most people won't ask you for one. Would it work here as well? Not with the cops, but maybe with the locals. Most of them were furious about the lockdown as it was; they might even see me as a vigilante hero.

Or, you know, shoot me.

I made another sprint to the next fence, threw myself over, and lowered to a crouch. Here was a driveway leading straight out to the road, but I had to check for police first. I crept forward, peering out and looking both ways. No cops. I slipped the knife into my leg sheath—a poor fit, but better than nothing—and then composed myself, carrying the rifle like a soldier on patrol and walking across the street like it was my job to be there. Halfway across I noticed an old man watching me through the open curtains of a house to my right. I saluted him and then immediately regretted it, wondering if it was too much. A wave would have been better. He did nothing, and I reached the next driveway and went back into hiding.

I crossed the rest of the town this way, jumping fences and hiding from cops. On the last street I had to wait almost ten minutes, crouched behind an old truck, while a police officer talked to a homeowner barely ten feet away. He asked if the man had seen anything and told him to stay inside. When the man left I held my breath, not daring to make even the tiniest sound. The cop got in his car and I moved around the side of the truck, out of sight from the street. He drove away, and I watched. The instant he disappeared around the corner I set out across the street.

"Not supposed to be out here," said a voice. I turned and saw the man the cop had been talking to, standing in his open doorway.

"Just watching for trouble," I said, gesturing with the rifle. "You really trust them to keep you safe?"

"Not at all," said the man, and he showed me a rifle of his own, just inside the door frame. I nodded, and he nodded, and I crossed the street.

Two yards later I was in a field of corn that was nearly shoulder high.

I stayed in the field for a ways, counting my steps and trying to calculate how many of them would make a mile. My steps were about two feet, maybe two and a half, which meant . . . twenty-six-hundred-something steps? I counted out two thousand, figured it was far enough, and then cut west to the main road, following it the rest of the way to Barkwood. There were no cops out here, and no traffic; I wondered if the police had barricaded the roads into Dillon as well as out. I realized Mrs. Butler hadn't told me which way to turn on Barkwood, right or left, but when I reached it I saw that left was the only choice. I turned and walked a few more miles, passing a couple of farmhouses. The sun was still high, but both houses had lights on. I'd come back to them later if I didn't find Beth in the rooster house.

And then I reached the rooster house—an old abandoned-looking farmhouse with patched shingles and a dead, sun-scorched lawn. The rooster on the mailbox looked like an old weather vane, rusted and bent and bolted to the top of the mailbox by a stick of old wood. It was at least a half a mile to the nearest neighbor.

I listened and heard crying.

I gripped the rifle tighter. I still didn't know how to kill this thing. Did it regenerate? Could it sense me coming? Would my own determination to kill it make it, in turn, determined to kill me?

Two voices crying now. Why two?

Because Attina had no will of her own and only wanted what the people around her wanted. And the only person around her now was Brooke, and there was one thing Brooke wanted more than anything in the world.

I almost started crying with them.

I crept forward, the dead grass crunching softly under my feet. The front windows were closed, the blinds drawn, but I found an unblocked window on the side. I stood on my tiptoes to peer inside, but the room and what little I could see of the hall beyond were empty. Not even much furniture, just a folding table and some old napkins. An old family house they only used for parties. I moved to the next window, listening to the wails as they varied in pitch—now softer, now louder, and suddenly a cry of pain and a whoop of terror. The second window I looked in revealed a view as empty as the first, so I moved to the back of the house. The door was locked. I went to the next window but stopped, seeing a glow by the stump of a dried-out tree. A basement window. I laid down on the dry grass to look inside, and there she was: Beth Gleason, eighty years old if she were a day, in the same old blue dress I'd always seen her in. Her hands, arms, chest, and entire lower body were covered with blood. I almost cried out, terrified that it was Brooke's blood, that I was too late to save her—but no. The inside of Beth's forearm held a long, deep gash, from elbow to wrist, sloughing out blood like a shaken trough. And then the gash healed, and the blood dried, and Beth wailed in despair and grabbed a pair of garden shears and slashed it open again. She bled, and screamed, and healed. Over and over.

She was trying to kill herself.

It was all Brooke wanted—the bottomless pit at the base of her mind, the horrifying legacy of Nobody. The Withered wretch who'd killed herself a hundred thousand times. Every setback seemed to trigger a new despair, and I'd pulled her back from the brink of more suicides that I could remember. When Attina had captured her, when she'd been separated from me, when it seemed that all was lost, she'd gone right back to it again, like the comfort of an old blanket, and Attina had been powerless to resist. She had no will but what she borrowed from others.

I had to act fast, before she borrowed one from me.

I tried the back door again, kicking it a few times, until finally giving up using the rifle to shoot the doorknob. The sound was deafening; I hoped that Attina's single-minded obsession would keep her from caring. In the depths of depression, Brooke wouldn't care—it might actually make her worse. Please let Attina be the same.

The stairs to the basement were right inside the back door, long and narrow. The rifle would be useless in those cramped quarters, so I left it by the wall and pulled out my knife, advancing slowly down the stairs with the blade in front of me. It didn't have the strength of Potash's old combat knife, but it was sharpened to a razor's edge, and it might buy me a few precious seconds, if nothing else. I reached the basement with my ears still ringing, the crying women only barely audible, and rounded the corner just in time to see Beth gash herself open again, bleeding copiously. The pool of blood at her feet covered nearly the entire cement floor of the basement, trickling in a steady stream down the drain in the center. How long had she been doing this?

How could I get away from her once this obsession cleared?

Attina ignored me, and I stepped through the sticky red mess to where Brooke was tied to a chair, watching the whole thing and numb with despair.

"Just let me die," she mumbled. "Just let me die."

"I will," I said. I needed to keep her sad, to keep her will for death as strong as possible. "I'm not here to save you—it's impossible to save you. You've been lost for too long."

"I know," she sobbed, "just let me die."

I cut her loose from the chair and helped her stand. She groped for my knife but I held it away in my left hand, holding her tightly to my side with my right. I just had to get her out of here—

—no. I couldn't think like that. I had to want to kill myself, too, to keep Attina occupied as long as possible.

Or maybe I just had to want to kill Attina.

I walked Brooke slowly to the stairs, searching for anything that might help. How could I kill a Withered who healed that fast? There was an axe leaning against the wall; taking off her head in a single stroke might work, but I didn't have the skill to pull that off. She'd regenerate so fast, anything less would be ineffective. I looked for more. A shelf full of dusty mason jars. A box of old decorations: Christmas and Thanksgiving and Halloween. Then I noticed the furnace, and had the answer: fire. It was the only way I'd killed Nobody—even the Withered soulstuff was vulnerable to it, and they couldn't heal fast enough to escape it. What else could I use? Mrs. Butler had said they held barbecues here—there had to be fuel, or at least charcoal.

"We'll never get out in time," I said to Brooke, trying to keep her thoughts focused on hopelessness, and I started knocking over boxes as we passed them, spilling their contents onto the floor, searching desperately for something to start a big fire. Finally I found a plastic jug of lighter fluid, but I had no free hands. I had to let go of Brooke or the knife. I dropped my knife and picked up the lighter fluid, popping off the cap and spraying it on the fallen decorations, on the shelves and wooden panels in the walls. I even sprayed some on Attina as she stabbed herself and howled again, ignoring me. Now I needed a flame. I dropped the half-empty bottle on the floor and eased Brooke upstairs, holding her with two hands, taking the steep steps carefully. She tried to throw herself down, pleading with me not to stop her again, not to keep her from her death, but I got her to the top and we stumbled into the kitchen.

"Look for matches," I said, pushing her toward the cupboards. "For gas lighters, for anything that will burn."

"Are we going to burn ourselves?"

"We are," I said, yanking open drawer after drawer. I couldn't help but feel a bit of eagerness, of excitement for a fire—I had never set one this big before, and it had been far too long since I'd set one at all. "All we need is—this." I opened the pantry door and found three miniature tanks of propane, dark green and each the size of a melon. I grabbed and shook them, finding them satisfyingly heavy. "Find matches," I said. "If you want to die, this is how you do it."

I set the tanks on the counter and ran from room to room, hoping to find a gas grill of some kind to hook them up to. Anything that would let the gas out. There was nothing in the house, and I didn't have time to search the garage. I found a sheaf of yellowed newspapers and grabbed it, rushing back to the kitchen to find Brooke holding a cardboard box full of matches, fumbling through her tears to light one.

"Is this enough?"

"It's perfect," I said, taking them away gently. I looked at her in sudden fear, terrified that my compliment had ruined everything: I needed to insult her, to tell her she had failed, that nothing she did would ever work. I needed her to want to die, or this whole plan could fail. I looked in her eyes . . .

. . . and I couldn't do it. "It's perfect," I said again. "We're going to make the most beautiful fire you've ever seen."

I tucked the matches under my arm and grabbed the propane and walked back to the stairway, back down to the basement. I turned the corner to see Beth standing in front of me, inches away, covered in blood and her eyes practically gleaming. I dropped my armful in shock, stumbling backward into the doorway as the tanks and matches clattered to the ground.

"You're building a fire," she said. The propane tanks were still rolling, carving slick pathways through the bloody puddle on the floor.

"Yes," I said. It was all I could say.

Beth stooped to pick up the newspaper, dropping the pages that had soaked up blood, and holding up the dry pages in her wrinkled fist. "We're building a fire," she said. "And I'm finally going to die." She picked up the fallen jug of lighter fluid and sprayed it on the walls and ceiling, soaking the carpet square that sat in the corner, drenching the rack of old clothes against the back.

I stood in the doorway and watched her build her pyre.

I never had to think about killing the first ones. They were monsters, and I was defending myself and my family and town. Now I was defending this town, doing something no one else could do, in a way no one else could do it, and it was good. It was the right thing to do—the Withered had to die. I knew that, in the same way I knew that stalking was unacceptable, that hurting animals was evil, that killing humans was wrong. That is to say: I knew it was true but I didn't feel it. I wanted to kill and slice and maim, but this was a cheat. A voluntary death. Tricking Attina into killing herself was . . . cruel, in a way. I didn't do this to be cruel. I looked at that frail old demon, trapped for years in a life it couldn't even recognize as its own, and I felt something I'd never felt before.

I felt pity.

"I don't want to do this," I said.

"I don't want to, either," said Beth, stopping immediately. She turned to look at me, holding the axe in her hands. Lighter fluid dripped from her hair and her dress, running down her arms and cascading off her elbows in tiny rivulets.

Five people dead and who knew how many more if I didn't stop her now. She'd held down Brielle and forced drain cleaner down her throat, choking her and burning her and eating her from the inside—not because she wanted to, not because she had to, but because she couldn't control herself. Because she was the worst of humanity given form. But she was also the best of it. She'd lived for so long here, never hurting a fly, making soup for her neighbors and organizing neighborhood watches. She could be good when the world was good around her. Did she really deserve to die just because I had come and ruined paradise?

But no paradise lasts forever. What would she do tomorrow, when a hundred national guardsmen showed up? They wanted to protect the town, so she'd protect it. They wanted to kill a bad guy, so she'd kill . . . I didn't know who. Someone. Unless I killed her now.

The demon king Rack had told me how the Withered began. Human beings, lost in antiquity, had given up their most hated traits to gain unimaginable power. Nobody had hated her body, so she gave it up forever; she gained the ability to take whatever body she wanted, but she'd lost that essential humanity that made it worthwhile. Forman had given up his emotions—why? He must have felt something terrible, guilt or loss or shame, and never wanted to feel it again. Attina had given up her own will, her own choices, I suppose because she'd made too many bad ones and didn't want the responsibility anymore. She didn't want the pain of choosing wrong. But choices still get made, whether you're the one making them or not, and all she had become was a slave.

I had to choose for her. I hated the choice more than I'd ever hated anything, but I had to make it.

"I don't want to do this," I said, and summoned all my will. "But I'm going to."

"We're going to," she echoed. Tears rolled down her face, and I wondered how much she really knew, or felt, or understood about what was happening. She couldn't make her own decisions, but was she aware of them? Was there something inside of her, like Marci inside of Brooke, that looked out and watched her body act, and cried and screamed and begged it to stop?

"We're going to kill ourselves," she sobbed. "And then we can start again." She raised the axe, turned toward the furnace, and shattered the valve on the gas line.

"Start again?" I repeated. That was something Brooke had said—a holdover from Nobody's old behavior. Possess a girl, live her life, and when you found a better one you kill yourself and take it. Start again. I looked behind me, but Brooke wasn't there. She was still upstairs.

With the rifle.

I screamed and ran as Beth lit a match, and the basement leapt into horrible, glorious, fiery life.

25

"A," said Brooke. "American Shipping."

The pickup jostled us, rolling across the blacktop of an old, flat highway. The wind seemed to speak as it whistled past us, half-formed words rippling past in invisible whorls. We were getting close to the end of our ride, and billboards were starting to appear. I saw a sign for a plumbing company and pointed it out. "B."

"Good for you!" she said, laughing and clapping her hands. They were still bandaged from the fire; I'd washed her burns as best I could, and stolen an old T-shirt off a clothesline to cover the wounds. She smiled at me. "I knew you'd like this game."

I looked at her, remembering those laughing lips wrapped around the barrel of a hunting rifle, those clapping hands trying to reach the trigger. I'd saved her just in time. And years too late. I saw a C on a road sign, but instead of pointing it out I distracted her by pointing the other direction.

"C!"

"Where?" She craned her neck trying to spot it, reading the sign as we passed it. "I don't see a C anywhere on there, but there's a J! Quick, find all the other letters up to J while we can still see it!"

"On the license plate," I said, still pointing away from the C sign. "There's a C, and then on the side of that truck there's a D, E. . . . I'm not seeing an F anywhere."

"Too late," she said. "The J's gone." She smiled at me, peaceful and contented. "We'll see another one."

"Yeah." The C sign was gone as well.

"Tell me where we're going again?" she asked.

"Nowhere special," I said, not meeting her eyes. "Just a place to relax for a bit."

"Rain was south of us," said Brooke. "We've been going north for two days."

"Agent Mills is still looking for us," I said. "And so is the FBI. We need to lay low."

"He still has Boy Dog," said Brooke.

"I'll get him back."

"F," said Brooke, pointing at a passing license plate. She laughed. "That's funny."

The town ahead was close enough to see now, a low mound of trees and buildings, and high above it all, the smokestacks of a wood plant. I looked at Brooke, just looking and looking. I didn't want to make this choice, and I did. Both at the same time.

"You're staring at me," she said.

"You're nice to stare at."

Brooke raised her eyebrow. "John Wayne Cleaver, you rogue."

"Brooke, I . . . " I took a deep breath, and blew it out slowly. "You're my best friend."

"You're mine."

"You're the most important person in my life. You're the two most important people in my life, all at once, and I want you to . . . to be safe. To be happy. I want you to grow up and get married and have kids and have a life. I want you to live a thousand years."

"I've already lived ten thousand," she said, and cocked her head to the side. "Why are you getting so serious all of a sudden?"

"Because I want to do what's best for you."

"You always do," she said. "And I want to do what's best for you."

"Those don't always line up," I said.

"I love you," said Brooke.

I sighed. "I think you probably do. And I think I . . . " I stopped, and closed my eyes, and said the hardest thing I'd ever said—not because it was false, but because it was completely, relentlessly true. "I love you too."

She moved across the truck to sit next to me, lifting my arm and snuggling in under it. The truck bounced us gently as we rode. The city ahead grew closer.

"Have we been here before?" asked Brooke. "It looks familiar."

"It's been a while," I said. "But yeah."

The C sign again: WELCOME TO CLAYTON.

Brooke smiled. "I remember this place. I grew up here." She sat up straighter, looking around, drinking in the familiarity. "Several of me did."

"This is where we're from," I said. "Brooke and John. This is home." We passed the gas station, the tire place, the old kitschy shoe museum. "You deserve a home."

"It seems smaller than I remember it," said Brooke. "Which is weird, because I'm not bigger than I was, I'm just older. But it all seems like it's . . . shrunk, maybe. Or maybe I'm just seeing it with new eyes. Like it all used to blend together, and now I'm seeing the gaps between the buildings, and the lines in the paint." She shook her head. "It's only been three years? Two years? It feels like it hasn't changed a bit. Or like it's aged a whole century."

The driver leaned out of his window. "The hospital, right?"

I nodded. Brooke didn't know it, but this was a chartered trip. Fifty-four dollars and ninety-six cents, every last scrap of money we had left plus everything I'd gotten for pawning the rifle, had been slipped through the window with a whispered plea when the truck picked us up.

"Why are we going to the hospital?" asked Brooke. She looked at her hands, and the bandaged burn on her leg. "They'll ask for ID."

"Your burns are fine," I said.

"Then why are we going to the hospital?"

I wished that idiot driver had just kept his mouth shut. This was hard enough without him spilling the whole plan early.

"G," I said, pointing at the sign for the Friendly Burger.

Brooke looked at me, thinking, her mind racing through the implications of my words, of our destination, of everything that was happening.

"No," she whispered.

"I'm sorry."

"You're going to leave me here," she said, pulling away. I grabbed her hand, holding her back, scared that she would jump straight out of the truck bed, trying to kill herself or simply trying to escape. "If we come back they'll recognize us, people will know us—we won't be able to hide anymore or finish our work with the Withered. And I know you're not going to abandon your war, so that means you're abandoning me instead! You're leaving me here!"

"I'm sorry," I said.

"I love you!" She cried. "I trusted you! We're a team—you said you'd never leave me, that we were partners, that you'd walk into hell to get me back!"

"You've already—"

"How could you!" She punched me in the shoulder with her free hand, only once at first, then over and over, pounding her fist into my arm and chest, digging her knuckles into my flesh. I grabbed her hand in mine, wrestling her to a halt.

"You've already been to hell," I said. "I'm the one who took you there. This life we've been trying to live, sleeping in alleys and living on stolen corn nuts from highway truck stops: this is hell. Dragging you from one murder to the next, forcing you to remember tragedies that aren't even yours, dancing along the edge of a suicide cliff and trying to catch you every time you start to go over: that's hell. If I love you, I can't put you through that."

"That's not your choice to make."

"I know."

"This is my life," she growled. "And if this is how I want to live it, I'm damn well going to live it how I want."

"You're ill," I said. "You need medicine, you need therapy, you need twenty-four-hour care of a kind that I can't give you—"

"I don't want care," she screamed, "I want you!"

"And I want you to be alive," I said. "And happy. Even if I'm not there to see it."

The truck stopped in front of the hospital, and Brooke wrenched away from me, leaping out and running.

"There she is!"

"It's Brooke! Thank God, it's Brooke!"

Brooke's parents had been waiting, probably for hours. It's hard to predict travel times when you're hitchhiking. I'd spent a dollar on a phone call, telling them the day and the place and hanging up. They streaked across the parking lot now, catching her in their arms, sobbing and lifting her up and holding on to something they thought they'd lost forever.

Brooke looked back at me, pleading, trying to break away. "You can't leave me!"

"She's a severe suicide risk," I called out, standing in the back of the truck. "Clinical depression and dissociative identity disorder. At least one of her personalities is bipolar. She needs a long-term, live-in care facility and intensive therapy, but she can come through."

"I'm not weak!" Brooke shouted.

"No you're not," I said. "You're the strongest person I've ever known. I could never have done what you did."

"Is that John?" asked Brooke's mother.

"He's saving her," said Brooke's father.

"He's hurting me," sobbed Brooke.

"Sometimes the right choice is the one that hurts the most," I said. "Good-bye Brooke." I sat down and knocked on the side of the truck. Time to go. I said the next one softly: "Good-bye, Marci." I started to cry, and the truck rolled.

"You're not staying?" shouted Brooke's mom. "What should we tell your aunt? Your sister?"

I didn't answer, and the truck pulled out of the parking lot, back onto the road.

I sat in silence for a mile or more before banging on the side of the truck again. The driver stopped.

"You want to go back?"

"Just let me out here," I said. I hopped down.

"What was all that back there?" he asked.

"You'll see it on the news," I said. "Look for the name Brooke Watson." I started walking away.

"What about you?"

I turned around, walking backward away from him. "The police are going to ask where you left me," I said. "Probably the FBI, too. Tell them I said hi."

I turned back around and walked away. I passed through the town I grew up in, wondering who might recognize me, what they might do. No one even looked. I was a drifter, here one minute and gone the next. I passed the school, empty in the summer; I passed the old apartments where my sister used to live. I passed Marci's house, still overgrown with trees and plants, and saw her little sister playing on the sidewalk, drawing pictures with thick sticks of colored chalk. I stopped half a block away and watched her. I couldn't see what she was drawing. I turned the corner and moved on. I passed the wood plant, and jumped a fence to the rail yard, and climbed aboard an empty flatbed as the train headed out for another load of logs.

The city disappeared behind me, and the wind whistled secrets in my ears.